A Cowboy & a Gentleman
by Ann Major

arm, wet kiss.

at one helluva kiss, Anthony silently amended
 red at Zoe, who was flushed and naked and
and begging him to get naked, too. As her big
yes flicked over him in awe, he felt something
dangerous luring him on.

He ped. 'This is crazy.'

wed against him. 'I don't know what I want,' Zoe
er voice lower, sexier.

maybe I do.' His finger traced along her soft
down her throat, down, down, circling over each
until they peaked into pert little beads of desire.

uddered. 'You think so, huh? Let's see if you're
hunky out of those clothes as you are in them.'

The she was peeling him out of his shirt, leaning into
him her slim fingers flying over those shirt buttons. She
yanked his shirt off his shoulders, then caressed
sculpted muscle.

Giggling, Zoe ran her hands down his naked spine. 'I
want to hate you. Did you know that's been my
ambition for nine years?'

'Mine, to
doing too

Beckett's Cinderella
by Dixie Browning

ꙩ ꙮ ꙩ

'We've talked. I've read your papers, and I'm not interested.'

As if to prove it, she crossed her arms.

His stomach growled, protesting its emptiness. Dammit, he needed to wind up this business and get back to his own life. He made the mistake of reaching out to lead her into the hall. The brief brush of his fingers on her arm created a force field powerful enough to set off mental alarms. If the startled look on her face was anything to go by, she'd felt it, too. Jerking her arm free, she led the way to the front door, held it open and stood at attention, waiting for him to leave.

Reaching past her, he closed the screen door. 'Mosquitoes,' he reminded her.

'Will you please just go?' Crossed arms again. The lady was at full battle stations. 'Whatever it is you're doing you're not doing it with me.'

Oh, but lady, I'd like to. The thought came out of nowhere, catching him off guard. And dammit, he didn't need that particular distraction. He made it a policy never to mix sex with business.

'I'm not interested,' she said flatly.

'You're not interested in ten thousand dollars?'

****

'A true pioneer in romantic fiction, the delightful Dixie Browning is a reader's most precious treasure, a constant source of outstanding entertainment.' —*Romantic Times*

Available in January 2004 from Silhouette Desire

The Playboy & Plain Jane
by Leanne Banks
(Dynasties: The Barones)

and

Sleeping Beauty's Billionaire
by Caroline Cross
(Dynasties: The Barones)

A Cowboy & a Gentleman
by Ann Major

and

Beckett's Cinderella
by Dixie Browning
(Beckett's Fortune)

Delaney's Desert Sheikh
by Brenda Jackson

and

Expecting Brand's Baby
by Emilie Rose

A Cowboy & a Gentleman
ANN MAJOR

Beckett's Cinderella
DIXIE BROWNING

SILHOUETTE®
DESIRE™

All the characters in this book have no existence outside the imagination of the author, and have no relation whatsoever to anyone bearing the same name or names. They are not even distantly inspired by any individual known or unknown to the author, and all the incidents are pure invention.

All Rights Reserved including the right of reproduction in whole or in part in any form. This edition is published by arrangement with Harlequin Enterprises II B.V. The text of this publication or any part thereof may not be reproduced or transmitted in any form or by any means, electronic or mechanical, including photocopying, recording, storage in an information retrieval system, or otherwise, without the written permission of the publisher.

This book is sold subject to the condition that it shall not, by way of trade or otherwise, be lent, resold, hired out or otherwise circulated without the prior consent of the publisher in any form of binding or cover other than that in which it is published and without a similar condition including this condition being imposed on the subsequent purchaser.

*Silhouette, Silhouette Desire and Colophon
are registered trademarks of Harlequin Books S.A.,
used under licence.*

*First published in Great Britain 2004
Silhouette Books, Eton House, 18-24 Paradise Road,
Richmond, Surrey TW9 1SR*

The publisher acknowledges the copyright holders of the
individual works as follows:

A Cowboy & a Gentleman © Ann Major 2002
Beckett's Cinderella © Dixie Browning 2002

ISBN 0 373 04972 2

51-0104

*Printed and bound in Spain
by Litografia Rosés S.A., Barcelona*

A COWBOY & A GENTLEMAN

by
Ann Major

ANN MAJOR

lives in Texas with her husband of many years and is the mother of three grown children. She has a master's degree and is a former English teacher. She is a founding board member of the RWA and a frequent speaker at writers' groups.

Ann loves to write; she considers her ability to do so a gift. Her hobbies include hiking in the mountains, sailing, ocean kayaking, travelling and playing the piano. But most of all she enjoys her family.

To Karen Solem, a truly great agent,
who was there for me long before she was my agent.

And to Tara Gavin, my wonderful editor,
who has faith in me even when I don't,
and who has infinite patience and wisdom, too.

And to Ted, for loving me and giving me the most
wonderful three weeks of my life in Greece.

And to Greece...

ACKNOWLEDGEMENT

I need to thank Patience Smith
for telling me about her job as an editor
and Caleb Huett for telling me what it's like
to be eight years old.

Prologue

What's a girl to do when she wakes up in bed married to the wrong man?

"I can't face Tony! I just can't!"

Zoe Creighton dashed up the ladder and flung herself onto a heap of hay in the loft. Her heart pounding, she moved into a crouch and peered through a crack in the barn's siding. She saw the snug, low roofs of Aunt Patty's ranch house and the windmill glinting in the late-afternoon sun below.

Anthony's truck was parked out front. The white cloud of dust that had plumed behind him when he'd driven up the caliche road so fast—and sent her flying out the back screen door in terror—hadn't quite settled over the thorny South Texas brush country.

The air was sweet with the familiar perfume of the barn—horses, oats, hay, leather and dung. She could almost smell the bluebonnets that had turned the mesquite-studded pasture closest to the house into a sea of undulating blue blossoms.

"Oh, if only…if only I could turn back time, just twenty-four hours…. I'd do it all so differently."

Zoe squeezed her eyes shut and tried to make herself believe that everything was the same. Only nothing was. Nothing would ever be the same again.

"Good Lord! What have you gone and done to yourself, Zoe Creighton?" she said aloud. "And Creighton's not even your last name anymore."

Brushing at her lashes, Zoe stared at the huge diamond on her left hand. Then, as if she still couldn't believe it was there, she held it up to that crack in the barn siding, so that the gaudy jewel shot white bits of glitter onto the wooden walls.

The ring was real all right. Only it was the wrong man's ring.

Quickly she fisted the hand and hid it behind her back.

Aunt Patty was always saying she was flighty and impulsive as a chicken. Zoe was only twenty, only a mere junior at the nearby branch of Texas A & M University, but she felt as if her life was already over.

"Stupid. That's what I am."

The barn door rolled, and just as she'd feared he might, Tony Duke stomped inside on a burst of blinding light, shouting her name so loudly the horses below snickered restlessly, their hooves clanging against the stall floors.

She stiffened. "Oh, why can't you just go on home and leave well enough alone?" she whispered to herself. "I came here to hide from you, you big, handsome idiot."

Used to be, when she'd see his truck roaring up to her gate, she'd rushed out to meet him.

"I can't face you. I can't tell you. Not after what we did here in this loft together yesterday," she added. The mere thought of her naked, virginal body under his warmed her like a fever.

"You have to tell him."

How had Tony known the exact moment Duncan had brought her back from Vegas?

Maybe if Tony couldn't find her, he'd give up and leave. Fearfully she peeped over the edge of the loft and stared down at his shiny, black head.

No doubt, because of the rodeo, he wore a red cowboy shirt and jeans. His wide shoulders made him look tough. The way he cocked his head back, so that his chin jutted out, made him look arrogant. He was so handsome every girl in the surrounding counties was in love with him. Why had he chosen her? Zoe had such a poor opinion of herself she'd never quite believed he loved her.

He strode about, throwing open the stall doors, calling the horses by their individual names as he searched for her.

"Give up, baby. Please…just go," Zoe whispered.

He slammed a stall door so hard she gasped. She must've jumped, too, because bits of hay sifted down and landed on his thick shoulders and black head.

"Oh, dear."

He peeled one out of his hair and another off his red shoulder. "So, you're up in the loft, are you?" He sounded angry but flirty, too.

"Don't you dare come up here! I don't want to talk to you ever again," she cried.

"You're wrong about that, baby," he rasped, striding toward the ladder. "Now, don't be shy."

Her heart pounded every time his boots struck a wooden rung. At the thought of facing him, she felt tears burning behind her eyelids. She was so scared, she began to shake.

First his big, tanned hands came into view, then the rest of him. For a long moment he simply stared at her. As always his carved face was dark and gorgeous, his sweet smile bold and white.

"I love that dress."

Her blue gingham.

"You're still wearing it," he said gently.

She remembered what he'd said yesterday when he'd first seen her in it, before he'd touched her, and her stomach did a crazy somersault.

She blushed. Everything was different now.

"Just go," she whispered, frantic now, as she backed toward the wall.

"Your aunt said you were in here. She seemed in some sort of snit."

No way could Zoe answer that.

"I missed you last night, baby. Looked everywhere for you at the rodeo. I'm sorry. It's not like you think." His voice was as soft as velvet, and because of what she'd done, it wrenched every part of her.

Could he be telling the truth? No!

"Too late to be sorry," she muttered, remembering what she'd done. "I'm sorry, too, and I have as much to be sorry about as you do."

"Rene means nothing to me," he whispered, slinging a denim-clad leg onto the rough flooring of the loft.

''That's not what she said.''

He laughed. ''She thinks she's hot. She's inclined to stretch the truth.''

Her best friend, Rene, had been after him for years.

When he stood up, he loomed over Zoe in the tiny loft. Her fear made him look even taller and more dangerously formidable than yesterday when his nearness and gentleness had made her melt.

''I don't care what she said, and neither will you when I'm done kissing you,'' he whispered.

''There won't be any more kissing. Not here. We already got ourselves into way too much trouble.''

''How come you ran away after we made love?'' he whispered.

''I was scared. I couldn't believe we did it.''

''Then you got up your courage and came back and found me with Rene.''

''How could you go from me to her?''

''I couldn't. I didn't. I love you.''

''That's just a word. I saw what I saw. She was all over you.''

''Baby, I won't say Rene didn't give it her best shot.''

''Are you saying that you didn't—''

One side of his mouth curved downward, and he gave her that lopsided smile she'd loved to think belonged to her alone. He was so tall and dark, so undeniably handsome. Just looking at him made her remember the thrill of his muscular body on top of hers. *Oh, dear.*

''I'm saying that I didn't,'' he replied.

She almost believed him. Her doubts shredded her heart.

In spite of everything, she still loved him.

"Last night I was a virgin."

"And that means everything to me."

Nervousness tightened her throat. Last night seemed so long ago. She couldn't tell him what she'd done. She couldn't.

"Go. Just go," she whispered.

"Darlin'," he murmured in that voice she'd thought belonged to her alone, too.

When he edged closer, she went still. When less than an inch separated his mouth from hers, he bent his head to hers and kissed her softly.

Before she could think, her mouth opened. His hands slid into her hair, down her neck, and then all over her just like they had twenty-four short hours ago. A lifetime ago.

"This time I'll go slower," he whispered, his breathing sounding rougher after just that one kiss.

For a second the tenderness and passion in his lips and hands made her forget everything that had gone so terribly wrong. It was as if it were all a bad dream. Now she was wide awake and Tony was here, and everything was all right again.

She wasn't the shy, plain girl, who read all the time. She wasn't in over her head, dating the most popular and the most handsome guy anywhere around Shady Lomas. Rene hadn't stolen him right after they'd made love for the first time. Zoe hadn't gone to the pig races and bumped into the town's most scandalous citizen, Tony's uncle Duncan Duke.

Uncle Duncan. If only he hadn't been so understanding.

Anthony's hands were sliding around her shoulders, down her spine to press her closer and kiss her again. The images of Duncan driving her around on those back-country roads in his red Cadillac blurred.

Was it only this morning that she'd awakened so woozily in Vegas next to the man? Reaching for him, she'd whispered Anthony's name only to scream when Duncan Duke had slung back the sheets and laughed at her.

"Mrs. Duke, when you wake up next to your bridegroom, and you don't know his name, it was a damn good wedding night."

She'd blinked at the old reprobate in horror. Good wedding night? How could he say such a thing? What was he talking about? His gray goatee had blurred. "We're not married! You're old enough to be my father."

He'd lifted her left hand. "That didn't bother you last night. Remember? Broken heart? Rene? My, but you were hell-bent on revenge."

He'd laughed again.

Revenge? No! She hadn't remembered the wedding or the wedding night at all. Indeed, she hadn't remembered anything much but those little pigs racing their hearts out for chocolate cookies stuffed with vanilla cream. She'd drunk a few beers while Duncan had listened to her talk about his nephew, Tony, in between races. Then when the races were over, Duncan had driven her around in his Cadillac and had taken her up in his plane. After that, the rest of the night was a total blur.

"We flew all the way to Vegas?"

"That and more." Duncan had kissed her left hand and made his obscene ring sparkle. "You proposed to me, said it would put the town in an uproar and take my arrogant nephew down a peg or two."

"I thought you loved Aunt Patty."

"Nothing like a surprise or two!"

"Take me home! This didn't happen! You aren't my husband!"

He'd climbed out of bed stark naked and produced the appropriate documents; photographs of the ceremony, too.

She'd stared at the photograph of herself wrapped in Duncan's arms and felt sick. "I kissed you? What else—"

The leer he'd given her had scared her. "No," she'd whispered. "Please, don't tell me!"

"I can fill you in on the details any time."

Well, maybe she was home again. But nothing could change the facts. She was married to Duncan Duke.

Worse! Here she was in her aunt's barn kissing her husband's nephew, Anthony, and moaning with pleasure, too. This was a nightmare! Only she wasn't going to wake up! This was a real life nightmare.

Placing her hands against Anthony's wide chest, she shoved. When he finally let her go, she fell backward a little.

Slowly she lifted Duncan Duke's big ring into a stream of light that sifted through a crack in the wooden siding. Turning her hand, she made sparks of light hit Tony's carved face.

Anthony squinted, but his dark eyes were on her wet, bruised lips and not on his uncle's ring.

"I've done something that can't be undone," she whispered brokenly. "It's like a nightmare. Only it's worse. 'Cause it's real. I can't believe I did it. But I was so hurt. I guess I wanted to get back at you."

"Baby, I love you so much there's nothing in the

whole world I couldn't forgive you. I've always loved you. Since you were a little girl in the sixth grade with those long, beautiful red braids. Why can't you ever just believe me?"

"'Cause I'm me and you're you. 'Cause I'm not popular or pretty."

"I've told you and told you that's all in your mind. You can be anything you want to be and have anybody you want."

Almost absently she moved her hand so that the diamond flashed fire across the coarse boards of the wall. "I was so mad at you about Rene that I ran off...and...and...well, I guess I got married. Truth to tell...I don't really remember."

"Married?" He grabbed her hand hard and stared at the ring on her finger. His mouth worked, but he couldn't speak. His eyes went cold as he studied her white face.

"I married your uncle Duncan," she murmured, staring down at his black boots.

"You what?" He cupped her chin and lifted it, so that he could look her square in the eye.

"I—"

"That old bastard's older than your daddy would be if he was alive! He's a scoundrel."

"I know that!"

"He was supposed to be courtin' your aunt Patty. The whole town watched him drive out here in that damned red Cadillac he wouldn't be able to afford if he hadn't stolen our land."

"Well, he married me. I don't know why he did it, but he did it."

"Because he's a bastard."

Usually the term bastard was an insult, but in this

case it was also a pertinent fact. Duncan Duke, who had long thrived on being Shady Lomas's number-one bad egg, had been born a bastard and pretended he was proud as hell about it.

Tony's grandfather, Harry Duke, had had two families, one on the wrong side of the sheets and one on the right side. He'd loved them both with a powerful passion.

Henrietta Duke, Harry's *legitimate* daughter, was Tony's strong-willed, straitlaced mother. Harry hadn't married wild, pretty Eva, Duncan's mother, but when Old Harry had finally died, he'd left the best part of the family ranch to his legitimate daughter, the stern Henrietta, his rightful heir.

Only, fate had played a wild card. Oil and gas had been discovered on the worthless marshland that fun-loving Duncan had inherited. Soon Duncan had become the richest man in three counties—three very huge Texas counties. He'd been buying land ever since his first gas wells had come in, and flaunting his wealth whenever possible. He'd had several wives, each one younger and prettier than the last. This was very upsetting to the town folk and especially to his two daughters.

Henrietta, who'd been hard-pressed to make it in the cattle business during the last drought, had been forced to sell Duncan the family's historical, red-roofed ranch house. She'd also sold him most of her prime ranch land, land that she leased back from him so she and Tony could run their herd on it.

"Every acre your husband owns should be mine—especially the house!"

"Is that all you care about—the house and land? The ranch?"

"What did you care about when you married my uncle Duncan?" Anthony's hair was blue-black; his face a livid, scary white.

"You slept with Rene, so it's your fault I went crazy and woke up married. I...I really don't remember it all exactly."

"You don't remember? Like hell! Let's get one thing straight! I did not sleep with Rene! But I will now! You were right! You've done something I'll never forgive! Neither will the town or the county! Neither will Uncle Duncan's daughters, my precious half cousins, Lana and Sue Ellen. They'll tear you to pieces. Why do you think he married you—to get back at all of us, that's why!"

Suddenly Anthony grabbed her by the shoulders.

"What are you doing?"

To her surprise, he circled her with his arms. "Don't I get to kiss the bride?"

She twisted and uttered an infuriated cry. "Not if you hate me so much!"

"There's no *if* about it, darlin'." He caught both her hands and held on tight, forcing her back against the wall. He was huge and powerful and determined to have his way with her. All too soon he had her plastered between the wall and the steel-hard muscles of his body.

Then his hard mouth was on hers, and his tongue inside her lips. Her breath caught in her throat as she began to ache for all of him and his lovemaking, but most especially his love. Remembering yesterday when their naked bodies had writhed, she moaned softly. He pulled away and laughed.

"Congratulations, *Mrs. Duke*," he whispered, wiping off her kiss with the back of his brown hand.

"I'm sorry," she sobbed quietly. "Make love to me."

"After Uncle Duncan's had you, too? Sorry. Maybe he wants my seconds, but I don't want his."

"Oh... How dare—"

She couldn't deny what he accused her of, so she closed her eyes, too ashamed to look at him.

He shot her a final, sardonic glance. Then he turned on his heels and leaped down the ladder, his boots crashing on the slender rungs, taking them two at a time.

She sank to her knees in the prickly hay.

Her mouth burning from his kisses, "Tony," she cried. "I'm sorry...."

"You got what you wanted—the ranch. The house...Duke Ranch."

"No. I got what you wanted."

"Gold digger." His final word rang sharper than a slap.

"Tony, you have to let me explain. I don't care what the others think of me...not even Aunt Patty. But...I have to explain to you."

"What's to explain? You made love to me. Then you married a rich old man—who hates his own family—for his money. You stole him from your aunt. I don't know what I was ever thinking of to fall so crazy in love with the shallow likes of you."

"Crazy in love? Were you really crazy in love?"

"Not anymore—Aunt Zoe," he said with malicious tenderness.

She crawled to the edge of the loft and began to cry in earnest. In the past her tears had always softened him, but today they had the opposite effect.

"Congratulations!" he snarled.

Then the barn doors slammed together behind him. He was gone, and she was alone in the dark. She heard his truck roar away, tires spitting white rocks and dust. She wrapped her arms around her waist and stayed where she was for a long time.

Then she touched her mouth with her trembling fingertips. She didn't hate him. No matter what he'd done or said, she never would. But that was only half her problem. She was married to the town's most disreputable citizen. It didn't matter that she had almost total amnesia about most of the wedding night and the ceremony.

The documents and photographs in her bedroom drawer were valid. The ring was real, too.

Slowly she climbed down from the loft and stumbled outside. She opened a gate and let herself into the closest pasture, which was ablaze with fluttering bluebonnets. The sun was hot pink against the distant horizon.

On impulse she peeled Duncan's big diamond off her slim finger. Her hand fisted around the hated gem. Closing her eyes, she spun round and round until she was so dizzy and breathless she could barely stand. Then she flung the ring as hard and as far as she could into the sea of flowers.

Trees whirled even after she opened her eyes. The earth beneath her feet felt uneasy. Hands outstretched, she groped at the air before slowly crumpling to the ground where she gagged and threw up.

She lay there in the thick blossoms for a long sickening interval before the will to live ebbed back into her body. Numbly she watched pink clouds float above her head and remembered lying on the ground like this, holding hands with Tony watching the clouds.

Tony… Ring or not, she was still married to the wrong man.

When it was dark, and she felt a little better, it became very important to find that ring. She stood up and began pacing the pasture methodically. Only, she couldn't find it.

She was married to the wrong man. She wanted out of this marriage, to give his ring back. Only she'd thrown the ring away.

But what did anything matter if Tony hated her?

What in the world was she going to do?

One

Nine years later

Anthony Duke felt so cold and alone that he shivered as the truck he drove hurtled through the high, wrought-iron gates of Memory Lane Cemetery.

"Slow down, son," his mother commanded.

"Hell." His boot tapped the brake.

Maybe he felt alone, but he wasn't. Henrietta Duke, his short, stout mother, who had an iron will, sat beside him, her gnarled fingers repeatedly rubbing circles around her kneecap. Noah, his hyper, eight-year-old son, was slumped in the back seat over one of his electronic games that made nerve-racking, beeping noises as he tapped the plastic keys.

Not that the illusion of solitude was strange to Anthony. He'd lived with it for years—when he'd been with Rene and Noah, as well as when he was out in some desolate pasture working cattle or in one of his breeding barns where he worked to improve deer stock to sell to other ranchers.

Something warm and bright had gone out of his life a helluva long time before Rene had died.

"Daddy! Do little boys ever get new mommies?"

Anthony hissed in a breath.

That same question again.

The lines around his mouth deepened. Rene had been dead a year. His ranch hands, his mother, and even his son were constantly pressuring to set him up with someone.

The cab of the pickup went deathly still. Was it that cemeteries seemed quieter than the rest of the world? Or was it just his guilty conscience? He had no right coming here.

"Do they get new mommies?"

Anthony's chest tightened. "We already had this conversation. No."

"What if you got married again? Would *she* be my new mommy?"

Anthony's fingers gripped the steering wheel as he headed toward Rene's grave. "We're here for your mother's birthday. You can't replace her. I'm not getting married again. Not in this lifetime. End of conversation."

But it wasn't. His mother, who was tuned in to him like radar, had her eye on him. Noah's questions and Anthony's answers lingered in the silence as Noah pressed his nose to the glass window to look at the orderly rows of tombstones.

"Why do people have to leave these junky artificial flowers and wreaths? Don't they know that they fade almost as soon as they put them out under fierce south Texas sun?'' his mother whispered.

''Because real flowers die.''

Anthony wished he hadn't said anything. When she turned to regard him, Anthony kept his eyes glued to the black asphalt. Still, he was aware of her fingers making those incessant circles on her knee.

''Well, except for the fake flowers, this place is one of the prettiest in the county,'' she exclaimed. ''Look at the trees! Except for the ebony and live oak, they've almost all lost their leaves,'' his mother continued.

Anthony gritted his teeth.

''The grass is mostly brown, but there's still quite a few patches of green,'' she continued, her fingers skimming her knee even faster.

''Do you think I'm blind? I can see trees and grass.''

The fingers froze on her kneecap. ''Edgy aren't we? You've been spending way too much time alone.''

''My life is none of your business.''

''What life? And don't tell me my son and my grandson are none of my business.''

Anthony slowed down as they neared the big gray tombstone that spelled out Duke.

''*D-U-K-E!* There she is!'' Noah cried.

Anthony shut the engine and opened his door, but the wind howled and slammed the heavy black door back in his face.

Guilt rushed through him. Who was he trying to fool with these visits to Rene's grave? He had no right to pretend grief for his perfect wife.

Well, he'd pretended for eight long years, hadn't

he? He and Rene had fooled everybody…except themselves. And except maybe his mother and Zoe's aunt Patty.

It was the first of February, yet this far south the afternoon was warm. The winter ice storm that gripped most of the United States had not reached south Texas. The temperature was in the eighties. He was wearing a white cotton shirt and a pair of old jeans. In another month, no telling how hot it would be. Or how cold.

"Looks like we've got the place to ourselves." Henrietta unsnapped her seat belt.

"Not many people make social calls to cemeteries," Anthony said.

"Shh," whispered Henrietta.

"Why is this necessary? There's nobody here."

"Mommy's here," Noah said quietly.

She's gone. Handle it. People die. Thousands, millions die, violently, peacefully or slowly and too young as Rene had. But the world keeps on turning. Time keeps passing.

People betray you in worse ways—they kill you and leave you alive.

Keeping his thoughts to himself, Anthony whirled around just as Noah stuffed his game into his sling pouch. The will to speak his mind died when he saw his son's grubby, little-boy hands with the black moons beneath the fingernails clutching a withered bunch of purple wine cups. How solemn his face had been as he'd knelt and picked them one by one, selecting the very best blossoms from the field in front of the house.

"How Rene loved flowers," Henrietta said.

"When do bluebonnets bloom, Dad?"

"March." Anthony bit out the word because blue-bonnets always reminded him of someone he preferred never to think about.

"'Member how she liked bluebonnets, Dad?"

A vision of a girl in blue gingham, not Rene, never Rene, sitting in a field of bluebonnets rose in Anthony's mind. He fought against the image, tried to dutifully replace it with Rene—fought and failed—as always.

Old girlfriends? Was everybody haunted by old girlfriends?

"Can we pick some and take 'em to Mom in March?"

"Sure we can." Anthony threw his door open and jumped out of the cab before it could blow back on him again.

"Are you all right?" his mother whispered.

Anthony shrugged. It was a test of his nerves when Noah shot out behind him and skipped eagerly through the tombstones with his bouquet and thermos toward Rene's grave. It was as if the boy expected her to rise up and hug him.

Daddy! Do little boys ever get new mommies?

"Why the hell does he drag us here every damn week?"

"Shh," his mother said.

What if you got married again?

"Just go with him," Henrietta said. "I know it isn't easy, but that's all you have to do."

"When is he going to get over her?"

"When are you?"

Their black eyes met and locked. Then a fierce gust nearly blew off his Stetson. He grabbed the sweat-stained, cowboy hat and pitched it into the back seat. When his longish, black hair fell against his brow, he combed back the thick strands with his callused fingers.

Why wouldn't his mother stop looking at him? He hated the way he always felt as transparent as glass around her.

As soon as he removed his hand, his hair blew back into his eyes. "Damn."

"'Bout time for a haircut," Henrietta said as he loped around the hood to her side of the truck.

"Don't nag," he said as he opened her door and helped her out.

Dead leaves crunched under his boots as he began walking. Soon he stepped up behind Noah, who was pouring water out of his thermos into the urns on either side of the massive gray tombstone. Carefully Noah knelt and tried to arrange the pitiful-looking flowers in the urns. He hadn't picked enough, and the wind caught the fragile blossoms and sent them tumbling across the brown grasses onto other graves.

Noah's face went white and stark. His pupils seemed pinpricks of black in the middle of blazing blue irises. "Dad—"

Noah was chasing after the flowers. The wind had scattered them in all directions. Soon Noah was back, his eyes brighter, his lashes wet. He looked up at his father, but Anthony stared at the two shredded flowers with the broken stems.

"I couldn't catch them."

The boy had straight yellow hair and big eyes that burned Anthony. Why did he have to look exactly like his mother?

Anthony knelt and beckoned Noah closer.

Noah, who used to fly into his mother's arms, held on to the flowers and hung his head.

Anthony flushed, not knowing what to do or say. So, he read the dates etched in the gray polished stone beneath Rene's name. She was buried beside his father, Anthony Bond Field.

"Your father died young, too," Henrietta said. "You were only a year old when they brought him home."

"I don't remember him. You wouldn't talk about him. Why did you take your maiden name back?"

"Because he ran off after you were born. He wasn't much of a husband, and he certainly wasn't much of a father. But the name Duke meant a lot more around here than Field, so I took it back. I had to be a mother and a father to you," Henrietta continued, "just as you have to be both for Noah."

Anthony stared at the dates on his father's tombstone. Then his gaze drifted back to Rene's stone.

Dates? Was that all a life added up to in the end? Rene was dead.

Noah backed away from him and ran to his grandmother. Slowly Anthony stood up.

He couldn't quit looking at those dates. Strange how he felt just as dead as she was. He closed his eyes and then covered them with his work-roughened palms. The wind rushed through the trees, battering his face, plastering his shirt against his broad chest. His hell went soul deep.

He stared at his mother who held his son.

When had it all gone wrong?

He knew when.

Again he saw *that* pixie face in the sea of bluebonnets. Not Rene's face. Never Rene's face. But a slim, young face with long-lashed, brown eyes and flyaway auburn hair, which she'd washed every day just so it would be shiny and soft for him. How he'd loved to wind that sweet-smelling silken mane through his fingers. Sometimes he'd used it to pull her close—the better to kiss her, to smell the lilacs in her shampoo, the better to love her.

Yes, he knew why. *She* was the reason he felt stripped of everything. He'd cheated Rene in so many ways…and all for a woman who'd betrayed him in the worst possible way.

He stared at his dead wife's tombstone. "What the hell can I do about any of it now, Rene? I'm thirty."

"Only thirty?" said his mother.

Anthony didn't realize he'd spoken aloud.

"You should start seeing new people," his mother said. She nodded toward Noah. "Make a life for him."

Noah, who looked thin and small, his golden hair spiking in the wind, was walking listlessly toward the truck.

"If you mean women…no way."

"You have to move on…for his sake," she said.

"You never remarried. I'll move on to dinner. But that's it. How about a steak?"

"You know you promised Noah we'd eat at Madame Woo's.…"

"That damned Chinese restaurant again! A man could starve on the mountain of grass flavored with soy sauce they serve there."

"Shh…"

Rene had been on a constant diet to keep her perfect figure. Madame Woo's had been her favorite Chinese restaurant.

"Why can't he let her go?" Anthony asked.

"Why can't you?"

For a second the pixie face wreathed in a garland of bluebonnets flashed with ghostly brilliance in his imagination. A flush burned up his neck and scalded his cheeks. He flinched with guilt. He turned before his mother could read him. Then he ran with long, impatient strides, as if a dozen demons were chasing him instead of one slim ghost in blue gingham, toward the big black truck on the asphalt drive.

Anthony scowled. "Noah!" he shouted. "Time to go!"

"Next time, can we bring her bluebonnets?"

"Sure. Sure. Just get in."

On the way to the restaurant, his mother told Noah stories and tried to maintain a cheerful atmosphere. From time to time she would pause and wait for Anthony to add something. When he didn't, her voice grew even brighter and her manner more determined at merriment.

Noah sat in the back, as silent as stone, his face glued to the back window as they sped away from the cemetery.

When they got to Madame Woo's, Noah ran ahead of the hostess and claimed Rene's favorite booth in the corner beside the windows. As the three of them settled into the red leather seats, the hostess started to remove the fourth place setting.

"No!" Noah cried.

"Will someone else be joining you?"

Nobody said anything. Noah grabbed the silverware and chopsticks and began trying to rearrange them on the black table. "I...I can't remember where the fork goes...." Blue eyes lasered in on Anthony.

"It doesn't matter. There's no fourth person. Take them away." Anthony scooped everything to one side.

Noah burst into tears. Before Henrietta could loop her arms around the boy, he jumped out of the booth and ran to the fish tank.

"Of all the insensitive…" Henrietta began.

"Rene's dead. It's a fact. I'm sorry about it," Anthony said. "But I didn't cause it, and I don't know what I can do about it. It's been a year."

"Today would have been her thirtieth birthday."

A waitress with two nose rings, an eyebrow ring, lots of ear studs and bunches of red pigtails appeared at their table, with a notepad and a big, toothy smile. "Can I take your drink order?"

"Water. We're in a hurry. I'll order everything at once," Anthony muttered. "Mother always takes number eighty."

"The vegetarian dish plus bean curds?" The waitress smacked a wad of gum and wrote laboriously.

"Without MSG," said Henrietta. "No sugar."

The pink wad of gum popped. "It doesn't come with sugar."

"I'll take sweet and sour pork," Anthony said. "And chicken strips for my son." Snapping the large, red menu shut, he went after Noah.

Noah was in no mood to return to the table, but he did. Not that he would allow his grandmother to pull him close. Not that he would smile or join in the conversation. When the food came, he stared at his father from beneath his brows and picked out the broccoli and mushrooms sulkily.

"Broccoli is good for you," Henrietta said.

Noah wrinkled his nose.

Finally even Henrietta quit her attempts at conversation. They ate in gloomy silence until the waitress with all the piercings slapped the restaurant bill and three fortune cookies on the table.

When Anthony reached for the last neatly folded cookie, an errant gust rattled the blinds.

Henrietta cracked her cookie open and directed a sharp glance toward her son. "A single kind word will keep one warm for years."

"Something wonderful is going to happen to you," Noah read, crumpling his fortune. "Like a new mommy, Nana?"

"Not that again," Anthony muttered warningly.

Noah leaned closer to his grandmother. "Do fortunes come true?"

"Sometimes…if you believe really hard," she whispered.

Noah shut his eyes very tightly. Again the wind gusted through the screens and made the blinds rattle.

"Don't feed him that pap." Anthony tore his cookie apart. One glance at the typed message had Anthony sucking in a breath and wadding the ridiculous fortune into a miniature ball the size of an English pea.

"What'd it say, Dad?"

"Nothing."

He got up from the table as his mother noisily unwadded his fortune. Her voice followed him as he made his way to the cash register to pay the bill.

"Reunion with a shady lady sets off fireworks."

"What's a shady lady, Nana?"

A pixie face in a sea of bluebonnets sprang to Anthony's mind. His hand shook as he slid his wallet out of his back pocket. His mother was watching him with that dangerous gleam in her eye.

"Zoe!" she said brightly. "Zoe Duke. Your Aunt Zoe. She's Shady Lomas's one and only shady lady! Anthony, remember that reporter who called her that when the scandal broke and your cousins sued her. This is great!"

"Don't mention Zoe Creighton to me—"

"Zoe Duke. Same as ours. She's your great-aunt, Noah."

"She is nothing to him." Anthony strode back to the table and ripped the fortune out of his mother's fingers before she could read it aloud again. "Don't give me that know-it-all smile, Mother." Angrily he stuffed the strip of paper into his pocket.

"You two want a ride home?" he demanded when they didn't budge. "Or is this a sleep-over?"

Before they could answer him, Anthony slammed out of the restaurant faster than if he'd been shot out of a cannon.

"Who's Aunt Zoe, Nana? What's the matter with Daddy?"

"Long story." Henrietta's mind was racing. Logic dictated she should despise Zoe for marrying her illegitimate half brother, the family's black sheep and the owner of Duke Ranch and the family house. But what woman worth her salt was dictated solely by logic? Zoe had the ranch and the house, and Anthony was still carrying a torch for her. Zoe was sweet and malleable. With proper training, she might make a perfect daughter-in-law. Besides, what other way could they get the ranch back? And then there was Noah, who wanted a new mommy.

"I like stories," Noah said.

"This one may be a doozie." What if Anthony still loved Zoe? What if she loved him back? What if there was a way to right all the old wrongs? What if a clever, liberal-minded woman tackled the problem?

Henrietta patted Noah's golden head. "Now you run along after your father. And don't you dare let him drive off without me."

When the glass door closed behind her grandson, Henrietta pulled her cell phone out of her purse and punched in the number of Patty Creighton, her maddening best friend. Patty had been lording it over the whole town, especially her, ever since Duncan had died and made Zoe the richest woman in several counties, even after all the lawsuits and settlements.

When Zoe had run off to Manhattan to play editor, Patty had installed herself in the Duke ranch house and pretended she was its mistress. Patty was every bit as flashy, maybe more so than Uncle Duncan had ever been even at his worst. She bought herself a brand-new red Cadillac every year.

"Why are all of them red?" Henrietta had asked Patty once in a showroom.

"So people won't forget him."

Aunt Patty had a dozen furs locked up in her deep freeze. She even had a younger boyfriend.

Money! What it did to people!

As usual, Patty, who was a total couch potato, didn't answer the phone.

"Patty, pick up," Henrietta harped when the machine came on. "This is Henrietta. Quit playing computer bridge. Get off your plump tail and pick up."

Patty had put on a couple of pounds a year since

they'd been girls. Thirty plus years at two pounds a year added up.

"Hello!" The single word of Patty's greeting was followed by heavy breathing.

"What's your darling Zoe, our shady lady, up to these days?"

Patty was still trying to catch her breath. "Plump tail…"

"Maybe you should see a heart specialist—"

"Is this conversation going somewhere? Or are you just stirring your long nose in my business for the hell of it?"

"I asked you about Zoe."

"I was just going to call her and find out."

"She's still single, isn't she?"

"Last I heard. She says New York is no city to catch a man."

"I've got the most brilliant idea."

"Oh, dear! This sounds like trouble."

"With a capital *T*. It has to do with your niece and my stubborn son."

Patty caught her breath. "Shoot!"

Two

"**W**ow! You've got another bestseller!"

"I'm just the editor," Zoe whispered.

"Spare me." Ursula, the editorial director of Field and Curtis Publishing, was black and gorgeous. More than gorgeous. Even though she was in her late forties, she had the face and figure of a supermodel. Usually she was self-contained and serene, sailing through hectic days at the office without a trace of visible emotion.

Not today. Ursula was weeping and laughing as she read Veronica Holiday's manuscript. Veronica had that effect on readers. The book was very late, months overdue—as usual—but it was another winner.

Ursula, who was an old friend of Aunt Patty's from her Vassar days, had an impressive corner office with views of skyscrapers as well as a wedge of greenery in the hazy distance.

Someday, Zoe thought, her gaze skimming her boss's sleekly modern desk with its neatly piled manuscripts. Mentally she compared it to her own cluttered, windowless cubbyhole littered with notes to herself, unopened mail and dog-eared manuscripts—not to mention the posters of movie stars tacked all over her walls. A bookworm by nature and a frustrated writer, Zoe loved working with authors. It was all the rest of it—juggling her correspondence, the deadlines and the editorial meetings that stressed her. And she was an absolute failure when it came to the politics of her department. Why couldn't she have been born with a gene for organization?

Zoe hovered anxiously over her boss's shoulder. Ursula continued dabbing her eyes. "More tissue?"

Ursula flipped the last page, turned it over. Then she shuffled through the mailer to make sure she hadn't lost some pages. "Not again."

"I…I'm afraid…"

When Ursula's perfectly shaped black brows rose ever so slightly in her boldly classic face, Zoe's stomach did a somersault.

"What? What happens next?" Ursula asked.

To cover her fear Zoe took her time lowering her damp tissue from her brown eyes. Smoothing a wayward tangle of auburn that had escaped her ponytail, she bought a few more seconds to mull on her answer. "What? What happens, er, next?"

"That's right."

Zoe tried to look innocent or suave or whatever it was a working girl—correct that—a working *person* in publishing was supposed to look like. Correct that. *An editor.*

Her mind began to race. Yes, she was an editor! No. Not just an editor. An associate editor—and a rising star in her own right. And all because she had discovered Veronica Holiday. Only Veronica hadn't been a household name then. She'd been Juanita Lopez, a plain, plump nobody with a chip on her shoulder. No, make those twin boulders on both her shoulders.

Zoe had discovered her in the slush pile…when she should have been at an editorial meeting.

Nobody would ever forget that day at Field and Curtis. Ursula had sent her secretary after her. Zoe had been on the floor of her office, pages everywhere, reading this weird, wonderful novel, *Bad Boyfriends.*

The novel, which was about a married woman who couldn't get over her old bad-boy boyfriend, had held Zoe spellbound. Apparently, the old boyfriend hadn't been able to forget about the woman either because he was stalking her. As usual, Veronica had sent that first book in without an ending. Only Zoe had known how it had to end. And she'd called her. The resulting book had been that year's sensation. Since then every Veronica Holiday book had done better than the last one.

The trouble was, Zoe's claim to fame, her job, her career, *everything* depended on Veronica, and if Veronica was anything, besides being famous, talented and highly neurotic, it was in a word—undependable. Oh! And superdifficult.

Take her hair. It was a different color every time she made one of her surprise trips to New York. Last night it had been orange. And spiky. And her weight. Six months ago she'd been a blimp in flowing, big-flowered gowns. Back then she'd hidden beneath big hats that had made her look even heavier.

Last night she'd been a Titian-haired wraith in a skimpy, see-through blouse and skintight, snakeskin pants. She'd had a slim, new nose that made her ever so much prettier.

"What went with the silky blond curls?" Zoe had asked while they'd sat in oversize highback velvet chairs. She and Veronica had munched figs from Venetian goblets bigger than their heads at the famous restaurant Veronica had demanded Zoe take her to.

"Blond curls weren't me."

"I can see that."

"Where's the rest of it?" Ursula now repeated, her silken tone barely concealing a steely edge of impatience.

Three police cars shot beneath Ursula's office, screaming toward the park in the midmorning gray light. Velvet chairs, gleaming gilt, mahogany wainscoting, orange hair and the slim, new nose dissolved. Zoe realized her mind had been a million miles away.

"What happens next?" Ursula whirled around in her chair, and stared at her.

Zoe had asked Veronica the same question last night. And Veronica had wailed. "We'll…we're…I mean Veronica's on top of that," Zoe said.

"She's really painted herself into a corner this time."

"That's what makes her books so great," Zoe murmured defensively. "Her characters are all so vulnerable and impulsive, and they get themselves into the most impossible jams.''

''The plots are as wild as her characters. The barge that contains enough toxins to destroy the ocean is breaking apart in a storm. The hero has been stabbed and is locked in the bowels of the ship. The bad guy, who's a sex fiend, has the girl and their baby. The hero…''

''When Czar went after him with a meat hook, I nearly died.''

Zoe had always had an overactive imagination. She loved stories and had a headful of fantasies. In fact, she still had fantasies about a certain cowboy from her own past.

''Don't think about him,'' said a silent voice in Zoe's head. ''You're doing it, anyway,'' said another.

Ursula ran long slim fingers through her sleek cap of straight black hair. ''What are you doing here?''

''This is my job. I work here.''

''Get to the Plaza Athenee. Get Veronica up. Get her writing.''

''But she has her heart set on lunch at the Russian Tea Room. She's got a new gold outfit that matches the decor.''

''Does she do anything but eat and sleep and shop for outrageous clothes?''

''Men. Since she got skinny and pretty, she's started chasing men. She's a walking disaster when it comes to men.''

''When?''

''When what?'' Zoe asked.

''Knock. Knock.'' Ursula rapped her desk.

"Hello. Lunch? Russian Tea Room? Bestseller with no ending?"

"Twelve-thirty."

When Ursula's dark-chocolate eyes fell to her designer wristwatch, she gasped. "You're late. As always. Find her! You're her muse! Get her writing! Now!"

"Two o'clock. No! Ten minutes past two!"

The snooty waiter in elegant black with a nose as long as a suicidal ski jump, was getting surlier by the second. He must've asked Zoe a dozen times if she wanted to order.

Zoe's stomach grumbled. "Veronica, where are you?"

When two stylish ladies at the next table turned and stared at her, Zoe cupped her hands over her mouth. Bad habit—talking to yourself. Besides that, Zoe was underdressed in a black skirt and rumpled sweater. She didn't ooze old money or new money, either, like most of the other diners did. "I'm on an expense account," she said under her breath. "A very large expense account."

Instead of reading the menu again, which she'd already memorized, Zoe's gaze flitted from the door to her own pale, disheveled reflection in the mirrored walls. Masses of auburn hair framed her stark white oval face.

She looked anxious. She was alone. In a word—she was pathetic.

"Girl, don't you know that big hair is a no-no in New York." She fluffed the unruly stuff. "I should cut it."

As always the other voice inside her head talked

back. Did everybody have voices in their heads? Or just frustrated writers who became editors?

"You've been telling yourself that, ever since you got here six years ago."

"Vanity. That's what's stopping me. I'm a Southern girl at heart. Why, every little-town Texas girl knows that big hair is power. Power over…"

Unbidden came the memory of Tony's hands in her hair.

Tony. Why couldn't she get over him? What was it with these fantasies about Tony?

Did women ever get over their old boyfriends? Or were youthful loves part of a woman's unique personal myth and mystery? Maybe Zoe identified with Veronica's work because she and Veronica shared an incredible vulnerability, an impulsiveness that got them into all kinds of trouble and into these disturbing fantasies about their old boyfriends.

Tony had loved her long hair. Loved to play with it and kiss it. Loved to watch it blow in the warm, south-Texas spring winds. She'd lain on top of him in the loft, and he'd wrapped it around his throat and made her feel like a goddess. Nobody in Manhattan had ever made her feel so adored.

It had been nine years since Tony.

"This is bad! Don't think about him!"

"But he's the reason I ran away after college and stayed gone. Not the scandal."

After Duncan's death and the vicious legal battles with his daughters over his inheritance, Zoe had finished college. Upon graduation, she'd wanted to get far away from Sandy Lomas and from Anthony and Rene and their new baby, from everybody in south

Texas who thought she was evil because she'd married the rich old reprobate.

Was it her fault Duncan had had a heart attack when she'd told him she'd lost his ring and wanted a divorce or an annulment? Apparently, a week before their marriage, Duncan had learned he had a huge, inoperable aneurysm. He'd confessed to her, "I decided if I was going to die, I want to go out with a bang! You're the bang!"

Duncan had pulled through that first crisis, only to get into a royal fight with both his daughters in the hospital over his marriage.

"She's got to be thirty years younger than you are," they'd screamed.

"Please—I'm a dying man."

Indeed, tubes were snaking from dozens of gurgling machines to various parts of his body. Bags of drugs were dripping into his thin arm.

"She's after your money, you old fool."

"Oh, is she?" he'd pulled Zoe closer, and dozens of red lights began to flash on his monitor. "Then I'd best give her what she wants, hadn't I?"

They should have known how perverse he was. First thing, he'd changed his will and left Zoe everything. Then he'd sent his girls and Anthony and Henrietta copies of the will just to stir them up. The girls had gotten so hopping mad, they'd accosted him again, this time on the main steps of the Methodist Church. He'd grabbed his heart and had a second attack and died in Zoe's arms on the spot.

His last words to Zoe as she'd knelt over him on those concrete steps had been, "I don't care what it costs, don't let them have a dime. They murdered me. Oh, and finish college.... Don't let our crazy marriage stop you from finish—'' He'd gasped, and his eyelids had fluttered. He'd smiled and was gone.

''Somebody help him! Please,'' Zoe had screamed.

Suddenly Anthony had knelt beside her. She'd caught his clean, male scent and had realized how everything about him had haunted her.

''I'm afraid he's gone,'' he'd said.

''It's my fault.''

He'd cupped her chin and lifted it so that she was forced to meet his blazing eyes. ''No,'' he'd said gently, surprising her. ''He was just a very sick man.''

''Oh, Anthony…''

Rene had called to him then. He'd gotten up and taken her hand.

''See you around, Zoe,'' Rene had said.

Of course Zoe had settled with his daughters, and the girls had gotten way more than a few dimes. But that hadn't stopped them from gossiping all over town about Zoe Duke being a gold digger. The talk was still so fierce Zoe couldn't go home without people turning their heads and treating her as if she was a scarlet woman.

But it was the sightings of a certain tall, dark cowboy and his darling little son that drove her back to New York with the fresh determination to show the world—to show him—she didn't need anybody's money.

She could make it on her own. She *had* made it.

Liar. She was still running from Tony. She couldn't forget the last time she'd seen him. He'd been smiling tenderly down at Rene in church. Rene had been so sick and thin, but her smile for her husband had made her radiant. How sad he'd looked then, how utterly devastated. How much he must've loved Rene, his perfect wife. And, oh, how lost and abandoned and petty and small Zoe had felt watching them.

Because of him, she'd come to New York broken-hearted, disillusioned but determined to make it big in this tough, tough city. Anthony was the one she had to prove herself to. She was still trying to show *him,* drat his hide. And she would. She would!

He'd had the perfect marriage to the beautiful, perfect Rene, who'd given birth to the perfect son. Now that Rene was dead, he couldn't get over her. Aunt Patty talked about him more than ever, telling Zoe about his weekly visits with his little boy to the cemetery.

"He always takes wildflowers. His heart is in the grave. He says he'll never marry—"

"I'm sorry for him, but please, don't tell me about him!"

"His little boy— He's a bright little monkey. A lot like Rene. He needs a mother."

"Don't."

"What about you? When are you going to get married?" Aunt Patty had asked slyly.

"Been there. Done that. Remember?"

"I am talking about a real marriage."

"I know you mean well, but that question is extremely annoying. Surely you've got something better to do than to meddle in my life, which is something you don't know anything about, Aunt Patty."

"Do you have a boyfriend?"

"Abdul."

"What kind of name is that?"

"His last name's Izzar. He's from Iraq."

"Oh. Don't guys like that have harems?"

"Abdul is an American citizen now."

"Abdul Izzar. Well, I wouldn't tell the folks here about him, honey."

"He's a commodities trader. Very smart."

"Why don't you come home to Texas where you belong?"

"Because I came to this city with a big dream."

"One you have yet to realize."

"Oh, Aunt Patty…"

"What's wrong with getting married and having babies?"

"We are living on an overpopulated planet."

"You just think that because you live in New York and read too much."

Zoe wasn't sure she'd accomplished anything in the years she'd lived in Manhattan other than fall on her face about ten thousand times. New York had a way of gobbling the unwary whole. At night sometimes she woke up feeling lost and all alone, her head spinning with dreams about Tony.

Her dream was always the same. At first, she was in the dark. It was misty, and she was all alone and trembling with fear. Then she felt someone there and the mist parted. Tony's brown hand was reaching for her, pulling her close. She wanted him so much and she could see the desire in his eyes. But she always woke up before they made love. Then she would lie awake—aching.

Nine years. How long did it take to get over somebody who hadn't even let her explain, who'd gone on with his own life as if he'd never much cared about her in the first place?

When she'd been unable to land a job in Manhattan on her own, Aunt Patty had called her old friend, Ursula, told her Zoe was a bookworm who had several unpublished novels in her attic, and Ursula had set up an interview.

Zoe was fiddling with her silverware and staring blankly at an enormous golden tree dripping with lighted eggs when her cell phone rang.

"It's me-e-e," Veronica drawled, her north Texas voice as whiny and twangy as a loose guitar string. Only last night she'd confided she was taking voice lessons to eliminate the accent. She didn't apologize for being late, Zoe noted. Bad sign.

"I can't do lunch," Veronica blurted. "I don't even know if I can live until tomorrow."

"Oh, dear."

"I pigged out at this deli, too. Three bagels. Cheese. Croissants, too. A cream puff even—"

"Croissants!"

"Oozing with butter and raspberry jam. Sugar! I ate sugar!"

Zoe's stomach rumbled. "This is bad. Where are you? I'll come...."

"I got on the Web."

Oh, dear. "I told you never to do that again."

"I...I was going to write. I felt a glimmer...you know, like the story was beckoning me. So, I turned on my laptop."

"This is good."

"But..."

"But..." Zoe hung on the word.

"Some bitch wrote *Lovers Don't Tell* stinks." Veronica burst into tears.

"*Lovers* made number one on every single list that

matters! There are lots of crazy, jealous people out there who need to get a life. Unfortunately, they all have keyboards and write nasty critiques.''

''She killed me.''

''Look, just come to lunch.''

''Food? Now? I can barely snap the waistband of my gold mini. My black mesh panty hose keep sliding under my belly the way they used to when I was so fat. I'm going for a walk in the park.''

''This is good. You're going for a walk in the park in a gold mini and black mesh stockings. I...I'll meet you.''

''I'm too suicidal for company.''

''Which is why—''

Veronica hung up.

Zoe stared at her cell phone. It was all she could do not to pound it on the table.

''Excuse me, madam—'' The snooty waiter stared down his impressive nose at Zoe's big hair and frumpy black sweater.

''I'm not a member of an alien species,'' she said tartly.

''Would you like to order, madam?''

''Check, please,'' Zoe retorted.

West of midtown, Chelsea, the heart of the garment district, Zoe's neighborhood, was like a lot of young, affluent areas in Manhattan. Only, lots of the attractive couples walking together in front of the nineteenth-century town houses, holding hands, were men.

It was late. The sun had disappeared behind the town houses, and the streets and sidewalks were engulfed in shadows. Zoe felt harassed, stressed and even more ineffectual than usual as she hurried past the Flatiron building toward home.

The day had gone from bad to worse. She'd walked in the park for an hour looking for Veronica.

No gold mini or black mesh hose. So Zoe had gone back to the office.

Ursula had caught her in the copying room. "So, how's the book?"

"She's working on it."

No sooner had Ursula walked out than Zoe had felt so guilty about her lie that she had put the manuscript in wrong and jammed the last antiquated copy machine that had still been working. All the other editors had snapped at her because everybody had deadlines and couldn't copy anything.

Every time her phone rang, Zoe had jumped. But Veronica hadn't called. Finally, Zoe had left work early and was headed home on the hope that Veronica might get bored with her own company and turn up on her doorstep.

The sidewalks were jammed as she walked past people pushing garment racks. She knew the rules. Keep to the right. Walk fast. No eye contact.

This city. So many people racing places. Were any of them like her, going nowhere? Faking it when they weren't fantasizing about old boyfriends and old loves?

"We're like ants spinning, going nowhere on this tiny mudball."

"Veronica, where are you?"

"Don't talk to yourself. Don't talk to yourself."

"You're doing it. You're doing it."

Ed and Gujarat, the guys who lived in the apartment below hers, came out of Zoe's brownstone town house, holding hands. They lived on the fourth floor. Sometimes they carried her groceries up and then stayed and drank wine with her on her balcony.

Ed raised his eyebrows and looked surprised to see her. Gujarat nodded slyly.

"Hey, guys," she said smiling.

"By the sound of that banging upstairs, we thought you were home already," Gujarat said.

"We were happy for you." Ed worked his brow again.

She stopped at her mailbox and then ran up the stairs without giving their remarks nearly enough thought. She was always doing that—missing clues any idiot would have picked up on and then catching them later.

She was only slightly out of breath by the time she'd climbed the stairs to her front door. The forty-block walk from her office kept her in pretty good shape.

"Patience," she whispered as she fumbled in her purse. It always took her a while to find her key in the scramble of dollar bills, credit card receipts and lipstick cases.

Finally she found it and opened the door. Abdul's computer monitor with all the little numbers that flashed constantly across the screen was on.

Abdul. Right! She stomped the floor. Her hands fisted on the straps of her purse. Then she flung it onto the couch. She'd promised to cook steak and make a salad. He was coming to dinner. Oh, dear. She'd forgotten again.

They didn't live together, but he'd installed the monitor so that when he was there, he could watch it out of the corner of his eye.

Well, she couldn't cook. Not tonight. They'd have to do deli.

"Super Cat! Kitty, kitty, kitty…"

Usually her big fat tiger-striped baby came running to meet her. Zoe stepped inside the kitchen, picked up a can of gourmet cat food and slid it under her electric can opener. When the opener buzzed, and the lid popped open, she blew tuna fumes and called him again.

"Tuna, your favorite. Super Cat! Where are you, sweetie?"

Genuinely worried when he didn't come, she dumped the tuna into Super Cat's bowl and stepped into the hall. When her toe snagged on something, she looked down. Gold fabric littered the hallway. She knelt and picked up a gold, uplift bra. A man's dark-blue tie and black mesh panty hose were tangled in the golden bra straps. Zoe fingered the soft blue tie and nearly strangled on her next breath.

"I know you. I picked you out at Macy's and gave you to Abdul. I looped you around his neck last Christmas."

"Stop talking to yourself."

She looked up. Clothes seemed to have exploded off bodies in her hallway. Her eyes followed a trail of slinky gold and the rest of Abdul's clothing—his dress shirt, two black socks, only one black shoe—to her bedroom door.

She didn't realize her headboard had been slamming rhythmically against the wall, until the banging stopped.

"Oh…oh…oh…" A woman was panting in the bedroom.

Then Zoe saw the gold mini.

Oh, dear. This was bad.

Mentally Zoe counted the months since she'd last had sex. And that hadn't been rambunctious, head-board-banging sex. Or meaningful sex. Or anything at all, really. Since then, she and Abdul had just gotten interested in other things. Funny, she hadn't even thought about sex—except when she woke up dreaming about Anthony—until now.

"Meow!" A striped, brown paw reached out from under the hall closet door and snagged her ankle. A claw sank into her flesh. Blood spurted.

"Sweetie!" In a daze, she opened the closet door, and a roly-poly blob of brown and gold fur with flattened ears brushed past her into the kitchen. Super Cat was frantic for his bowl of tuna.

The bedroom door cracked, and Abdul stuck his black head out. "*Habeebti,* you're home early."

Zoe's tongue hit the tip of her front teeth and stuck there. Her throat froze. She tried to say something, but somehow she was so upset, all she could do was mouth soundless gulps of air.

Then she exchanged a wild, panicked glance with Super Cat before the cat wisely hunkered down to lick at his tuna.

Without a glance toward Abdul, Zoe sucked in an indignant breath. Then she whipped the clothes off the floor, went to her kitchen window and threw them out onto the street.

"*Habeebti!* What are you doing?" Abdul yelled.

"Don't you dare *habeebti* me!" He'd taught her that *habeebti* meant darling in Arabic. When pedestrians looked up, she waved his jockey shorts at them.

"Not my jockey shorts!" Abdul shrieked.

She dropped them and turned to smile brightly as Abdul, who, wearing only a towel, stomped barefoot into her kitchen.

"Out!" she purred, turning on him.

"This woman with red hair came here. Said she was looking for you. She attacked me."

"And you surrendered. Out!"

Green eyes slitted, Super Cat stopped eating tuna and glared at him for good measure.

"You locked Sweetie Baby in the closet."

"I can't believe I did that."

Zoe went to her front door and opened it for him. "I can't, either. If you don't go, there's going to be blood."

He scooted past her out into the hall. "You sure about this?"

She went over to the table, ripped the plug out of the wall, and carried his monitor to him.

"Take your monitor thingy." She rammed it into his hands.

"This city. What it does to people."

"Not this city—you. And her. It's been a crazy day—even for me!"

In a flash of impulsive brilliance, she yanked her towel from his waist, took a final glance at his sleek brown body that had reminded her of Anthony's and slammed the door in his startled face.

"Be honest. You only dated him because he sort of looks like Tony."

"Liar."

"Hush. You're doing it again. Hush."

Abdul banged on the door and screamed, "You'll be sorry!"

"No. I won't. You don't even read."

"What? I can't stand here naked and scream through your thick door."

"Then go get your jockey shorts. They're out on the street." She shot her dead bolt. "You tricked me. You read book reviews. You don't know anything."

"I know how to make money!"

"The less said at such times the better. Just go home." She stomped down her hall and yelled, "Veronica!"

No answer.

When Zoe opened her bedroom door, Veronica, clad only in bedsheets, was curled up like a sex kitten, scribbling frantically on a yellow legal pad she'd stolen from Zoe's desk.

"I was writing on that tablet."

"Go away," Veronica whispered desperately. "I've got it! Eureka! I've got the ending! Wow, you were wonderful when you came home! All that passion! You're gonna love my ending!"

"No, I won't. Because you're not going to write it! I'm going to part that orange mop of yours with...with..."

A big black umbrella stood in her corner. Zoe grabbed it and stalked toward Veronica. "With this umbrella."

Veronica leaped out of bed, trailing sheets and the lavender bedspread. "You're sore about Abdul?" Veronica was scrambling to pull her train of sheets through the bathroom door. "That dud, who can't talk about anything but positions in deutsche marks and Swiss francs...even in bed—I did you a huge favor."

They stared at each other.

"Huge," Veronica repeated.

She had a point.

Not that this was any time to concede high moral ground to the *other woman*. Still, Zoe dropped her umbrella an inch or two. Slowly she stepped out into her hall, closed the door and sagged against it.

"I'm a failure in every department. As a writer. As an editor. As a woman. As a New Yorker."

"Oh, and don't forget, you still have fantasies about your old boyfriend."

"You're doing it again."

"Shut up."

"I can talk to myself if I want to."

Zoe's kitchen phone began to ring.

Still muttering to herself, she walked back down the hall.

"How's single life in New York?" croaked Aunt Patty.

"Bad question," Zoe admitted.

"Bad timing?"

"Don't gloat."

"Who me?" A thoughtful pause. "How's Abdul?"

"He's history."

Aunt Patty emitted what sounded like a sigh of pure bliss. "Why, this is great timing. You sound as miserable as Tony."

"Tony's miserable?" The thought was too dangerously comforting.

"Why, Henrietta was telling me just yesterday," Aunt Patty continued.

"Stop right there! I'll hang up if you talk about him. He and I are not, hear this, we are not orbiting the same sun anymore."

"He's single. You're single. You're both miserable."

"Reality check. We broke up nine years ago. He lives in Texas. I live in New York."

"One of you has to make the first move."

"Not me—"

I still dream about him. I never date anybody who doesn't look like him.

"Aunt Patty—"

Neither of them said anything for a long moment. Twisting the phone cord, Zoe sank to the floor. "What's wrong with me, Aunt Patty? I messed everything up with Tony. I married Duncan to get even. Duncan married me for a lot of harebrained reasons, too. I was so stupid. Stupid. Stupid. And ever since…I haven't gotten one bit smarter. Why can't I do anything right?"

"It's not too late to start over."

"You got me this job. But I'm no good at it."

"Ursula loves you."

"I never meet my deadlines. I turn all my authors into prima donnas. I can't file. She's always telling me I can't prioritize. I…I can't say what I really think in editorial meetings…. Oh, and I break all the machinery."

"But you discovered that…that—"

"That monster!"

"How can you call her that? I've read all her books! Her characters are as crazy as all the people I know. And she dedicates all her books to you!"

"Let's not talk about her! I'm quitting. I'm leaving New York for good."

"Great. You can come home."

"Who was I kidding? I can't make it here. I can't

make it anywhere. If I didn't have Duncan's money, I'd be worse off than those homeless people sleeping in cardboard boxes in the park.''

''Just come home.''

She thought about Tony, about her crazy dreams. She'd never get over him if she went home. ''I have to forget Tony.''

''Why?''

''I can't come home, and that's final.''

Another long, pensive silence.

Aunt Patty's voice was different, cautious. ''Maybe, then, maybe you just need a little vacation. I could give you a week of my time share… anywhere in the world. I've already got a week traded for Greece.''

''Greece?''

''Henrietta and I traded our time-shares for a week next month. And now we can't go….'' Her voice trailed off.

Aunt Patty sounded a little funny, but Zoe didn't really pay attention.

''No way am I going to Greece.''

''I'll fax you the brochure.''

''I love the ending!'' Ursula cried, elated. ''Yes!'' She made a fist and punched the air above her head. ''Yes.''

''Good. Maybe you can be her editor from now on.'' Zoe leaned across her desk and laid a rather wordy letter of resignation in front of her boss.

Ursula got halfway through the first paragraph and tore it in two.

''You can't quit. I won't let you.''

"I am a complete failure. I've failed at everything."

"You're Veronica's muse."

"No."

"She said she was sorry. She sent you bushels of roses."

"She's too crazy for me."

"Her endings make her crazy. They make us all crazy. Take a month off. Go to Greece. You've earned a vacation."

"Did you talk to Aunt Patty?"

"She called me last night. She's very worried about you. Go to Greece. The time-share in Rhodes sounds wonderful. Think about your life. Figure out what you want to do with it. Don't throw your career as an editor away just on an impulse."

"Impulse?"

"That's your weakness. You're always leaping before you look...like Veronica's characters. You married Duncan.... Go to Greece."

"Greece? Why Greece? What's in Greece?"

"Your future. Trust me." But Ursula wouldn't meet her eyes.

Again, some instinct warned Zoe that Aunt Patty had told Ursula more than she was telling her, that Greece was somehow dangerous.

"Why Greece? What's in Greece?"

"Maybe the man of your dreams," Ursula replied.

Three

"**A**thens. Why can't I get excited about Athens, city of dust, bougainvillea, roses and short, boxy buildings?" Zoe wondered as her bus rolled through dry, red hills out to the airport on the edge of the city.

"This is the capital of Greece. You'd think somebody would think to build at least one hotel by the airport?"

"Hello? I had to take a bus into the center of town to find lodgings, an hour-long ride through thick traffic. I want Manhattan. Chelsea. Super Cat. And somebody besides me to talk to."

In a word, her vacation hadn't even begun, and she was already homesick and sick of her own company.

The bus she'd caught this morning at Syntagma Square in the heart of Athens rolled to a final stop.

Zoe, who was at the front of the bus, grabbed her backpack, leaped off and headed inside the terminal.

With difficulty she read the Greek signs. This country was like a perpetual eye exam. Traveling by herself was no fun, either. She felt so alone, so cut off and so dangerously vulnerable somehow. But at least most of the men left her alone. Greece reminded her of Mexico, only it felt safer. Still, it was a long way from Manhattan and everything that was familiar.

"Being alone is the whole point," Aunt Patty had said yesterday when she had called to wish Zoe a safe journey. "You'll have time to think. About your future."

"You never go anywhere by yourself. You always go with Henrietta Duke," Zoe had replied.

"Who never shuts up and refuses to play games with me."

"Wasn't she going to Rhodes with you? How come you two canceled?"

Aunt Patty had coughed nervously, mentioned doctors and changed the subject rather quickly. Which seemed odd now that Zoe thought about it. Yesterday Zoe had been in such a hurry to finish all her last-minute chores so she could make her plane. Why hadn't she paid more attention to Aunt Patty's evasive nonanswers?

Henrietta owned a time-share, and usually the two of them traded for the same week in the same locale. Zoe should have asked about her aunt's little cough. Had the two of them had a fight? Would Henrietta be in her time-share?

When Zoe got to the gate for her flight to Rhodes, she was three hours early and spacey from jet lag.

She sank down into a plastic chair and pulled out a paperback novel. The words blurred.

Even after a restful night's sleep in a small hotel in the Plaka with views of the Acropolis, she still felt strange and disoriented. It was weird to step on a plane in the U.S and get off in a foreign country. It was like some vital piece of herself hadn't arrived. It was probably 2:00 a.m. back in New York. Super Cat would be curled up on her pillow waiting for her to come to bed.

What was she doing here? Zoe hadn't had one coherent thought about her life on the endless flights to get here. Or her future.

If you ignored the columns and all those glorious naked male statues and the olive trees, Athens reminded her of west Texas. Dry, red dirt. West Texas had never been her favorite locale.

Her Greek hotel had been tinier and stuffier than a roadside motel in west Texas, too. She'd had to put her key in a slot in the wall just to turn on the electricity.

She opened her book and was soon lost in the story. She didn't look up until it was almost time for her flight and the lounge was filled with people.

Thinking she'd better go to the ladies' room, she slid her book into her purse. Then she got up and rushed down a wide hall. She was heading for a sign with a little fat lady above the door, when a small boy with straight yellow hair and loose shoelaces streaked out of the men's room and slammed into her so hard she almost fell on top of him.

''Oops,'' she said gently.

He'd been juggling a video game and sling pouch filled with little stuffed animals in one hand and a cola cup in the other. She caught the video game just as his soda sprayed all over her black skirt.

"Sorry," he whispered.

She helped him to his feet. "Careful." She handed his electronic game to him. "Are you okay?" she quizzed softly.

He was beet red. When he was done stuffing his game into his sling pouch, he stared up at her, his blue eyes desperately intense. "I've lost my daddy."

He rubbed at his eyes, and for a minute she was afraid he might cry. So she took his hand and pressed it reassuringly. "It's okay. I promise."

He gulped in a big breath of air, and she nodded.

He had thick straight yellow bangs, slim pointy ears, freckles and a gap between his two front teeth, which seemed huge compared to his baby teeth.

"We'll find him," she said.

She was about to stand up when a pair of long, black pointy-toed cowboy boots planted themselves on either side of the boy.

On either side of her, too.

Before she had time to look up, an all-too-familiar voice made her shiver. "There you are you little rascal! Damn it. I've been looking everywhere—"

"Do not cuss. He's just a little boy," Zoe said.

"My little boy! My son, damn it!"

Instantly the boy's blue eyes brimmed with tears.

"Oh, dear. I really do know that voice." She gasped as her eyes ran upward from his boots, up his long legs, up, up, up to his grim, dark, chiseled face.

Recognizing her old boyfriend instantly, she froze.

"Tony!" Then the thought came, *Aunt P! You witch!*

Zoe's heart thudded wildly as she stood up to confront Anthony Duke. "Oh, dear. Oh, dear," she murmured to herself.

He cocked his head to one side. His brows arched.

"Hello, Tony," she whispered in the chilliest tone she could manage.

In that long moment before he spoke, the seconds ticked by one by one, as slowly as hours.

A jet rumbled down the runway. The floor beneath her shuddered. A blush heated her cheeks.

"*Zoe Duke?* Aunt Zoe?" he mocked.

"Oh, dear."

"What in the hell are you doing here?" he demanded.

"I asked you not to cuss in front of your son."

"I want an answer." His cold black gaze filled her with dread. "Don't bother. I can guess." He gave her a slow, insinuating appraisal. "Of all the low-down, sneaky…"

"Wh-what are you doing in Athens?" she stammered.

Had he always been so huge? So intimidating?

No. He'd been tall, but he'd been more boy than man. Now he was filled out. He was a big man, whose broad shoulders were heavily muscled from real work on the range and not from some expensive, Manhattan gym. He was dark from the sun and long hours in the saddle. His large brown hands were rough.

Oh, dear. And he was handsome. Too handsome. Her pulse was racing just because he was standing so close. She hated the way she was overreacting to him.

"I fell down, Daddy," the boy said. "I hurt my knee."

When Tony knelt, his large, masculine, brown hands ran gently over the boy's legs to make sure he was all right. Just watching those hands made the world slow down and other conversations die away.

Old boyfriends. She was always buying novels that had to do with old boyfriends.

The little boy, Rene's son, was staring up at her. His big eyes blazed as startlingly blue as Texas bluebonnets, just like Rene's used to, and yet he looked so vulnerable.

"Rene," Zoe murmured. How sad it must have been for her to get sick and know she had to leave such a beautiful little boy.

He was wearing a torn beige T-shirt and long, wrinkled shorts. All his clothes were too big. His athletic shoes were too big, too. He needed a mother to dress him, a mother to cut his hair, to make him wash his hands, to tie his shoes, to scrub his fingernails.

"You know my mommy, too?" The little boy looked up at her, his intense eyes bewildered.

"You…must be Noah—" Zoe tried to look anywhere but at Tony and his darling son.

"Should he call you Auntie Zoe?" Tony drawled in a cocky tone that set her on edge. "Technically, he's your great-nephew and I'm…I'm your nephew."

"By marriage!" she exhaled the word.

"Yes. *By marriage.*"

She felt a wealth of regrets.

"So, what are you doing here, Zoe? When my mother talked me into this trip, I should have suspected a trick," Tony accused.

"Me?" She stiffened. "I'm the one who's been

scammed. Ever since Rene died, Aunt P can't stop talking about you.''

''Any more than my busybody mother can stop talking about you,'' he murmured, his deep voice softening in some subtle manner that was highly disturbing. And did he have to rake her body with those hooded black eyes of his?

''Wh-why can't they accept the fact that we hate each other?'' she asked.

''Apparently they never got over us breaking up.'' His gaze lingered on her swelling bosom beneath her dark sweater.

''I would have forgotten you years ago if…if…''

''So, you haven't forgotten me,'' he mused dryly.

''How could I, er, when…when Aunt Patty brings you up constantly. But that's beside the point. I didn't plan this. They're a pair of stubborn, meddlesome old fools.''

''Is this lady really my aunt, Dad?''

''She's just someone I used to know,'' Tony muttered.

''Just someone?'' Zoe groaned. *I was a virgin, you jerk.* ''Just someone? That's rich.''

''Did you know my mommy?'' Noah persisted.

''She was my best friend.'' Zoe studied the beautiful boy with new wonder.

''So, have I heard of you?''

''Probably not. She and I were friends a long time ago.''

''Nine years ago,'' Tony said in that voice that chilled her.

''I'm eight.'' Noah whirled around, holding up eight fingers.

''See. Ancient history. Before you were born.''

Zoe ruffled his hair affectionately. The boy moved closer to her as if he craved being touched by a woman's loving hand.

"So, what are we going to do about this?" Tony demanded of Zoe.

"What do you mean?"

"This disaster? Who's not going to Rhodes?"

"I didn't lose two nights of sleep, fly all the way over here just to fly all the way back to Manhattan."

"Neither the hell did we."

"So—"

"Why can't we all go, Dad?" Noah whispered in a small, shy voice.

Tony glared at her until Zoe blushed. His eyes were so piercing she began to wonder if her sweater and skirt had suddenly become transparent. Was he assessing changes in her physical appearance as swiftly as she was assessing them in him?

He was taut, tall and lethally magnificent. His carved face had a few more lines, especially around his mouth and eyes. He was huge, and he exuded male virility and anger—lots of anger, all of it directed at her.

His black eyes blazed. Well, at least she had his full attention. She remembered how jealous she used to be of him. She'd been so insecure. So young.

It bothered her to realize that she'd measured every boyfriend to Tony, and none of them had come close.

"Can we sit by her, Dad?"

"What?" Tony growled.

"No!" she whispered, just as frantic as Tony.

"On the plane?" Noah queried insistently.

"*No,*" both adults chimed.

"But you don't talk to me, Dad. And you won't play games—"

"Because they last for damn ever."

"You're cussing," Zoe chided gently.

"They're adventure games. Mommy wouldn't let him say bad words, either."

Zoe took a long, slow breath. "You sound kinda lonely, little fella. It's rough losing your mom. I know because I was just about your age when I lost mine."

Noah handed her his electronic game. "Do you know how to play?"

She shook her head. "But you could teach me."

"How'd your mother die?" Noah whispered.

Tony sucked in a deep breath. "Of all the low-down, dirty tricks to tell my kid about your—"

"In a wreck," she said simply.

Noah's blue eyes widened. He placed a hand on her knee.

"Only, I lost my daddy, too," she said.

Black boots shifted impatiently.

"How?" The word trembled on Noah's lips.

"Same car accident," she whispered. "They'd gone to a movie they said I was too little to see. When they died, I went to live with my mother's sister-in-law, Patty." Zoe spoke matter-of-factly, covering a wealth of pain. As a little girl she felt so lost and alone, so afraid that if she ever loved again, she'd suffer the same loss.

"Patty Creighton, who takes me for rides every time she gets a new red Cadillac?" Noah asked.

"Which is every damn year, thanks to you," Tony muttered savagely. "That money could go into the land."

"My land," Zoe reminded him.

"I lease it."

Zoe ignored Tony and nodded at Noah. "Only, back then Aunt Patty was an old maid and didn't know much about kids. But she had lots and lots of cats at her ranch. Seventeen. Maybe more. To keep the snakes away, she said. And she was a librarian, who didn't make much money or ever have a new car. But she took me with her to the library. That's when I began to read. All the time. To forget about my parents...."

"But it's hard to forget, and I don't want to forget," Noah said.

She'd read books instead of making friends. Then Tony had come along.

"You know what my favorite thing in all the world is?" Zoe asked.

"No," Noah whispered.

"To lie, curled up with a cat in my lap, reading a book."

"You have a cat?"

"Super Cat," she explained. "He's home with a cat-sitter."

"Dad won't let me have a cat." When Noah slanted his eyes toward his father, Zoe gave Tony a long, hard look, too.

"Cats make him sneeze," Tony said.

"'Cause I'm allergic." Noah sucked in a breath. "But I like to play video games. 'Specially adventure, warrior games."

"And you'll teach me if we sit together," she said eagerly.

"Stop it. Both of you," Tony roared. "This budding friendship ends now. She won't be playing games or sitting by anybody.'' He turned on Zoe with a vengeance. "I don't give a damn what scheme you hatched with my mother.''

"You're cussing again. He's a child.''

"My bad habits are none of your business.''

"You're a father. You have to try—''

"I said—don't lecture me about—''

"I wouldn't have met him if you hadn't lost him.''

Tony moved so close to her she could smell the hot, masculine scent of his powerful body as well as his minty cologne. She would've retreated, but she wasn't about to show cowardice.

Fortunately, the flight attendants called her row number.

"You and I were done with each other nine years ago, and you know it!'' Tony muttered heatedly. "Let's keep it that way!''

"Fine.''

She caught her breath as he grabbed a bewildered Noah up in his arms and stomped off to a far corner of the lounge.

Noah's game was on the floor forgotten. She started to call to them and then thought better of it. Instead she slipped the game into her carry-on and rushed to the gate.

In spite of seat assignments, there seemed to be great confusion in boarding. Nevertheless, Zoe found her seat, which was a middle seat between a fat lady, who sat by the window and reeked of garlic, and an empty aisle seat. Hopefully, the flight wouldn't be full, and she could move into the aisle seat.

Lowering her head, Zoe pulled out her paperback and began to read. Thus, she was minding her own business, thank you very much, Mr. Big, Bad Cowboy, when suddenly Noah sprang into the empty seat beside her and buckled his seat belt.

"Hi," he said, flashing his toothy grin at her.

"Hi, yourself." She hesitated. "Where's your daddy?"

"Right here," drawled that deep, husky voice that made the bottom drop out of her stomach. "You're in my seat."

"My seat!" she snapped back at him.

His long, tanned fingers flapped a boarding pass in her face.

"Oh, dear, it does seem to have my seat number printed in bold black." She sighed.

"So, get up."

"There has to be a mistake."

Passengers stacked up behind him while she rummaged in her messy purse to find her mutilated boarding pass. When she got it out and unfolded it, she gasped.

"It's the same as mine!" he said.

"I got here first," she muttered. "So, the seat's mine."

"I need to sit by my son. Don't make me bodily remove you." He leaned across Noah. Her smile died when blunt fingertips unhooked her seat belt.

"Don't you dare touch her, Dad."

"He's right." She was shivering again from his nearness and from the accidental brushing of his hand against hers. "Be a gentleman and go ask the flight attendant for help."

"She speaks Greek."

"Your problem. I got here first."

Everybody glared at him. Even Noah.

"All right." Tony vanished toward the back of the plane.

All too soon he was back with a pretty flight attendant, who seemed to have a weakness for lethal, male beauty of the rugged, cowboy variety.

"Ma'am, I'm afraid you'll have to move," she said. "We've found a seat for you in the back of the plane."

"Where it's bumpy. Let the gentleman sit back there."

"But this little boy is his son."

"He's…my, er, my great-nephew," Zoe fought back tartly.

"And I want to sit with my aunt," Noah said, inspired. "We don't see each other very often, and we're going to play games."

"Sir, I don't understand. Duke? Her name *is* the same as yours."

"Noah!" Anthony barked. "She's no aunt! You never saw her before in your life."

"She's my aunt Zoe, and you know it!"

"Noah!"

"You said so yourself! And how come she's got my game, then, Dad?"

"The hell she does."

"Don't cuss at my great-nephew—nephew!"

Two more flight attendants appeared only to add to the confusion with dramatic hand gestures and rapid Greek. Both women batted their lashes at Tony, which made Zoe go green.

When Zoe still refused to move, the flirtatious blond flight attendant rushed to the front of the plane. Almost immediately the captain's deep voice boomed over the speaker system in English.

"We can't take off until all passengers are seated."

Zoe pulled Noah's game out of her bag, waved it at the boy. "You were going to teach me how to play."

"Oh, boy!" Noah said brightly as he deftly punched the on button. "First, you gotta know that there are all these warriors you can unlock. You want me to describe them?"

"Great!"

"Sit down, mister," said another passenger.

Tony gave Zoe another long appraisal, his eyes burning through layers of thick sweater with such scathing intensity that her nipples tingled.

"Be a gentleman," Zoe whispered.

"Okay. You win," Tony said. "For now."

Had she? Then why did her nipples feel as if they'd been burned with ice cubes all the way to Rhodes?

"Why can't Aunt Zoe go in our taxi?"

"She is not your aunt!"

"Yes, she is," Noah shrieked, circling round and round his father. "Remember, Nana told me about her at Madame Woo's."

"She can't go with us, Noah."

"I like her, Dad."

"That's because you don't know her as well as I do."

"She played with me the whole way over. She doesn't yawn and shift around in her seat like you do. She found me a pillow and a blanket when I got sleepy."

"She made me sit in the back of the plane."

"So?"

No way was Tony about to admit flying made him nervous, especially when the flying got bumpy.

"Because of her I was squeezed into a seat that wouldn't recline. The cushion was as hard as a rock and the size of a postage stamp. I had a fat man on either side of me...."

Noah yawned, so Tony didn't tell him that the fat men's beefy arms had overflowed into his space. Or that one of them had bad breath and had crunched potato chips the whole way. Or that when the flight had gotten bumpy, Tony had clenched the armrest so tightly, the men had laughed at him.

Glass doors of the terminal swung open, and a slim woman with auburn hair walked out into the bright sunshine with her backpack. That skintight, short, black mini clung to her shapely hips. Full breasts jiggled beneath her black sweater.

She'd walked like that in high school.

Do you have to make 'em bounce, baby?

"Shh." Tony knelt over the kid. "Here she comes. Look the other way. Don't you dare say anything about sharing a taxi."

She beamed when she saw Noah.

"Nephews!"

Tony thought of his uncle Duncan, and the word galled.

Noah waved wildly.

She took that as an invitation and stepped toward Tony, into his space. God, she smelled sweet. Lilacs. Way better than the fat men. And, oh, how her auburn hair flashed in the sun.

"Is this fate?" She ruffled Noah's hair, and the brat smiled from ear to ear, showing off his brand-

new permanent teeth that were going to cost a fortune to straighten.

"Or is this fate?" she purred softly against Tony's
ear. When he tensed, she whirled away, breasts
bouncing. Then she smiled so flirtatiously at their
dark driver the old fool's tongue nearly lolled out of
his mouth.

"What do you bet we're all going to the same
hotel?" She flapped her hotel voucher at the driver
with a bright smile.

Noah pulled out an identical voucher.

"What'd I tell you?" she said.

The taxi driver grinned from ear to ear. "You
could share—"

"You win the second round," Tony conceded.
Bowing low, he opened the door for her.

"Romantic holiday?" the driver queried. "Second
honeymoon?"

"We're not sure what it is yet," Zoe answered
brightly as if the flight with Noah and their new
friendship had made her overconfident.

But, oh, her hair was the color of spun flame beneath the bright Greek sun. And those breasts! And
she smelled so good.

"Just get in the back seat," Tony growled as he
took her luggage.

"My pleasure."

Then she winked at him.

"Don't flirt!"

"Maybe I can't help myself."

Four

"Nice," Zoe murmured.

Deliberately avoiding the dark eyes of the tall, dark man sitting on the patio next to hers, she slid her glass door open. She felt dangerously inspired to do mischief as she pranced past Tony in a skimpy black bikini and a loose, overlarge, white shirt that was sheer and soft after years of washings. She leaned against her low wall and eyed the blue-green Aegean and the mountains of Turkey and then stretched with feline grace, breathing in the cool, salty, humid air.

The shirt whipped around her, revealing her belly and slim waist.

"Too nice." Bitter sarcasm coated Tony's compliment.

Even though she didn't look his way, Zoe had the disquieting sensation he was watching her as she leaned back against her wall. She shaded her face with her hand so he couldn't see her blush.

"You're enjoying this," Tony accused crossly.

They had checked in together. Since they shared the same last name, the entire staff had assumed they were married and had just wanted lots of room. Then Zoe had explained everything in vivid detail that had made Tony turn the most darling shade of purple.

"So, you see, guys, I'm actually Tony's beloved aunt Zoe."

She'd rung a little bell and insisted Tony share her bellman, saying it was the least she could do since he'd been such a gentleman about the taxi. Then she'd given Noah her key and invited him inside to explore her unit, which he said he preferred to his father's.

"Am I staying with you, Aunt Zoe?"

"No," his father growled.

"You can come over anytime," she'd told Noah as Tony was dragging him away by the collar to their unit.

"The hell he can."

"You're cussing—"

"If you don't stop, you'll drive me to do worse...."

"I am breathless with anticipation. But why don't we both change into something more comfortable first?"

"What is that supposed to mean?"

"Whatever you want it to."

When she'd smiled, he'd stared at her, stunned. She'd shut her door in his face, her heart pounding. What in the world had gotten into her?

Their condominiums were located on the bottom

floor of a boxy, multistoried building that was painted a dazzling white. Both units looked out on a grassy lawn, an aqua swimming pool, a jewel-white strip of beach littered with blue and white umbrellas and chaise longues on the shores of the Aegean.

You're enjoying this, he'd said right before she'd gotten lost in her own thoughts.

Zoe inhaled a long breath. "What's not to enjoy? I don't have a problem with purple mountains of Turkey misting across the Aegean. Did you know they are exactly eleven miles away?"

If he'd been reading his guidebook as diligently as she had, he didn't say so.

"Or a problem with red bougainvillea dripping from all the balconies," she went on. "Or yellow roses and sprigs of basil frothing at my window boxes."

"Frothing." His chair legs grated against tile. "You've been editing too many novels."

"What if I have?" She plopped herself down in a chaise longue. "I am on vacation. One is supposed to enjoy one's vacation. Did you know Ulysses once sailed this very same sea on his way home from Troy?"

Tony leaned over the low white wall that separated their patios. He wore cutoffs and nothing else. He was dark all over, and his teak-brown belly was still as flat as a washboard. A strip of black hair ran up his middle and flared across his broad chest. He didn't used to have that much hair.

He looked too good, so doggone good and primitively male that her nerves skittered as if she'd taken a heady jolt of electricity. In nine years she hadn't felt this alive.

"Why, he looks good enough to eat."

"You're doing it. You're doing it."

His black eyes made a tour of her long, shapely legs. "What?" he muttered.

"I didn't say anything," she replied on a quick blush.

"Yes, you did. You were muttering to yourself. I used to think that was cute."

"Your imagination, cowboy."

His handsome mouth quirked. Oh, dear, there was that beguiling lopsided smile she used to think belonged only to her.

"You still talk to yourself, don't you?" he whispered in that raspy voice that had once belonged only to her, as well.

"Do not."

"Still make up stories?" he taunted. "Still want to write?"

She had brought a yellow legal pad and several pens. She had planned to try her hand while she was here. Not that her unrealized dreams were his concern.

"Is it true what they say about editors being frustrated writers?" he persisted.

"My life is none of your business."

"How about other frustrations?" His eyes burned over her body again.

Her color heightened. "I said mind your own—"

One black brow arched. "And if you'd minded yours, we wouldn't be here together. Did you or did you not set me up?" he demanded.

"Did you or did you not set me up?" she mimicked, winking at him flirtatiously. "You know *I* didn't!"

''Mammalian trickery.''

''What is that supposed to mean?''

''That anything's possible especially where women are concerned. Especially a woman who married an old man who was her aunt's suitor.''

''An old man who'd just discovered he was dying and wanted to exit Shady Lomas with a real bang.''

''…A woman who became a millionairess when her husband obliged her by dying so fast.''

''I told you—he did what he did on purpose. He used me to get back at you and his daughters. If his own family had accepted him—''

''So your marriage is my fault?''

She wet her lips nervously. ''Look. I could have gone home to Shady Lomas if I'd wanted to be slapped in the face with my life history every time I turned around. We're here. And it wasn't easy to leave the office or my cat or be hand-searched in half a dozen airports. I for one intend to make the best of it—even if you're here, too.''

''Even if I'm here. You got my mother to get me here.…''

''You are too conceited to believe. True—you're kinda cute.''

''Kinda?'' He actually looked hurt.

''But, kinda cute or not, you are—understand this once and for all—you are the very last person I would choose to take a vacation with. I did not conspire with my aunt and your mother. They must have cooked this wacky plan up all by themselves because we're both single. We can either make the best of it or the worst of it. It's a long way home, so I suggest that you sit down and be quiet and pretend you know how to be a gentleman and let me enjoy these purple mountains across our wine-dark sea.''

"Wine-dark?'' He snorted.

"Homer. Hello? Do you read? *The Iliad.*''

"And *The Odyssey.* That water is blue, Miss Know-it-all Bookworm.''

"I wish you'd quit looking at my legs.''

"I would—if you'd stop blushing every time I do.''

"Quit looking, and I'll stop.''

Obediently he stared out to sea, too. She tried to imagine ancient Persian war galleys, their oars driven by shackled slaves, racing across the waves.

"You really didn't set me up?'' he persisted.

"End of that discussion. I am trying to relax and enjoy my vacation.''

"The only way to do that is to avoid each other.''

"So punish me,'' she said. "Avoid me. Go inside.''

"Why don't you? We could take turns.''

"Turns? We sound like children. We've got adjoining condos, adjoining time-shares, whatever—thanks to your mother and my conniving aunt. You and I have known each other since the beginning of time. We could try just to make the best of a bad situation. After all, you are my nephew.''

"Just stop with the nephew bit.''

"Okay.'' She held up her hands in a defensive gesture. "Okay. Truce. Your precious Noah, nimble-fingered Noah, is my new best friend. All I'm saying is that just because our high school romance went sour—''

"You slept with me and married my rich uncle, who I don't claim, by the way.''

"Because you slept with me and the next time I saw you, Rene was all tangled up in your arms and legs."

"Any girl with two eyes could've seen that I was trying to get loose. You accused me to get yourself off the hook."

"No. Because of Rene and you, I did what I did. I know I was stupid, but that's why I did it."

"You're not off the hook."

"Okay, but do we have to hate each other for the whole week? Maybe the only week we'll ever be here?"

He stared at her and then at the Aegean. Maybe the sheer, spectacular beauty of this idyllic paradise was beginning to get to him as it was to her.

"I came here to figure out my future," she said. "If you don't hush and leave me alone, I'll never be able to think about anything." She smiled at him. "How about some ouzo?"

"I will not drink ouzo with you."

"Your loss." She poured herself a glass, shifted her chaise longue so she couldn't see him, stared at the mountains and began to sip.

Even before he spoke, she was burningly conscious of his gaze on her legs again. He laughed when she blushed.

"You can just feel me looking at you, can't you?" Her cheeks got hotter. "Would you quit?"

"It's called chemistry."

"I don't care what it is called. Just quit."

"Where'd you get that?" he demanded. "The ouzo, I mean."

"I ordered it off a menu last night. It was so good I bought a bottle. I was jet-lagged as all get-out. After a sip or two, I felt absolutely mellow. It tastes weird, like licorice, but it's great."

Noah skipped out onto the balcony and ran up to the wall beside Zoe. Blue eyes peered over into her patio. "Can I have a drink, too?"

"No," Tony replied.

She got up. The wind sent her shirt sailing above her head. When it fell back into place, the blaze in Tony's eyes made her feel so positively naked, she shuddered and then rewarded him with an all-body flush.

"O-of course you can, Noah, dear. I have juice and soft drinks in my fridge." She smiled at both her male fans before heading inside.

"He can get his own damn drink out of our fridge."

"He's cussing at me again," Noah tattled as he shoved a plastic chair over to the white wall that divided their balconies. He climbed onto the wall where he sat, skinny legs dangling over her side.

Zoe returned with a tall glass of frosty orange juice.

"I'd rather have a soda," Noah said, poking a straw into the bubbles.

"You'll drink what she brought and say thank-you," Tony growled.

"Thank you." Instead of drinking, Noah set the glass on the edge of the wall. She touched his knee that was red from his fall, and he smiled at her bashfully.

Noah was incredibly adorable. Oh, dear, dear. She had it bad.

"Your father's afraid of flying. Did you know that?"

Noah shook his head and made his bangs flop.

"That's why he's so grumpy."

"But he doesn't fly in Texas."

"You mean he's grumpy like this all the time?"

Noah looked at the ground sheepishly. "Well, most of the time, I guess."

Tony slammed a chair against the wall so hard, Noah's glass fell and shattered on Zoe's red-tiled patio. "It's hard to be happy, damn it, when—" Tony stopped, appalled by his outburst and the mess he made.

Zoe rushed toward him, her gaze on his ravaged face.

"When the wife you loved more than anything is dead," Zoe finished softly. "The only woman you ever…"

"Don't put words into my mouth. You don't know a damn thing about me anymore. Enjoy your precious balcony to yourself. Oh…sorry about the glass."

I know you go to the cemetery every week.

"Come on, Noah. We're going inside—"

When she'd cleaned up the breakage and was alone, she felt adrift and far lonelier than she had after she'd thrown Abdul out of her apartment a month ago.

Why had she pushed Anthony? But flirting with Anthony made her feel alive. His pain devastated her. How was that possible…unless…

She had seven days here. Maybe it was good in a way that this man who had haunted her for nine years was next door. Maybe if she faced him, she'd see him for the macho, pigheaded redneck he probably was. Then she'd get over him and be happy when she found some sophisticated, gentlemanly man more to her taste in Manhattan. One way or another she needed to grow up and move on.

She finished her ouzo and decided to go for a walk on the beach. The sand was fine and white and littered with perfect, round, white rocks. Clear, turquoise water lapped against the shoreline. Blue and white umbrellas had been lowered and were folded against their poles. Cushions had been stashed in a cabana, and the chaise longues were stacked under the building's eaves. A sea breeze whispered through her hair. She hadn't walked far before Noah dashed up to her.

"Does your father know where you are?"

He shook his bright head. "I think he's mad. He's just sitting in the kitchen not saying anything."

"You really shouldn't run off from him like this, you know."

He knelt in the sand and began inspecting the rocks that littered the beach.

"Look at all the perfect, round rocks." He built a mountain out of them while she stood over him and watched.

Soon, it was getting dark, and he'd stuffed his pockets until they were bulging with rocks. It would have been fun to romp with him in the sand, to take him to dinner, to play another adventure game with him. But he didn't belong to her. She wasn't his mother.

"I really think we should go find your father," she said.

"He likes being alone."

"We don't want him to worry, though."

"I don't care." Noah crossed his arms.

"You know you don't mean that."

She took him by the hand, and he wove his fingers through hers and clung tightly, as she led him home. They were halfway across the lawn to their condos when Anthony rushed up to them.

"I've been looking everywhere—"

"He followed me to the beach. I was just—"

"You should've known I'd be worried—"

"I did. I was just—"

"Dad, she was bringing me—"

"Home," she said gently.

"Then, thanks. Thanks a lot for being so nice to him." His eyes clung to her face for a long moment. Then he seized the boy, turned his back and abruptly left her.

She stood in the dark and watched them until they disappeared into the golden glow of their doorway. The door shut behind them. She leaned back against a tall palm with rustling fronds, staying there until the stars came out and the beach was quite dark. The lights went out at Tony's condo. They'd probably gone out to dinner.

Never, ever had she felt more alone.

Wrong.

The worst night of her life had been Tony's wedding night. She'd been a widow. And he'd married Rene, anyway.

Would she ever get over him?

Yes! She clenched her hands together. Her fingernails dug into her palms. She was going to dinner all by herself. She'd take her book. She'd eat grilled octopus and have a Greek salad. She was going to do what she'd come here to do—think.

If it was the last thing she ever did, she would

figure out how to rid herself of her hangup about Anthony Duke.

Old boyfriends. Who needed them? She, for one, was not going to be haunted by hers for the rest of her life.

Zoe had ruined his evening. It was late. All through that feast of souvlaki, Greek for shish kebabs, and grilled fish, which Anthony had washed down with too much retsina, wine flavored with pine resin, he'd moodily thought about her.

Zoe's condo was dark, but her patio doors were open. Her long white curtains swirled in the wind. It was just like her to go to bed and forget to close her doors.

What she did was none of his business. Still, Tony had knocked at her front door four times and grown even more worried and frustrated when he'd gotten no answer. If she were home, you'd think she'd answer.

He'd even called her. She hadn't answered her damn phone, either. Again, he reminded himself, she wasn't his concern. Still, he couldn't go to sleep with those patio doors open.

Anybody could see those curtains and go in and do anything to her. Maybe she'd picked somebody up. A stranger, a madman capable of anything.

A madman? Anthony knew he was losing it. But what if she'd fallen and couldn't get to the phone? He imagined her injured, semiconscious sprawled out on that gleaming, white-tiled floor.

On that happy thought, he jumped their wall, threw back her billowing curtains and stomped across her slick floor to check on her for himself.

He called her name in the darkened condo. Again, she didn't answer. When he punched at a light switch to get his bearings, the lights didn't come on.

Their condos were mirror opposites, so he knew the layout. Swiftly he made his way across her tiny living room, dining room, and kitchen. As he turned to the left and stepped into the hall, he heard her shower go off. A faint crack of light glimmered beneath her bathroom door.

Before he could retreat, the door opened, and he was enveloped in a warm, golden mist.

Run! She's fine.

His bare feet rooted themselves to the cold white tiles. The mist cleared. Like Venus in her seashell, Zoe was naked and more beautiful than ever. In one hand an apricot towel dangled to the floor.

He gulped in the scent of lilacs. Then he whispered her name. Before she could scream, he had her against the pink tile wall, his hand over her slick, hot lips.

"Shh. It's just me, Tony," he murmured gently. "I wouldn't hurt you. Not for the world. I was just making sure you're okay."

Her damp breasts mashed into his chest and soaked his shirt. Without really knowing what he was doing, his long fingers wound into her thick wet hair. Her heart beat wildly, but no more wildly than the drumbeats in his own chest. Instead of fighting him, she went still.

He knew he should let her go and apologize for scaring her, but he felt the mad need to touch her and hold her and make love to her. Suddenly she was melting into his heat even as he melted into hers.

"Tell me this is a dream. Tell me we're not really

doing this," she whispered even as she dropped her apricot-colored towel and arched herself into his body.

His whole world became hot, wet, flame-haired woman with the pixie face.

"It's a dream," he muttered roughly. "The same nightmare that's tormented me for nine damn years."

"You, too?"

"Yeah. Even down to the shower."

"Apricot towel, too?" she purred.

"I'll have to add that detail."

"So will I. And I didn't realize the mist was from the shower."

Her luminous brown eyes widened, whether with fear or desire, he didn't know. He was too far gone to care. He simply lowered his mouth to hers.

He knew he should stop, but his quickening breath told him it was already too late. Even before his lips touched hers and he caught that first delicious taste, he had to have more. Still, he waited a heartbeat.

"Stop me, why don't you?" he muttered. "Fight. Writhe!"

"Would you stop?" She moaned and went limp. "Can you stop? Can you?"

Her lush, warm body felt glued to his.

"Oh, Zoe…" His voice was thick with need.

She opened her mouth and wet her lips and then his too with the tip of her tongue.

That second little taste of her even before he kissed her pushed him over some edge, and he was lost.

Then she said, "Let's get you naked."

He felt violently aroused, totally at her mercy.

"This is torture," he muttered.

"But sweet, mad torture," she promised, teasing him with a saucy grin. "So...enjoy."

He answered with a soft chuckle.

Their tongues touched. Then they kissed.

Five

One warm, wet kiss.

Make that one helluva kiss, Anthony silently amended as he stared at Zoe, who was flushed and naked and alluring and begging him to get naked, too.

This is wrong!

Maybe so, but as her big, brown eyes flicked over him in awe, Anthony felt something hot and dangerous luring him on. How the hell could he stop now? What man made of flesh and pumping blood could have?

She drew her tongue across her lips and then lifted a fingertip and toyed with the top button of his shirt, undoing it.

She married your bastard uncle. She got the ranch, the house, everything. Her aunt drives red Cadillacs just like Uncle Duncan used to, and that

*irritates the hell out of you. You lease her land—
land that should be yours.*

His body was sending him a different message as
her hand moved beneath his shirt. Then she leaned
forward and kissed him again.

Her lips clung to his, and he tasted her and reveled
in doing so. Licorice? Ouzo? Whatever it was, his
blood buzzed with desire.

"What are you doing here?" she whispered
drowsily a few dozen kisses later as she levered herself forward into the hard, masculine strength of his
body.

"You left your back doors wide open."

"And you took that as an invitation to…?" There
was no mistaking the husky timbre in her voice as
she slid her palms down his shoulders.

"Anybody could have."

"But anybody didn't. You did." Her hands moved
over his muscles lovingly.

"I was worried."

"About little ol' me? You could've knocked."

"I did," he replied with quiet gravity. "I phoned,
too. You didn't answer."

"Well, I'm okay, cowboy. You can go." Her teasing voice was deep and velvety.

Talk about mammalian trickery. She said one
thing, but in the next breath she gave him that wide,
lush smile.

"Is that really what you want?"

"What I want?" she purred. As if mesmerized by
him, she threaded her fingers through his hair. "What
I want—"

"Awhile ago you asked me to get naked."

"Are you sure you didn't maybe dream that up on your own?"

"Did you drink more of that ouzo stuff?"

She nodded and buried her face against his throat. "What I want? What I want is…so wrong." Her hot tongue flicked at the pulse beat in the hollow of his throat. "But now that you mention it, why don't you get naked."

His heart sped up. The tongue kept at it—flicking, twirling—until he couldn't breathe and his body was swollen and lava hot.

He gasped. "This is crazy."

She wiggled against his groin. Her voice was lower, sexier. "I don't know what I want," she said thickly.

"Well, maybe I do." His finger traced along her soft cheek, down her throat, down, down, circling over each nipple until they peaked into pert little beads of desire.

She shuddered. "You think so, huh? Let's see if you're still as hunky out of those clothes as you are in them."

Then she was peeling him out of his shirt, leaning into him, her slim fingers flying over those shirt buttons even faster than his, loosening, tearing. She was the one who tugged at the white sleeves, yanking his shirt off his brown shoulders. Then she ran her hands over sculpted muscle.

"So, the years have been kind. Oh, Anthony, why do you have to be built like a hunky god?"

"Talk about ego gratification," he muttered.

"Psychobabble from the big, bad cowboy." Giggling, she ran her hands down his naked spine. "I want to hate you. Did you know that's been my ambition for nine years?''

''Mine, too.'' He pulled her closer. ''We're not doing too good.''

''So, you thought about me?'' she asked.

''Not happy thoughts.''

''Then you think we're going to regret this in the morning?'' She rubbed her breasts back and forth against the black bristly hairs on his chest.

''Definitely.''

''But this sure feels good tonight.''

''Definitely.'' The soft feel of her naked flesh rocked him to the core. With a thudding heart, he whispered her name and put a question mark at the end of it. ''Zoe? Zoe?''

''Who's afraid of the big, bad cowboy?'' she hummed, letting him go. She leaned back against the wall and drew a deep, shuddering breath. ''Not me,'' she whispered in a tiny voice. ''Not me.''

The silence between them thickened.

''Are you afraid?'' he whispered.

She didn't answer for a long time. Did he only imagine that she shivered? ''You know me. I leap off the cliff and then look for a safe place to land.''

''While you're in the leaping mood, wrap your legs around my waist and hang on,'' he murmured dryly against her ear.

''Oh, dear.''

''Just do it.''

She leaped, and he caught her.

Her legs around his waist felt too good. She was sleek and slender, but he said, ''You've put on a pound or two.''

''So have you, buster.''

"In all the right places," he murmured.

She ran her hands over his muscular shoulders again. "Ditto."

Gripping her tightly at the waist, he carried her into the bedroom.

"This better be good," she challenged as he lowered her to the bed.

The mattress dipped beneath their weight. "Or what?"

"I have this thing for your hunky body."

"Just my body?"

"It'd be terrible to have a thing…and…and…"

"Shut up," he whispered gently as he ripped the sheets back. "Just shut up." He threw the pillows onto the floor.

"This isn't fair. We should be messing up your bedroom.…"

His mouth crushed down on hers. And it wasn't long before she quit trying to make conversation about idiotic things like housekeeping details. He kissed her everywhere just like in his dream. And just like in his dreams, she kissed him back.

She wasn't as experienced in reality as the vixen he dreamed about, but her shy, awkward fumbling turned him on even more. Maybe she didn't do this with every guy on the block.

A surge of jealousy shook him at the mere thought of other men. Nine years. How many had there been? What about Uncle Duncan? He'd been a sick man when he'd married her. Had he even been able to consummate their marriage?

Don't think about it. Not now. Not when you've got her right where you want her, under you, writhing and twisting.

She moaned and arched her body against him. "Now. Now."

He laughed and slowed their pace and made her wait. When he wouldn't speed up, she kissed the middle of his chest. Then she bit him.

"Ouch."

"Now," she urged. "Now."

"You little wildcat…"

"Now. Get inside me. I can't wait."

He peeled a condom out of its wrapper and put it on. Straddling her, he thrust deeply.

She went still.

So did he.

"You okay?" he whispered.

She smiled, her face radiant.

Oh, the joy…the pleasure of those breathless, silent moments. He felt himself swell and heat up inside her. She gasped with pleasure. Then he began to rock back and forth and let the ecstasy build. She was soft and hot but gentle and loving too, and her hands were all over him.

Awkward with each other no longer, their bodies moved in that ageless, perfect rhythm. She felt so good. So damned good. So damned incredible. So perfect.

Nine years he'd gone without this. Nine years. He wanted their lovemaking to last forever. And it seemed that it might for a while. Then the pressure inside him built, but he held back, waiting for her even as passion swept through him. Waiting, his fists wound so tight they hurt, waiting until he was mad with desire and still she couldn't seem to—

He opened his eyes. Her lips moved. She was staring past him up at the Venetian chandelier. "Ten, eleven, twelve little lightbulbs..."

Lightbulbs? Was she counting bulbs to herself under her breath?

"Stop it," he muttered savagely.

She gasped. Then he kissed her hard. When her body went wild, he spun crazily out of control, too. A second or two later, she exploded. He came after she did.

He wound his hands through her hair. "Did I ever tell you I loved your hair?"

She was still trembling all over. "Oh, Anthony...what have we done?"

"Counting? Those damn little lightbulbs? Why did you do that?"

"To make it last."

"I thought I wasn't doing it right." His voice was oddly rough. He felt so damned vulnerable, and he hated that. She would use it...maybe to destroy him again.

She kissed the tip of his nose. "How could you think that? You were too perfect to believe."

She laid her head next to his shoulder and fell asleep.

"Too perfect...."

With her warm body cuddled against him, and his desire sated, his brain went into overdrive. He remembered every sordid detail of the past, especially the details involving her marriage to that scoundrel, Uncle Duncan, and her inheritance, the Duke inheritance.

His inheritance.

She and her aunt had made him the laughingstock of Shady Lomas. He'd plunged into marriage with

Rene, the prettiest girl in town, just to prove he hadn't cared. But he had cared, and he'd made Rene so unhappy. She'd loved him, and he'd hurt her so badly he'd have Rene's unhappiness on his conscience forever.

Zoe slept as blissfully as a baby in his arms while he lay beside her, staring up at the ceiling for hours. It wasn't so easy to forget those red Cadillacs Zoe's aunt Patty bought every year while his own mother had to drive an old truck that had over two-hundred-thousand miles on it. Or to forget that he leased Zoe's land, prime Duke ranchland, from her aunt to run his cattle on.

When he finally fell asleep, he dreamed he was in a red Cadillac convertible. He and Zoe were parked in a pasture choked with mesquite and aflame with bluebonnets. They were making love in the back seat.

When he woke up, it was dawn. Zoe's cheek was pressed against his hair, and he was breathing hard.

A damned red Cadillac! They'd done it in Duncan's damn red Cadillac!

Careful not to disturb her, Anthony got up, grabbed his clothes, pulled on his slacks, locked all of Zoe's doors and stalked back to his own condo.

"A damned red Cadillac!" he muttered as he stripped and got in his shower.

No way in hell was he going to get involved with Zoe Creighton. Make that Zoe Duke! Make that Aunt Zoe! After all, she'd married Uncle Duncan!

Zoe's bedroom glowed gold with a magical light. For a hazy moment she had no idea where she was. All she knew was that she felt warm and cozy and incredibly wonderful. Maybe Aunt P and Ursula had been right to advise Greece.

Then she sat up and realized she was naked and her bed was a mess. Her vision was a little blurry. Was that her apricot towel all tangled up in the door-way? Whatever was it doing there?

An image sprang full-blown into her mind. She was naked, and Anthony was pushing her hot body back against that icy wall.

"This is bad.... It's a dream." Her voice grew softer and more desperate. "Please let it be a dream...." For no reason at all she couldn't stop looking at that towel.

She saw her hand opening, and felt the towel slip-ping out of it, right before he'd grabbed her.

Why did her body feel so...so different...somehow...so complete?

Oh, dear. She'd drunk several glasses of ouzo at dinner.

More visions rose to torment her. In her dream...was it a dream...well, whatever...she'd crawled on top of Tony and kissed her way down, all the way down from his broad, brown forehead to...to his shaft.

She remembered a mat of thick, black whorls at his groin. He'd been so huge. Huge! She put her hand to her lips. What was that funny taste in her mouth?

"Oh, dear! You didn't!"

"You did!"

"You're doing it!"

"Shut up!"

She wrenched the sheets up to her neck. Even so, she couldn't stop shaking. After a dream like that, how would she face him today? And Noah?

"It was only a dream!"

But when she got up and went to the bathroom and picked up her damp, apricot towel, certain delicate tissues of her body felt raw and used as they rubbed together. She clutched the towel to her breasts. Then her legs went limp at the knees when she saw her face in the mirror.

"Oh, God...oh, God..."

Her hair was a mess. When she pressed a fingertip to her swollen lips, her temples began to pound.

No dream! She'd done it with him!

Warm sexual afterglow mixed with wild panic.

"What are you going to do about this, big girl?"

"Get your skinny fanny on a fast jet back to Manhattan!" said a wise sassy voice.

"You're doing it."

"Shut up! Shut up—both of you! I've got to think!"

She grabbed her white, terry-cloth robe off a hook, put it on and stumbled into her kitchen where she made coffee and boiled herself an egg. Then she opened a container of yogurt and poured honey and walnuts into the rich stuff.

She sat down to eat, but just as she dipped her spoon into the thick, velvety yogurt oozing with honey and walnuts, her phone rang.

Her hand froze, her spoon sinking slowly into the golden goo.

No way could she face Anthony so soon!

Maybe it wasn't him. Of course it was him.

On the fifth ring she placed her hand on the receiver, but she just sat there, her pulse racing, as she stared unseeingly out the window at the aqua pool and sea and those incredible lavender mountains. The sun was already brilliant in a cloudless blue sky. Again, the water was that same shade of dazzling blue green. Indeed, the whole world seemed to sparkle.

Scarcely had the phone stopped jingling and she'd lifted her spoon again than her doorbell rang. She dropped her spoon with a plunk, splattering little globs of yogurt all over the table.

Would the big lug ever give up?

She stomped to the door, clutched her robe around her neck and shouted through the thick wood, "You got what you wanted last night! Now go away!"

"It's just me," said a soft, crushed voice.

She unlocked the door. "*Noah.* Oh, dear! Darling, I'm sorry."

She meant to crack the door a mere inch, but the minute she turned the knob, Anthony shoved the toe of his black boot in it.

She slammed the door.

"Ouch!"

"You're hurting him, Aunt Zoe."

Zoe decided there was nothing to do but open it wider. She stepped back as Anthony stormed inside.

"Talk about mammalian trickery!" she whispered in a goaded undertone.

Blue eyes bright, Noah smiled up at her. "We want you to spend the day with us, Aunt Zoe."

"Doing what?" she replied, her voice raw as she held the edges of her robe together.

"Anything you want," Anthony murmured so sexily she itched to slap him.

"You should be ashamed," she pleaded.

"Me? About last night? You have no room to talk!"

"I meant to use your son to get through my door."

"Oh, this was his idea."

"I'll bet."

"It was," Noah confirmed. "Just like it was my idea to sit by you on the plane and to get you to share our taxi!"

"See!" said his father, grinning down at her.

Oh, dear. As always Tony's lopsided smile got through all her defenses.

"You're incorrigible," she whispered, her voice cracking.

"Ditto."

She glared up at Anthony.

Again, his triumphant smile was so charmingly crooked, it took her breath away.

Noah stared at them both. As if sensing he was out of his depth, he squinted and then looked away, wary all of sudden.

Oh, dear. Anthony's black eyes shone even brighter than they had last night. They were so hot and dark, she felt consumed in the same crazy flame that had devoured her.

"I...I..."

"We knew you'd say yes, so I've rented a little car and ordered three picnic lunches from the resort cafeteria."

She'd been trying to forget Anthony Duke for nine long years. "I couldn't possibly," she said forcing an edge in her voice.

"What will it take to change your mind?" Anthony demanded softly.

"Nothing. You couldn't possibly—"

"Noah, why don't you go play your adventure

game in our condo while I talk to your Aunt Zoe…in private.''

''Sure, Dad—''

''Noah!'' she cried desperately. ''Don't you dare leave me alone with him.''

''Noah!'' His father's tone was stern. ''Remember our deal?''

Father and son exchanged a look. If Noah had been a magic genie capable of vanishing in a puff of smoke, he couldn't have disappeared faster. The door soon slammed behind Noah, and she was alone with Anthony.

Six

"We hate each other," Zoe said, her pulse accelerating now that she was alone with Anthony in her kitchen.

"Did you sleep well?" he asked, his deep tone laced with polite concern. "I had some disturbing dreams."

"Just leave. You know we don't even like each other."

"I told myself that too when I got up this morning."

"See, you dislike me, too."

Still, just a few hours ago, they'd made love in the adjoining bedroom. Oh, dear. Why hadn't she made the bed?

"My heart's thundering like a jackhammer. Is that what I feel—dislike?" he whispered.

When his possessive gaze raked her naked shoulder, she clutched the edges of her robe together again.

"What are you wearing under that robe? Not much, I hope."

Zoe swallowed. A dull red crept up her neck as she adjusted her robe again to cover herself.

"Mmm. Does anything in the whole world... maybe besides lilacs...smell as good as fresh coffee brewing? Do you mind if I pour myself a cup?"

"I just wish you'd go."

Instead of leaving, he opened her cabinet and banged cups madly before pulling one out. She felt strange, all mixed up as he moved about, making himself at home in her kitchen, rummaging in a drawer for a spoon and then dipping it into the sugar bowl.

Was he staking a claim? Or had he done that last night? His every assured movement as he poured milk and stirred in sugar implied all the new intimacies that bound them and yet tormented her, too.

"No way can I go anywhere with you today," she said as primly as she could manage.

He sat down and added more sugar to his coffee, his spoon clanging so vigorously against the delicate cup, she was afraid it might shatter. Abruptly he dropped his spoon just as noisily in his saucer.

"What about last night, Zoe?" His eyes went dark and intense as if he were searching into her heart.

She lowered her lashes so he couldn't read her secrets. "What about it?" she whispered in a trembling tone.

"What did it mean?" he demanded.

"Mean?" she repeated, picking up her cup and

twisting it round and round in her fingers. She felt shaky, so she pulled out a chair and sat down beside him.

"So you sleep around in Manhattan, do you?"

"Why, how dare you accuse—" She set her cup in her saucer and flashed him a hot look.

He laughed. "Then there must've been some reason that you…that I…"

She could feel the vein in her neck throbbing. "You came into my condo. I…I was naked."

"Delightfully so." He smiled as if he relished the despicable memory, but one glance into her huge, luminous eyes, and his smile died.

"You grabbed me," she accused. "You took advantage—"

"So…you're saying that what happened meant nothing to you, and that it was all my fault." His deep voice was dangerously quiet.

"That sounds good. Really good." She nodded her head briskly, hoping he'd buy it and go.

"You little liar. We made love for hours, and you know it. If anything, you were more enthusiastic than I—"

"I certainly was not!"

She shoved her cup and saucer across the table and got up. She meant to run from him and get dressed in her bedroom, but his hand snaked across the kitchen table and grabbed her wrist.

"You were wild about me, and I'll prove it!"

When he drew her closer, her robe fell off her shoulder again. She fought to readjust it, but his hand got there first.

"A gentleman would go," she said.

"I'm a cowboy, remember?" Sliding his rough

palm across her bare skin, his fingers heated as he pulled the robe lower. "You're naked under this, aren't you?"

"Why are you here this morning?" she pleaded. "Why won't you just leave me alone?"

"Would you have preferred me to have treated last night as a one-night stand and gone off somewhere with Noah and just ignored you?"

No! Yes! No!

Instead of answering him, she bit her bottom lip until it bled. He was impossible. Every single answer was impossible. The whole situation was...

She notched her chin upward and eyed him defiantly. "Are you just after more sex?"

"Are you suggesting more sex?" He smiled.

"Stop." She bit her tongue, and the taste of copper in her mouth grew stronger. "I...I shouldn't have asked you such a leading question."

"I didn't mind. If you're thinking about sex, I want to know." He burst out laughing. Then he pulled her closer. "You've still got the hots for me, and that makes you madder than hell."

Fingers splayed, she pushed against his chest, but he was strong and had no intention of releasing her.

"More sex sounds good." He grinned. "It's been a while. Rene and I...we weren't—"

"I'm sorry...about Rene." Zoe remembered how sick Rene had been. Last night hadn't been special to him. Zoe had just been a convenience after a long, forced abstinence.

"And you were really, really good," he murmured. "*We* were good."

"There is no 'we.'" Why couldn't she speak normally? Why was her voice so choked?

"You sure about that?"

"Just go. Please…just go."

"Then how will *we* ever know?" His dark gaze roamed her face, lingering on her naked shoulder.

"Know what?"

"What it all meant."

"I told you. It meant nothing."

He sighed. "I wish you were right. Maybe you do, too. I don't think it's that simple." His arms wound around her waist. Instead of fighting him, she stood perfectly still as she had last night and let him mold her against his muscular body as if she belonged there.

It all felt strangely right and thrilling to be in his arms. Her nerves sang. How she'd loved him when she'd been a girl.

Oh, dear. She had it bad.

"You hate me for marrying your uncle," she accused. "And I hate you…for choosing Rene. For being so deliriously happy with her…while I—"

Anthony cursed under his breath, but he didn't release her. "Yes, I hate that you married Duncan and made me the laughingstock of Shady Lomas. I was pretty self-righteous back then, and I guess folks needed a laugh. Maybe this whole thing was good for my character."

"You? The laughingstock? You were married to beautiful, perfect Rene."

"Why do you think I married her?"

"Because she was beautiful and perfect… and…and…"

"Too damned perfect," he muttered.

"It's me, the black widow, the shady lady of Shady Lomas, that everybody gossips about."

"Not just you, honey. They take me down a peg or two every chance they get. They said you went from me to him. You should hear Guy Pearsol's jokes on the subject when he ties one on."

"Guy's gross."

"But he's funny…when it's at someone else's expense."

"He really makes jokes about you?"

"Why'd the bookworm leave you, Duke? The only thing stiff about Duncan was his joints? Answer—new dollar bills are stiff. How do you feel about her being the owner of Duke Ranch and a glamorous New York editor to boot?"

"Oh, dear.…" Zoe hesitated. "I'm sorry. I don't go home because I can't face— And you have to live there.…"

"Sometimes I envy you because you got out. Rene was perfect, but I wasn't the perfect husband for her. Far from it. Then I've got Mother and my cousins to take care of. And there's Noah, too."

"So, will you go back and tell everybody that you've had the last laugh?"

"What do you mean?"

"Will you tell them we did it?"

"Is that what you think? That this is some kind of game to me?" His voice was deep and dark. So were his troubled eyes. "What we did… Well, it's nobody's damn business but ours what we did."

The way he said it, the way he looked at her made her feel so special.

Then his roughened hands were in her hair. "Zoe. I woke up this morning hating you…and wanting you. Mostly wanting you and hating myself because of it. Baby, you've damn sure got me in a tailspin."

"I know the feeling."

He lifted a strand of silk, and the Greek sun turned it to flame. "Then Noah said he wanted to spend the day with you and that I'm not as much fun as you are."

"That's brutal."

"Yeah. From the mouths of babes. But the truth is, I'd have more fun, too, if you came."

"You would?"

"If it was only about sex last night, I wouldn't feel that way, would I?"

"I never was very good at reading minds."

Before she could really get going on her argument, he drew her closer. Without even a thought to resistance, she lifted her lips to meet his.

His mouth closed over hers, sweetly, gently. Not hungrily like last night. Her lips parted with matching, heartfelt need. It felt so good to be held and kissed at breakfast the morning after.

"What is going on here?" whispered one of those little warning voices inside.

"Shut up. Shut up."

"You could write off last night. This morning is serious."

"Shut up."

"You're doing it."

Anthony's mouth on hers silenced the voices. Soon her whole body was trembling with sensual delight as his lips continued to kiss hers tenderly. She half opened her mouth, and his tongue slid inside. Her breathing was soon as uneven and harsh as his.

Her arms came around his shoulders. She couldn't resist winding his soft black hair at his nape around her fingertip. Nobody ever had made her feel even half as wonderful as he did.

She still loved him!

Love?

That word covered a lot of bases. Still, whatever she felt…

This was bad.

Oh, dear. Oh, dear…dear…dear…

"Let me go," she whispered pleadingly, knowing that if he picked her up and carried her to bed she, spineless ninny that she was—no, make that sex-starved nympho, at least where he was concerned— she wouldn't do anything to stop him.

"Let you go? Now that I have found you? I have a much better idea."

"I'm afraid to ask."

"Let's play show and tell."

"I don't know what you mean."

"Not to worry. I'll show you.…"

Gently he lowered her back into her kitchen chair.

"What are you doing?"

"Not to worry," he muttered with a wry smile.

Then he was down on his knees and crawling under the table toward her lap before she could protest. When she tried to get up, his hands clamped around her waist, holding her in place.

"What—" She stiffened and brought her legs together.

"Relax," he whispered, putting his hands on her knees and opening her legs.

Before she could think of another ploy to stop him, his mouth blazed a trail from her knee up her thigh. Up…up… He was going all the way.

He spread her legs, his expert lips lingering in all

those intimate spots a nice girl would never let a man anywhere near. His tongue found forbidden lips and made nerves she'd never known she had flame and tingle and come to life full of new needs. He kept kissing her until the pleasure down there grew nearly unbearable.

She gasped, squirming in her wooden chair. Then her hands cupped his black head. Every flick of his tongue, every wet, darting kiss made her blood pulse faster. She was soon so hot, she felt steam must be seeping out of every pore.

This is bad. I can't blame this on ouzo.

Then his unerring mouth found her most sensitive spot and toyed with it, taking her to some rosy nirvana, a paradise beyond thought and doubt. The perfumed air of this insanely delicious heaven smelled of spring roses. She was near the summit, flying weightlessly, melting and moaning softly, when his tongue and callused hands stopped.

Abruptly, she fell to earth like a brick.

Faster than she could blink, he had scrambled into his chair and was stirring his coffee with a well-practiced air of gentlemanly innocence.

She took her cue, pulled her robe together and sat up ramrod straight in a more ladylike posture. Her heart was still knocking, and she couldn't look at him without blushing. Still, she stuck a spoon into her yogurt and lifted her cup and swallowed her cold, black coffee.

The front door slammed open and Noah came running in.

Anthony must have ears like a lynx.

"Dad, is she coming? Is she?"

Coming? Her skin flamed at the word.

"No," she said, not daring to look at Anthony for fear she'd really turn beet red. "And, Tony, tell him that's definite. Please…tell him…and…and just go."

"Noah, it's your turn to ask her. I did my best…to work my…er…charms on her." The incorrigible beast smiled at her in that lopsided way that made her heart flip. "Now it's your turn, son."

"You're dangerous," she muttered to Anthony. "You know that, don't you?"

"I try."

"You don't play fair."

"Who's playing?" he murmured silkily.

She could still feel his tongue rasping over her silky sex, still feel his roughened hands doing all those delicious things to her lower body that had her wet with desire.

As if he read her mind, Anthony smiled at her wickedly. Then he downed a long swig of coffee as Noah popped into the kitchen.

"Did you say please, Dad?"

Anthony's black eyes seared her. "In my own special way I said pretty please. But it didn't work."

Didn't work? Her whole body was boiling mush. She'd been on the verge. She was still wet. And hot. Burning up. Every nerve in her body was screaming for him. She wanted him so much. And the handsome snake knew it.

"You did this deliberately!" she mouthed to Anthony.

"It was fun, wasn't it?"

A half sob bubbled up from her throat.

Then Noah looked up and began bouncing from one foot to the other. His eyes were so bright and intense, she swallowed the lump in her throat and tried to calm down.

"Please come," Noah whispered. "Please. Pretty please…"

"I tried to make her," his dad said with *that* smile. *Kill.* "I really can't," she demurred.

Noah's eyes clouded with real pain. "He was mean, wasn't he?"

"Not exactly…."

"Not exactly?" Anthony winked at her.

"Then why?" Noah persisted.

"I just can't…."

"Make her come, Dad!"

"Believe me, I tried!"

"Just go—both of you!"

"All right. You win," Anthony said to her.

Why did she feel such loss as he stood up to go?

"But, Dad—"

Seven

Zoe was walking briskly along a narrow sidewalk in the bright sunshine past palm trees and tourist shops on her way to the bus stop. Determined to put Anthony out of her mind, she'd spent the past hour or two reading tour books on Rhodes. Not that she'd really been able to concentrate all that well on her reading. She could barely think about anything other than Anthony and their wonderful sex last night, and then their latest little adventure in the kitchen that had left her so restless and edgy.

Not that two hours would have been nearly enough time to read and understand about the Knights, who'd built their impressive fortress in Rhodes Town, even if she hadn't felt distracted by Anthony. What had those fighting monks who'd been so determined to fight Islam been about?

Motorcycles jammed the sidewalk in front of a

café, so she hopped down into the street to walk around them. The sun felt wonderful on her back and arms. Yes, she was definitely on her way into Rhodes Town to get her mind off sex. She was going to see the Knights' fort and think about ancient wars between Moslems and Christians instead of a certain handsome cowboy.

As she walked past a minivan, a motorcycle came out of nowhere and whipped past her so close she screamed. Dropping her books and purse, she tripped over them. Not that the rider looked back.

Picking her things up, she scrambled back onto her sidewalk as fast as she could, just as another motorcycle roared past her.

What was this thing Greeks had with motorcycles? They were such nice people—until they got on motorcycles. Didn't they have mothers to tell them that motorcycles were dangerous?

A horn tooted. Scared it was another motorcycle, she turned. A square, little red car she couldn't identify swerved as recklessly as the motorcyclist toward the curb beside her. She was about to scream when a brown, work-roughened hand that she most certainly could identify—hadn't it been all over her thighs just an hour or so ago in the kitchen—thrust the red door open.

"Sure, you won't go with us?" rumbled that deep, sexy drawl that made her homesick for Texas and turned her stomach to mush.

"No. Definitely. No. I'm not going with you." She spoke loudly and clearly even as she felt his gaze sear her naked legs.

Too bad she made the mistake of leaning down and meeting his burning gaze.

"You're blushing," he whispered.

She lost herself in the coal-bright depths of his eyes, which were deep and dark and spoke to her on some unfathomable, ungentlemanly level.

Noah's were white-hot with innocent eagerness. "Please, please, Aunt Zoe."

A tremulous silence hung over the three of them. She licked her lips. A dozen motorcycles roared past them.

"Don't go, girl. Sex last night. Then the kitchen…"

Much to everybody's surprise, especially hers, she ignored those worried little voices and slid a long bare leg inside the little car, slamming her door with a great deal of zest.

"Eyes on the road," she commanded saucily. "Oh, and by the way, where are we going?"

Anthony tried to hide his lopsided grin as he turned around and hit the accelerator.

"Dad! You know what the man said!"

"What man?" Zoe wanted to know.

"The man who rented Dad this car," Noah answered.

"The poor devil only owns three cars," Anthony explained. "He couldn't stop polishing the front bumper and the headlights even after he gave me the keys. He nearly wept when I put it in too high a gear as I drove off the lot. Yelled at me not to drive into *Rodos*."

"What? That's where the Knights' fortress is. Where else would any self-respecting tourist want to go?"

"Exactly."

"He said not to park by rocks," Noah chirped from the front seat.

She leaned forward. "Why on earth not?"

"Because," Noah said, "the goats will jump on it."

They all laughed.

"Where are we going?" she asked.

"Lindos," Anthony replied.

Soon they were driving along the east side of the island where the cliffs were high and rocky and plunged to the sea. An hour or so later they reached Lindos, which was a white jewel of a village, its sun-drenched, boxy houses perched high above the sparkling, aqua sea on sheer rock ledges.

Anthony parked outside of town near rows of tour buses. The threesome headed down a steep, narrow road. They had to stay to the side to avoid dozens of motorcycles that zipped past them. When one roared too close, Zoe grabbed Noah's hand instinctively.

The little boy clasped her fingers tightly and looked up at her and smiled.

Her heart fluttered with strange longing when he held on to her so trustingly. He was so darling. And he needed a mother so much.

"I want one of those when I grow up," Noah said.

"A motorcycle? Do you remember that one-legged boy we saw in Athens?" Anthony countered.

"Don't scare him," Zoe whispered.

"I'm glad you came," Anthony said quietly when Noah loped ahead.

"I don't think I have a brain cell working."

He smiled. "Good. That's the way I like you."

She was dangerously glad she'd come to this charming town of small white houses that lined narrow, winding streets. But it wasn't being in Greece that was so wonderful. It was being with them.

She felt so alive and happy as they climbed past shops and vendors and tourists who spoke a babel of tongues, all the way to the ancient acropolis that crowned the village.

Sometimes Noah held her hand. Sometimes he rushed ahead. And always, always, she was too aware of Anthony at her side, the back of his hand lingering at her waist. It seemed he was constantly finding some excuse to touch her.

She knew she shouldn't be with them. She was here to forget Anthony. He belonged to the past. To Shady Lomas. To Rene. To scandal. Zoe had burned her bridges when she'd married Duncan. The whole town thought she was some sort of black widow or scarlet woman. She couldn't go back. She couldn't be in love with Anthony Duke…her nephew. Why was she even thinking about impossible possibilities?

The rocky path grew smooth and slippery. When Zoe paused in their climb to look at an embroidered tablecloth a woman had spread out on the rocks, she nearly stumbled. Instantly Anthony's dark hand was at her waist. Steadying her, he drew her closer to his own body.

His fingers burned through her sundress. As always, it was as if a jolt of electricity had passed through her. She jumped, startled.

Then his leg brushed hers. He stood so close she could smell him…his cologne…the laundry detergent that clung to his fresh, white dress shirt…and him…that clean male scent that was his alone. In one second she was back in the kitchen, her legs open, his mouth, his tongue…

Her palms grew damp. So did certain other un-mentionable parts.

Oh, dear.

"Do you want the tablecloth?" Anthony's voice was a husky whisper against her ear.

"No." She bit her bottom lip. That wasn't what she wanted. She couldn't have what she wanted. She was the black widow, the shady lady of Shady Lomas. She'd become too rich, too unforgivably rich, when her older husband had died.

She'd loved Duncan at the end. Maybe not the way she'd loved Anthony. But then he hadn't hurt her the way Anthony had, either. Knowing that his death could happen at any moment, Duncan had been determined to live life to the fullest.

"I want all the old Goody Two-shoes to know I'm still kicking," Duncan had said one night. "And you and the stuffed-shirt-who-won't-own-me-as-his-uncle are too young and too serious to appreciate each other. People need to suffer a little before they marry. Mark my words. One day you'll be glad you married me."

Duncan hadn't made her crazy with jealousy and insecurities that drove her to— No, Duncan had been wise and understanding. In a strange way, he'd been the father she'd never had. But nobody wanted to hear that, least of all Anthony.

Well, all she knew was that there was no going back for either Anthony or herself. She belonged in Manhattan now. She was a big-city editor.

Right. You're like a scared little mouse in every editorial meeting. You dumped Veronica. Who are you without Veronica?

It was hot when they reached the ancient city. The

acropolis was crawling with sunburned tourists. Noah climbed up onto every rock and had to be watched and chased. Every time Noah looked at her or grabbed her hand, Zoe ached because she knew it was Rene he really wanted.

Rene belonged with them. Not her. Never her.

And yet...today the impossible felt almost possible.

Beneath them the windowpanes in the boxy, white houses caught the sun and shone like gold. Anthony came up to her.

"It's so beautiful here," she said to him.

He nodded, saying nothing, simply staring into her eyes. When the wind blew her hair into her face, he smoothed the tendrils back. Then he smiled. Her heart pounding, she turned away.

Later they found a roof garden with awnings to shade them and stunning views of the sea, acropolis and village. There was even a cat that looked sort of like Super Cat to throw scraps to. On the way home, Noah and she sat in the back seat and played adventure games. Then they opened the sunroof and stood up together, letting the wind blow through their hair as Anthony drove on the narrow, winding road.

The day was perfect. Unbearably perfect, and every perfect moment had made her want one more moment.

The little car raced through the two-lane streets of the last Greek village before reaching their suburb. The sun was low; the glowing light magical. And, oh, those misting, purple mountains in the distance, they were magical, too.

A few minutes later Tony pulled into the resort

parking lot. He cut the motor and smiled at her. She didn't know what to say.

"Thank you," she finally whispered.

"Thank you," he said.

He got out and opened her door. She put her hand in his. He helped her out, and together they gathered her things.

One day down and six more to go, she thought when they reached her door.

What about the nights? She couldn't stand it. She was head over heels in love with both father and son. Impulsive, impossible relationships were her specialty.

"What about dinner?" Anthony whispered against her ear.

"Tonight?" she squeaked.

"I've got that camp-out on the beach," Noah said, "with all the other resort kids. I can't eat supper with you."

"I know, son. I was asking Zoe for a date."

"Wow!" Noah's smile was so big, she saw every one of his new teeth. As he studied them both, his huge blue eyes became fever bright with eagerness.

"Of course, I…I should say no," she said.

"Neither one of us has been doing what we're supposed to lately," he murmured.

Remembering their interlude in the kitchen, she couldn't speak.

"Your place or mine?" Anthony whispered.

"Seven o'clock," she said. "My place."

Zoe was scared. Feelings of vulnerability had her shaking every time Anthony looked at her or got too close. The air in her kitchen seemed to sizzle, now that they were alone in it again—and there was nothing in the frying pan.

Dinner, which had been carryout Greek salad, roasted chicken and red wine was over. She and Anthony were seated across the table from each other again.

He glanced at his watch and then at her. "We have an hour and a half before camp-out ends. What do you want to do next?"

Her gaze left his handsome face and wandered around the room, avoiding *the* chair where he'd made her melt. "We could go for a walk on the beach."

"Yes." He got up from the table, stacked the dishes and put them in the sink. "We could."

"Noah loves all those perfect little rocks."

When she arose, he was right behind her.

"I'm not Noah." Anthony's hands touched her hair. Before she thought, she tilted her neck to gaze up at him. He took that as an invitation and slid his arms around her. His slightest touch held magic warmth and brought profound comfort and need. She felt his lips in her hair, and their heat burned all the way to her scalp and sent little shivers down her spine.

Oh, dear.

"How do I know you're not just after the ranch?" Her lips barely made a sound.

He cupped her breasts. "How do I know you're not just hot for my bod?"

"This is insane."

His hands moved lower, circling her waist. "Wildly so. Maybe that's why it's so much fun. I like the way you shake every time I touch you or look at you. The way you blush when I look at your legs.''

She liked it too. That was the trouble. ''Well, *I* don't. It makes me feel…'' Vulnerable and out-of-control…crazy with want to have the one thing I've been running from for years.

''My whole life has been about forgetting you,'' she said.

''Maybe we've both been on the wrong track. Do you know I've spent years and years working and taking care of people, doing what I'm supposed to. Years not giving in to any of my own feelings. I shouldn't have married Rene. I should have faced what I felt for you.''

''But you had the perfect marriage.''

''You can believe that myth if you want to.'' He paused. ''This week, when I first saw you, I was furious. So furious I began to realize I hadn't really felt much in years. Then I run into you in Athens and feel this powerful thing for you…. Why?''

''The black widow at work.''

''Don't call yourself that. What I'm trying to say is that you make me feel alive.''

''You've made me feel alive, too,'' she admitted. ''Why do you suppose that is?''

''Maybe it's just that you're dangerous and forbidden and I know I should know better than to trust you.''

''Ditto,'' she said, hardly daring to breathe.

''Or maybe…maybe we should stop analyzing it. Something tells me to just go for it. Let's see what happens…where this takes it. Let's find out why we feel the way we do. Life can get too predictable.''

''Not mine,'' she whispered.

He laughed. "I want to make love to you. But this time you have to admit, beforehand, that I'm not forcing you."

"I'm supposed to be here thinking about my life. And…and writing."

"Maybe being with me is the same thing. You're living it. Your body is making up your mind for you."

She drew a breath to steady herself. "Not good."

"Your body was always smarter than your brain, bookwormella."

"Thanks a lot."

"You've got a great body, and I've got a question."

She waited.

"Do you want to finish what we started this morning in your kitchen?"

"What you started, not me."

"There you go, blaming me—"

"Okay. Okay," she admitted.

"Well, do you—"

"Well, I'll have to ask my great body."

"What?"

"You said my body was smart." She went to the kitchen counter and turned on the radio. Greek music filled the condo, and she began to sway back and forth to its beat.

"What the hell are you doing?"

"You asked my body a question. It's making up its mind. Does it or doesn't it want to make love to you?"

"I'm waiting."

"Just watch," she whispered. Lowering the strap of her sundress, she whirled to the music. After a minute or two, her hand went for the zipper at the back of her dress. In the next instant the dress slid off her breasts, waist and hips to the floor, and all she had on was her black bra and black, lacy, thong panties.

She turned the music louder and began to undulate to the frenzied tempo. Soon the beat throbbed in every cell of her body. Or was it his narrowed, brilliant eyes that made her blood cells boogie?

She unhooked her bra. As her body swayed, her breasts bounced. Oh, man, the heat in his eyes and his obvious arousal when she threw her bra at him turned her on big-time.

When the music began to wind down, she danced her way to the bedroom. He followed. Last thing, she stripped off her panties and threw them at him, too. Then she bolted her door in his face.

He jiggled the knob. "Was that a yes or a no?" came his ragged voice.

"You tortured me this morning. Now it's my turn."

"Let me in, you sexy witch."

"The bod's thinking about it."

It didn't take the bod long. With shaking hands, she opened the door.

He stepped inside, her black thong panties dangling from a finger. He let them fall onto the white tiled floor. For a breathless eternity, their eyes devoured each other. Then he swept her in his arms. "Where did you learn to strip like that? What other tricks do you have up your sleeve?"

"No tricks. I just want you more than I can bear."

"Me, too." He slid his tongue into the honey-sweetness of her mouth, and she felt herself do a slow burn as he kissed her.

"I'm melting. I'm melting," she said.

"Me, too. Shut up. End of conversation. And..."

"And what?"

"No counting," he ordered.

"Okay," she whispered against his mouth. "But you have to promise to go slow and..."

"And?"

"And be tender."

"Tender? Like this?" When he traced the contours of her breasts with the tip of his tongue, she gave a long, drawn-out sigh of pure pleasure.

"You're off to a great start."

He began teasing her with little love bites on her throat and shoulders. Then he played with her hair the way he used to, winding it through his fingers and lifting it to his lips. "How beautiful you are."

"We're running out of time."

He drew her closer. "You said go slow and be tender."

"You promised to finish what you started this morning in the kitchen."

He made love to her sweetly and tenderly, satisfying her in every way. When it was over and she was nestled in his arms, feeling as limp and pliable and lazy as a well-simmered noodle, her telephone rang jarringly.

"Don't answer it," he whispered.

She picked it up. When the caller said hello and she recognized the voice, Zoe shot to a sitting position, her hands gripping the receiver like claws.

"Oh, dear." She let out a little moan of pure misery.

Anthony dove under the covers and put his tongue between her thighs.

Zoe gasped, "Who gave you this number?" Then she put her hand over the receiver and pushed at Anthony's broad warm shoulder.

But the distracting velvety tongue continued to flick and cause rapture. The voice on the other end of the line babbled frantically.

"Anthony, I can't concentrate." To the caller she said, "Up? You're here in Rhodes? Now?"

The tongue made thrillingly slow circling motions. In the next breath she shuddered in pure bliss.

"You can't come up! No!" she said to the caller. She patted Anthony's head, "Darling, you'd better go—now—"

"Who is it?" he demanded gruffly from under the sheet.

"I…I can't tell you! It's a secret! No! It's an emergency!"

He pushed the sheet out of the way and frowned at her. "Is it about Noah? Is he okay?"

Shaking her head, she cupped her hand over the receiver. "Go now, darling. I'll call you later."

"Is it a man?"

"Worse." She waved at him to go with her free hand. "Business. Please, just go."

He looked puzzled and a little worried as she pointed to his clothes and motioned to him to get dressed.

He stood up. "You're going to tell me what's going on—"

"Later." She nodded.

He was scowling as he pulled on his slacks. "Is it a man?" he demanded again.

"I already answered that question."

"You'd better be telling me the truth."

"I am. I swear."

"With our history, it's not so easy to trust you, you know."

"That was low."

He grabbed the rest of his clothes and stalked out of her condo.

"I'll call you," she cried.

With Anthony gone, Zoe lay back against her pillows and tried to give her full attention to her exasperating caller.

Eight

"**I**s someone else there?" Veronica was so over-wrought her Texas drawl was way more pronounced than usual. The word *there* came out tha-a-a-a-re. "Did I call at a bad time?"

Oh, boy, did you? "Don't be ridiculous," Zoe said crossly. "This is a great time. What's wrong?"

"Is someone there?" Veronica demanded. "When I heard you were in Rhodes staying at some hideous time-share, I rented a villa on a mountain with olive groves and lemon trees that go down to the Aegean. It reminds me of Delphi."

"I haven't been to Delphi."

"Well, you should go. It's magical. The muse liked Delphi. Anyway, ancient history. I'm here. You can move into the villa with me…help me get this novel started.… It's called *Vanished*. This woman looks up her old boyfriend."

''You still hung up on the old-boyfriend theme?''

''Aren't we all? So, my characters have this big date, sort of a reunion. Sex. Everything is too perfect. Except…then she vanishes. Her twin sister gets worried and starts looking for her.

''The twin meets this man. Only I can't get started, and there's no spark. I keep writing the same sentence over and over.''

''No. I cannot help you. Manhattan. Abdul. Super Cat—remember?''

''That dud. Not your cat—Abdul! He locked your precious cat in the closet and then he pounced at me in your hall. Honest! You're not going to let that worthless dud come between *us*. You know you're better off without him!''

''End of conversation.'' Zoe hung up on her.

The phone rang again. Only this time it was Anthony.

''What is going on?''

There was a loud knock at her front door.

''I really can't talk right now.''

''Is this about a man?''

''No. Goodbye.''

''Don't hang up—''

''Goodbye.''

''Don't…''

''Sorry.'' Gently she placed the phone on the hook.

While Veronica pounded, Zoe took her time getting dressed. She found a pair of soft jeans and grabbed a white pullover cotton sweater out of a drawer. She even combed her hair and put on lipstick. And, of course, she had to make that bed. That took a while since all the sheets had come off and were in wadded tangles on the floor.

Only when the condo was immaculate did she open the door. Veronica's mouth fell open. "You…you look great! New nose? Or?"

Zoe fluffed her hair. "Same old me. But, hey, you look great too."

"How do you like my new boobs?"

Veronica bounced through the door in a skin-tight pink jersey top.

"Impressive. And you've gone back to blond."

Veronica shook her loose curls. "To go with my new movie-star figure. I'm having fun with it, too. This is definitely the real me."

"Okay. But after this, no more plastic surgery. Stop right there. Enough already."

"That's what my mother says. The nose is good. And the boobs are perfect. But she's always sending me pictures of these plastic surgery disasters. Faces of stars in tabloids who look like wax dolls melting."

"Your mom's right. No more surgery, okay? There's nothing wrong with you, Veronica. You are okay just as you are. Someday you are going to realize that."

"Since you dumped me, I'm into therapy." Veronica headed toward the kitchen. "Lots of dishes—" she whirled, and her voice went silky "—for a woman vacationing alone."

"Veronica, why did you come here?"

She whipped around. "You have to forgive me."

"I forgive you, but that doesn't mean I have to work with you. You betrayed me."

"Never again. You matter more to me than anybody…except my mother. I swear I'll never do anything to hurt you again. I was awful. I know. I wouldn't forgive me, but you're sweeter than me. And I'll go all to pieces if you don't.''

''That is emotional blackmail.''

''I know. I don't care how low I have to stoop to get you back. Just listen.''

''Okay.'' Wearily Zoe went to the stove. ''Hot tea?''

Veronica nodded, and Zoe set a kettle of water and lit a burner.

''In my defense, I was all alone in New York. I couldn't face Ursula or you without the ending of my book. But I couldn't write. What kind of writer misses all her deadlines? I had that huge advance—which I'd already spent. So much was riding on that ending. And then that creep wrote all those awful things on the Internet. I felt alone and desperate.''

''You're repeating yourself.''

''Okay. The point is I was just so crazy. The sex was awful. It made me really hate myself, and that was before you came in and found out. Please…please try to understand. I really am totally, truly, forever sorry.''

Zoe couldn't help smiling. ''As apologies go, yours is pretty inspired, but then you are a writer.''

''I'm so sorry. Really—''

''All right,'' Zoe murmured as the teakettle whistled.

She poured tea. They both sweetened it.

''But you can't stay here now,'' Zoe said. ''I have things going on in my own life. And I can't move in to your villa.''

''But my book—''

''Hello?'' Zoe took a long sip of hot tea and then

looked Veronica dead in the eye. "Are you listening? I have a life, too. I had an agenda of my own when I came to Rhodes."

"But...what about me—"

"We'll do a long lunch. Tomorrow. In Rhodes Town." Zoe grabbed a yellow guidebook off her stack on the table and thumbed through it until she came to a rooftop restaurant in the Knights' fortress she'd read about. "This place is supposed to be quiet, and it has lovely views. Bring your legal pads. We'll be inspired."

Veronica pulled out her address book and jotted the name of the restaurant down. "What would I do without you?"

"You'd be fine."

"Not without my muse."

She got up. They went to the door and hugged.

"I'm really glad to hear you're in therapy," Zoe said.

Zoe was dressed and needed to leave if she was going to be on time for lunch with Veronica, but Anthony wouldn't get off the phone.

"Why won't you tell me who this mystery lunch date is with?" Anthony demanded.

"I said I'll see you tonight."

"Lunch with this mystery person is going to take most of the morning and all afternoon?"

"I'll explain later."

"Is it a man?"

"No...for the fourteenth time!"

"Zoe—"

"Trust me."

"Trust Shady Lomas's black widow?"

"That's a low ball and you know it. How many times—"

"Sorry."

"That apology doesn't sound even a tiny bit sincere."

"Because it isn't."

"Because you're too macho and pigheaded."

"Any more of my flaws you'd like to list?"

"Oversexed."

"That's a flaw?"

"A fun flaw." Zoe glanced at her watch. "Look, I've got to go, or I'll be late for lunch."

"It's only ten."

"The person I'm meeting is extremely impatient."

"I want to meet this…this impatient person."

"And I want you to mind your own business."

"You are my business."

"One night of sex and you think you own me."

"Two nights and one morning. You know what they say about three being a charm."

"You don't own me, Tony."

"Zoe—"

"Goodbye."

"Zoe—"

"Take your mind off this. Play adventure games with Noah. And while you're at it, give him a kiss on his forehead for me."

"I'd rather give you a kiss somewhere else."

"Tonight. I can't wait." She blew him a kiss and hung the phone up slowly.

With Noah gone to resort camp again, Anthony couldn't contain himself. He had every window of the condo open, so he could smell roses and the salty

Aegean. But the lush setting only upset him and made him all the more edgy. Every time he thought about Zoe going to lunch with this mystery person in some romantic locale, he cursed silently. What was she pulling this time?

He stalked out to the patio and stared blindly at those infernal blue mountains across the aqua water. One minute he'd been kissing her between the legs and, damn it, she'd been melting, and then the next she'd sent him packing and all because somebody had called her. Would she tell him who? No! And now this mystery lunch date!

When they'd had hot sex as teens, Zoe had gotten neurotic about it and run off. When she'd caught Rene coming on to him, she'd believed the worst without even listening to him. Then the next thing he knew, she'd run off with Uncle Duncan and created the scandal of Shady Lomas.

Bookworm? Sexpot? Black widow? Who the hell was she? Had she and Uncle Duncan even had a real marriage?

Noah hardly knew her, but he already adored her. Like dogs, kids had highly honed instincts about human character. Kids hadn't been properly indoctrinated, so they saw through lots of bull. Thus, Anthony trusted Noah's instincts more than he did his own.

Bottom line—do you want the shady lady of Shady Lomas, who once utterly humiliated you, in your life…maybe forever?

Hadn't Aunt Peggy and his own mother set this up? They must think such a match was okay. Noah adored Zoe. Anthony adored her. Who else in Shady Lomas mattered?

So—who the hell was Zoe going to spend the day with when she should be with him?

"Trust me," she'd said.

Anthony did trust her. Well, sort of. He just had to know who she was with and where she was. When he heard her door open and close, he pulled back his window curtain just as she stepped out in a skimpy red sundress slit to the thigh. She was wearing strappy red sandals that made her legs look long and curvy.

Those legs. His legs. He had to follow those legs. Even as pride and indignation slammed full force into his conscience, he hid behind the curtain just long enough for her to disappear down the walk behind a tall green hedge. Then he grabbed his wallet and keys and raced after her.

"You have no right…"

"Damn it. I bedded her. She melts every time she looks at me. No matter what she's up to or who she's with, she's mine."

Anthony thought of the last nine years without her. They'd been dead, lonely years. Everybody but his mother had thought he was so happy with Rene, but he'd been living a lie.

He slid into his rental car when Zoe flagged a cab. When the taxi tore off, Tony turned his key in the ignition.

Nobody was taking her away from him again. Period. Because he loved her.

He loved her.

Anthony didn't have much time to reflect on that shocking thought. Nor did he want to. Her cab driver was a maniac. The madman ran lights, passed in no-passing zones. In the middle of Rhodes Town, Anthony got caught at a light and lost the jerk.

Anthony drove aimlessly for a while. Rhodes Town was so packed with tourists, it took him an hour even to find a parking place in a park under a palm tree. By then he felt so frustrated, he banged the steering wheel with both fists. Then he looked up at the colossal battlements, huge watchtowers and bridges of the Knights' fortress. Zoe was alone somewhere in that very romantic old fort with her mystery date.

Oh, God.... *Love?* He loved her? Such questions made Anthony feel like he was on a ship that was riddled with holes, a ship that was sinking really fast in a very deep ocean. He slid the key out of the ignition. He had to find her and start patching the holes in their relationship before they both drowned.

Real relationships weren't ever easy. But how could he possibly convince Zoe to leave her glamorous job in Manhattan and come back to him and face the narrow-minded people in Shady Lomas, who loved to gossip about her?

Determined to find her before she did something impulsive, Anthony got out of the car and started walking toward the magnificent golden walls of the old city. The Knights' fortified castle with its thick walls and wide mote filled with huge cannonballs was very impressive. If he hadn't felt so consumed with jealousy and uncertainty, he might have enjoyed stepping back into history.

If only Zoe had been at his side with Noah trailing along, he might have gladly paused to stare up at the high crenellated walls. He would have leaned against a low bridge and lifted Noah for a better view of all the cannonballs stacked up in little pyramids every-where—in the mote, on the bridges, on the lawns.

The fortress was huge and made one think of the age of chivalry, of knights and armor. The Crusaders had been dead serious about not wanting Jerusalem to fall into Moslem hands. In a way that war was still going on.

Anthony trudged up the narrow, rocky streets for two hours, walked until his stomach was rumbling with hunger, and he felt crazy as hell.

Damn it! Where was she?

If she'd run off with another man…

Anthony imagined her in bed, melting beneath an-other man's lips, and rage and hurt shuddered through him.

"Trust me," she'd whispered.

He held on to that plea as if it were a lifeline and kept walking along the crenellated walls and stone towers.

He had to find her.

Nine

"**Y**ou're really something!" Veronica said.

Veronica's golden hair was blowing about her naked shoulders. Voluptuous pink bosoms seemed to explode out of her tight green dress. "What are you—my spark plug!"

Zoe laughed. "I think I prefer the word *muse*."

The rooftop Greek restaurant was as charming and as quiet as the guidebook had predicted. It had views of the marina and fortress. If Zoe stood, she could see the two bronze deer at the harbor's entrance.

Zoe had her usual Greek salad with a diet cola, so Veronica, who had a guilt complex about her voracious appetites, had dutifully followed suit.

They'd brainstormed an hour before lunch, and Veronica had written twenty pages of notes on her yellow pad. Instead of being scared and depressed, now she was excited about her book. Repeatedly she said she'd found her spark.

"You're a natural at dieting," Veronica said. "Me, I have to watch my figure."

"Which is spilling out of your chartreuse halter dress."

"After the surgery, I had to buy all new clothes. Or at least tops."

When Veronica polished off the last scraps of lettuce out of both their salad bowls, she called the waiter over and ordered more ouzo.

"You've had two glasses," Zoe reminded her.

"You're always counting. If I can't eat, I have to do something."

"I'm a counter." *Oh, dear.* For no reason at all, Zoe's mind turned to sex with Anthony that first night when she'd counted to prolong the ecstasy.

"Why, you're blushing," Veronica said. "Have you met somebody here?"

"If I were you, I'd watch the ouzo," Zoe cautioned in a dry tone. "It's too good."

"That sounds more like a recommendation than a warning." Veronica sipped the dregs from the glass the waiter had just set before her and then ordered another.

"It is and it isn't…a recommendation."

Zoe thought about her first night in Rhodes when she'd eaten alone and had drunk too much ouzo. Would she have fallen into bed with Anthony—the man she was supposed to be here to forget—jumpstarted if she hadn't been so mellow from ouzo?

Oh, well, that horse was out of the gate and galloping toward the finish line.

"I love him," Zoe whispered under her breath as she toyed with her fork.

"You're in lust."

"You're doing it. You're doing it."

"I want to *do* it with him tonight."

"That's not what I meant."

"You're talking to yourself again," Veronica said.

Zoe bit her lip and put down her fork. "Bad habit."

"And blushing!" Veronica said slyly. "I talk to myself all the time. That's how I start all my books. Then I start writing down what the voice says. I hate it when it stops talking." Veronica swirled her glass of ouzo. "I think this stuff is inspiring me. Or maybe it's just you—my muse. Hey! Back to the blushes. You didn't answer my question. Did you meet somebody?"

Zoe felt her cheeks heat again. "I told you I came over here to think…and to write a little."

"And have you written?"

"The same sentence over and over."

"I know that feeling. So, what have you been up to?"

Again heat crawled up Zoe's neck. "We're supposed to be working on *Vanished.*"

"You're blushing again."

"It's the sun."

"You're in the shade, love. And it's pretty cool out here with all these wonderful sea breezes."

"Rays are everywhere," Zoe siad. "I have a very delicate complexion."

"I know a blush when I see one. Who is he? Can I meet him?"

"After what happened in my apartment? Are you

crazy? Do you think I'd want you to meet any of my friends…if I had a man friend I mean.''

"We're talking romance here. Not friendship. And it hurts me that you don't trust me.''

"Veronica! We've discussed that until I'm sick of it.''

"Okay. I know. It isn't an easy thing to forgive.''

"What you did hurts more than what Abdul did. You really meant a lot to me. I went on the line for you. I had faith in you.''

Veronica's face softened. She reached across the table and took Zoe's hand. "I'm very sorry about what happened in your apartment. You are so precious to me. I couldn't stop eating after I did that to you. I gained fifteen pounds in a week, and I've been on the most terrible diet ever since. I love you so much. I'm sorry. I swear I will never betray you again. Not even if you date Prince Charming!''

Zoe swallowed. "Okay. I think I'm starting to believe you, at least in this fleeting second. But trust takes time, understand? At least with me. You're not the only neurotic around, you know. I can be very jealous…when it comes to certain people.''

"Your new boyfriend, you mean?''

Zoe nodded.

"I love you. I won't betray you again.''

"So, let's get back to work. We only have a few more hours.''

"And why is that? What are you doing tonight?''

"I have a life. Why is that concept so hard for you?''

"Boundaries? Right? My therapist is trying to drill that concept into me. All right. You have a life. No more questions. Work.''

But while they brainstormed and scribbled on legal pads, Veronica kept watching her slyly and toying with her glass of ouzo. Like a bloodhound tracking a scent, Veronica couldn't let go. She was a writer and that made her too curious about people.

"I have to stretch," Veronica said. She got up and moved languidly over to the wall and looked down at the flagstone street.

Her face lit up. "Get up, Zoe! Have I got a sight for you!"

Zoe rose and moved toward Veronica.

"He's the one!" Veronica pointed down at a tall, broad-shouldered man in the street.

Anthony looked up as Veronica leaned over the wall, bosoms spilling out of her green dress as she waved to him wildly.

Zoe gulped. "But he's taken," she whispered. "He's mine."

Veronica didn't even hear her. Anthony waved back at her with equal lusty enthusiasm.

"Rene was blond and big on top," said a vicious little voice inside Zoe's head.

"You said if I was dating Prince Charming," Zoe whispered.

"Talk about Prince Charming. He's coming inside. Oh! Oh! He's coming upstairs. Oh! Where's my lipstick?"

"Veronica, there's something I've got to tell you—"

"Not now! I've got to go to the ladies' room and put myself together."

"Veronica, he's mine!"

Veronica had raced away. If she'd heard, she paid Zoe no attention.

So much for trust.

* * *

Anthony was so happy that Zoe was with a woman and not a man that he couldn't stop grinning at Veronica, who was a looker, if you went for the flashy, flirty type.

"My, my! So this is your long lunch date?" he asked Zoe.

"You two know each other?" Veronica wanted to know.

Anthony stared at Zoe. "You could say that."

"We have adjoining time-shares." Zoe's voice sounded dry. She felt as if she'd swallowed a lime whole and couldn't get it down.

"I asked her if she's met somebody here?"

"And what did she say?"

"Nothing. She didn't mention you at all. She used to have this boyfriend in Manhattan—Abdul. He looked a lot like you. I guess she goes for dark, handsome guys."

"Shhhh," Zoe growled at Veronica.

"I'm starving," Anthony said. "Do you mind if I join you?"

"Not at all," Veronica said in a thick, syrupy voice. She shot him a lush smile and leaned closer, pointing her pink bosoms at him.

He grinned again so broadly, Zoe wanted to slap him. "Stop slobbering," she whispered.

He arched an eyebrow her way. "Did you say something?"

"No!"

Veronica began to tell him that she was a big, important writer now but that Zoe had discovered her in the slush pile.

"For a long time she was the only person who believed in me," Veronica said. "Until I met Zoe, nobody ever thought I was much. Since I met her, I've been a star. But I've never written a book without her help. That's why I followed her here. I couldn't get my new novel started."

Anthony studied the thick legal pads. Maybe this woman had overdone the peroxide and the implants, but she was serious as hell about her work. So were a lot of people...like Zoe's boss. And Zoe herself. She'd run off from him in the middle of hot sex to deal with this blocked writer. That was really sweet of Zoe.

Anthony made up his mind that if Veronica was important to Zoe, he'd be nice to her even if it killed him. When Veronica put her hand on his knee and made a pass, he pushed her fingers away and smiled at both women awkwardly.

He had to be nice.

At some point Zoe bowed out of the conversation, so it was just him and the pushy blonde engaging in witty repartee. He finished lunch and said he had to go.

"No," Veronica pleaded. "This is just starting to get fun."

Zoe stood up. "We're through working, aren't we?"

"Oh, yes!" Veronica said. "This is definitely playtime."

Anthony was about to get up, too, but the hand with the long fingernails was back on his leg, clawing. If he sprang to his feet, he didn't trust what Veronica would do next. So he stayed put.

"Then I'm going," Zoe said.

"I've got my car," Anthony said. "Can I drive you back to the resort?"

"No. I'll get a cab. You two stay and enjoy yourselves."

"Zoe—"

"You two have fun!"

"Zoe!"

Zoe ignored him and ran toward the stairs. When he sprang to his feet, Veronica tackled him. By the time he'd gotten himself untangled and downstairs, Zoe's cab was speeding away.

The waiter came out and said, "Sir, your friend…the lady upstairs…that blonde…in the green dress…she's passed out."

Anthony raced back upstairs. Sure enough, Veronica was doubled over the table, blond hair spilling over the salad bowls and silverware. She was face-down in the breadbasket, her hand still gripping her last half-full glass of ouzo.

Five waiters circled him. When he glared at them, they shrugged their shoulders and looked up at the deep blue sky. Anthony cursed silently under his breath. He wanted to find Zoe, but Veronica was Zoe's most important writer. He couldn't just leave her here at the mercy of whoever found her.

Gently he shook her bare shoulder. "Veronica…"

At his touch, she muttered something incoherent. He lifted her head out of the breadbasket. Her lashes fluttered. She shot him a lush smile. Then she saw her waiter and waved her ouzo glass. "Empthy. Anotha-a…"

"You've had enough for one day, sweetheart," Anthony whispered, carefully lowering her head to the table.

"Get her downstairs," he said to the waiters. "I'll go get my car."

"And the check, sir?"

As Anthony slid his hand in his back pocket for his wallet, the biggest waiter leaned down and lifted Veronica over his shoulder. With her head hanging over his torso, her blond hair sweeping his knees, he carried her caveman style toward the stairs. She had a skinny waist, a big butt, long legs, not to mention incredible breasts.

She was a picture. But too loud and pushy. She didn't do it for him. Zoe did.

He had to take Veronica to her hotel and get back to Zoe.

When he returned to the restaurant in his red, rental car, the waiters placed a limp Veronica in the front seat. When they shut the door, she opened her eyes and gave Anthony a sexy smile that scared the hell out of him.

"What hotel?" he asked.

"Villa-a-a."

"Where?"

"Where do you want ith to be?"

"No games."

She laughed. Then she gave him another dopey smile.

"Where…"

"I heardth you," she lisped.

"You need to sober up."

Her sensual mouth curved. "I've got a better idea."

"Where is your villa?"

"I forgoth." Giggling, she put her hand on his leg.

He shoved her hand away. ''I'm serious about Zoe.''

She laughed as if this was deliciously amusing and leaned toward him—bosoms first.

''Thas what Abdul said.''

''Who the hell is Abdul?''

''Zoe's boyfriend.''

Ten

I swear I will never betray you again. Not even if you date Prince Charming!

Zoe picked up one of those perfect little round rocks that littered the beach and threw it as far as she could at the water. She should have sent Veronica packing.

When the rock she'd thrown vanished, she watched the water until it was smooth and glimmering like glass again. Then she threw another.

"How could you, Veronica? I told you he was mine."

But was he? That question made her chest hurt. With a savage flip of her wrist that made the little bones in her hand ache, Zoe sent another rock sailing high into the air. She watched the circle of ripples expand outward on the water.

How could he?

With a vengeance, Zoe whispered every bad word in her vocabulary. Some of the expressions were so gross, she smiled. Her repertoire was pretty awesome. She read a lot. Some of her writers could get colorful.

Not that the cussing or the rock throwing helped much. Zoe was upset with both Anthony and Veronica, but *his* betrayal hurt the worst. She remembered losing him to the beautiful, perfect Rene, who'd told Zoe so often she wouldn't be able to hold on to him. Was that still true?

And how dare Anthony follow her to the restaurant today! How dare he flirt when Veronica had thrown herself at him? Couldn't he see how mixed-up and vulnerable Veronica was? She didn't know who she was, much less what she wanted.

"How can you be worrying about Veronica? She's the other woman."

"You're doing it."

"I always talk to myself when I'm crazy and out of control."

Furious and hurt, Zoe sat down on the beach. As the sun sank and the air got cooler, she huddled beneath a towel some tourist had forgotten, her gaze fixed on those magical mountains across the sea. Slowly they went from gray to violet and then to glowing orange as the sun plopped into a hot-pink sea.

And still no Anthony.

When it was dark enough for the stars to pop out in little pinpricks of brilliance through the velvet blackness, she wrapped the towel around her and slunk back to her condo like a wounded animal.

In her kitchen she walked past her fruit bowl and

fridge without glancing at them. It was way past the dinner hour, but she was in too much pain to feel hunger.

Alone in her bedroom she sat down at her desk and faced her empty yellow legal pad. She lifted a pen, uncapped it and then stared at her pale reflection in the mirror. Not that she really saw the glazed brown eyes or her lank, windblown hair.

No, she was back under that arbor on the rooftop in the middle of the Knights' fortress. Veronica's lush bosoms were bobbing up and down like apples in a barrel, and Anthony's grin was growing bolder and whiter every time she jiggled them.

"You're wallowing."

"You're doing it."

Zoe chewed the tip of her pen. Then she bent over the yellow pad and began to write. Words flowed in scrawls of black ink as she spilled her raw pain onto paper. An hour or so later when she was done, she felt a little better, but when she read the first sentence, she was so horrified by her maudlin dribble, she nearly got sick.

Why had she ever thought she could be a writer? She was an editor. She never came close to really expressing what was in her heart the way Veronica could. Zoe was in awe of people like Veronica. That's why she'd let Veronica run over her. Veronica was this megatalent, this big author.

"But as a person, she's so fragile and lost, and she's a miserable human being. The slightest little thing reduces her to less than nothing."

"She got your man, though."

"The new va-vooms got him."

''The only man you ever loved was positively drooling over them.''

Zoe ripped the pages out of her tablet, wadded them into a tight yellow ball which she pitched into her trash can. Then she just sat there, staring at herself for an endless time until the phone rang.

Anthony? She hated herself for feeling the slightest bit of hope. Then she dived across her bed to get it.

A lady with a British accent said, ''Your nephew called and said he was in a bit of a jam.''

''Who is this?''

''Bridget—at the front desk.''

''Right.''

''Seems Mr. Duke can't get back to pick up his son from our camp on time. He asked us to call you—''

Zoe repeated some of her most colorful expletives under her breath. *The jerk didn't have the nerve to call her himself.* ''Of course, I'll come get Noah—''

Noah was waiting for her just inside the resort camp gate clutching three drawings, his lunch box and his electronic game. ''Where's Dad?''

''Out with a friend.''

''Who? You're his only friend here.''

''He made a new friend today.''

''Who?''

''Hey!'' she whispered, determined to distract him. ''What are these pictures?''

''We went to a taverna. I drew fishing boats.'' Noah was not to be distracted. ''When's Dad—''

''He'll be here soon. What did you do at camp all day?''

He told her with immense, highly animated detail,

his hands waving as he spoke. He'd met a biker from Germany at the taverna, who smoked a lot of cigarettes and wore a black bandanna. The children had gone to the ruins of Kamiros, the smallest of the three ancient cities on the island of Rhodes.

"Zoe! There were all these tiny rooms with no roofs. What happened to the roofs? How did dirt get in the houses? Where's all their chairs and tables and beds? Would the roofs come off our houses? Will our houses fill up with dirt someday? Where did all their furniture go?"

She laughed. "So many questions." She thought for a moment. "I'm not really an archeologist, but I think houses made of stone are better preserved than the kind we live in now."

He listened as she tried to answer him. When she was done, his blue eyes grew laser bright. "Who?"

"Who?" Zoe played stupid.

The bright eyes refused to look away.

"What?" she whispered.

"Who's he with? How come Dad isn't with us? How come you won't tell me why? How come you look sad? Is he—"

"Oh, Noah…Noah…" She wrapped him in her arms.

He shuddered and drew away. He paled and seemed to grow smaller. Then his cheeks flushed cherry bright. She'd frightened him. He was remembering Rene and worrying that his father might be dead, too.

"He's okay. Nothing's happened…. Noah, your dad's fine."

"Really? Nobody would tell me about Mother at

first. They just looked at me funny the way you're looking at me."

"Really?" She pulled him into her arms again, and they snuggled close. Her fingers brushed his hair back from his hot brow. Nobody had told her about her parents' death for a while either.

"Why would he go out with somebody else when you're here?"

"Oh, Noah." She hugged him even tighter. "Let's not worry about him anymore. Let's just have fun."

"Like, can we play some games?"

"You bet. And for as long as you like—"

"Oh, boy." He dug in his backpack for his electronic game.

They had dinner together at her kitchen table. Then they played games until Noah's bedtime.

"You're not very good at this," he said, yawning sleepily after she'd lost a fourth game.

It had been hard for her to concentrate. "Maybe you're just very, very good," she said.

"Really?"

"You're a champ."

She gave him a glass of milk and boiled her toothbrush so he could use it to brush his teeth. He took off his clothes and she loaned him one of her big T-shirts. When he was dressed for bed, she tucked him beneath the sheets and blanket and tried not to remember that this was the same bed where Anthony and she had made passionate love only last night.

She sat down by the bed in the dark and tried not to think about Anthony at all as the clock on the dresser ticked mercilessly.

She hugged herself and tried not to imagine Anthony in Veronica's bed. Of course, her overactive imagination refused to cooperate. Visions of Anthony and Veronica rolling over and over on a Turkish rug in a luxurious villa bedroom with views of olive groves that went down to the Aegean danced in Zoe's brain. Soon she was half-crazed with jealousy. And still the clock ticked relentlessly.

At midnight her doorbell rang.

Zoe ran to the door and stared through her peephole. The curve of the little glass distorted her view. Anthony and the golden woman hanging from his arms looked like two fat dwarfs captured in a weird, glass bubble.

"Don't open it," warned a voice.

Zoe flung the door open. "Good evening, Anthony," she said.

Their gazes locked. She saw the dark circles beneath his black eyes and read his silent plea for help and understanding. His shoulders drooped. He looked as if he'd been in a fight or worse. Instinctively, Zoe's heart melted with sympathy for him. Then the visions of the couple on the Turkish rug started dancing, and her heart iced over.

"Now I understand why you were so upset last night when she called," he said. "You'll never believe the stunts she pulled."

"Try me," Zoe whispered in a faint, tortured voice.

"It's late. You don't want to know."

She nodded. "You're right."

Even in this moment of utter betrayal, Zoe wanted him. Even though he held a half-naked woman in his arms, a woman who was her protégé and friend, even though visions of them making love cavorted in her mind, Zoe still ached to be in his arms.

"Fool."

"You're doing it."

She bit her tongue and bent her head so he couldn't see the raw need in her face. Stepping back from the door, she let him pass.

"Noah's in my bed. You can put her on the couch," Zoe said crisply.

Zoe held her head high and tried not to show the slightest sign of her true feelings as he carried Veronica inside. None of the shock, none of her exquisite hurt must he see. Yes, even these moments when he held another woman, even these fresh insults had to be endured with no sign of the pain she felt. She was not going to let him humiliate her again and make her do something impulsive and crazy.

He laid Veronica down on the couch. Then he pulled a pair of green high heels, a bra, and shiny green thong panties out of his pocket. He placed the shoes on the floor beside the couch and stuffed the underwear into them.

Oh, dear. The visions started dancing again. Only this time the costumes were different. The woman underneath Anthony rolling on the carpet wore nothing but green thong panties.

Zoe rushed to the shoes and yanked out the thong panties and waved them at him.

His dark face was contrite and embarrassed. "Your friend is…is…confused."

"P-please—"

Zoe waved the thong panties wildly. He grabbed them. For a ridiculous moment, they played tug of war. Then she let go, and they popped into his brown hand.

"They're yours," she spat. "You earned them."

"What?" He stared at her, reading her too easily. "You think I—"

"I have eyes."

"I guess it looks bad," he admitted.

"She took off her clothes, didn't she? She attacked you, you'll probably say."

"Worse."

"You surrendered…after a long battle?"

"How dare you say that? You know her. And you know me."

"And I know what I see."

"Listen to me, Zoe. I love you."

"Love? You must think I'm a pea-brained idiot."

"I love you," he repeated.

"Don't say that!"

"I—"

"I don't care."

"You don't mean that," he whispered.

"I don't want the man I marry to sleep with a friend of mine and then say he loves me. That makes me feel crazy. And I've spent enough of my life feeling crazy about you."

"You have?"

"Nine impossible years. Not to mention when we were kids."

"You've been crazy about me while you were in Manhattan?"

"Yes! Yes! Yes!" She threw up her hands in disgust. "Well, no more. I came here to get over you. And now I have. We're through. I was a dumb, innocent girl the first time. I loved you so deeply. I hurt so much."

"You hurt? I can tell you about hurt. And about

guilt—'' The scorn and anguish in his voice made her heart tighten.

''I married Rene, a woman I didn't love, to get even because you'd made me the laughingstock of the whole damned town. You'd married my uncle Duncan. I thought people would stop laughing if I married Rene. And you know what, they did.''

''Oh!''

''But I paid a hellish price. I never loved her. I married her because she was your best friend. I made her miserable. Oh, I tried to be a good husband. I tried to love her. But trying wasn't good enough for either one of us. Without love, she sort of withered. She put on weight, let herself go. Then she got sick. I know everybody said I nursed her faithfully at the end. But I owed her a lot more than that. She knew it and I knew it. She was my son's mother and a wonderful mother, too, but behind closed doors, where it really counts, our marriage was hell. We stopped sleeping together years ago. She'd asked me for a divorce right before she got sick. Then we got the diagnosis, and I swore I'd take care of her. She agreed because she wanted to be with Noah as much as possible. I haven't told anybody any of this but you.''

''Oh...I'm...sorry.''

''Apparently, she'd always loved me, so I really hurt her. She was a wonderful cook...sweet... maternal... Rene would have made some man a perfect wife. But not me. Because of you, you little fool. I loved you then, and I love you now.''

''What about Veronica?''

''What about me?'' Veronica said, yawning, sitting up like a cat getting to her haunches. She ran her hands through her wildly tangled hair.

The hands froze in midair when she saw Zoe. "Oh, no, no! Not again." She turned on Anthony. "I told you not to tell her about us. She's my muse. I need her. I told you she's insanely jealous."

"I don't care what you told him," Zoe said firmly. "Get your high heels and your damned thong panties and your fake va-vooms back to your own villa. Write your own darn books from now on."

"But I can't!"

"You should have thought about that before you made love to Anthony on that Turkish rug."

"What Turkish rug?" Anthony demanded.

"The rug doesn't matter! Out! Both of you!"

"But nothing happened," Anthony said.

Zoe went to her door and slung it open for them.

"You have to believe me," he said.

The door banged against the stopper. "I don't have to...to anything." Zoe drew a breath. "Oh, you'd better get Noah. He's asleep on my bed."

When Veronica and Anthony and Noah finally left together, Zoe resisted the impulse to slam the door. Because of Noah she shut it very gently, but when she got to her bedroom she began throwing all her makeup and clothes at her backpack.

"What are you doing?" the voices began.

"Packing! Shut up and leave me alone!"

"You're doing it. You're doing it."

The phone rang.

"For what it's worth, I love you," Anthony said softly.

She took a deep, agonized breath. "When my parents died, I hurt so bad for so long, I went numb. I never wanted to love you again because I never wanted to feel like that again. I don't want to marry you. I just want to feel numb again. Don't call anymore.''

She slammed the phone down.

Eleven

Even at this early hour, the Greek sun was dazzling.

Zoe tapped her room key against the counter in the lobby. "Hello? Somebody? I need to check out!"

A slim woman in a burgundy-colored suit with a gold pin that said Bridget came out of a back office and smiled at her. When Zoe returned the smile, her lips froze.

The young woman wore wire-rimmed glasses and had her blond hair pulled on the top of her head in a Tinkerbell knot.

"That was some hot date your nephew had last night," the clerk said in a beautiful British accent.

"Do you take Visa, Bridget?" Zoe's voice was crisp as she snapped her credit card onto the polished mahogany and then shoved it toward her.

As Bridget zipped the card through her scanner, she looked almost wistful. "When your nephew barreled into the parking lot, his date was standing up in the back seat. That little window in the top of his car was open.''

''You mean the sunroof?''

Bridget nodded. ''Well, she was topless. Her blond hair was blowing and she was having a lovely time waving her arms at the sky. I was afraid somebody would see them and call the police and get your nephew arrested.''

''If I'd seen them, I would have made the call myself.''

The clerk shot her an odd look as she printed Zoe's bill and handed it to her. Without a word Zoe signed it. Slinging her backpack over her shoulder, she raced out to the little side street behind the resort to hail a taxi.

A yellow cab rushed up just as Noah came running up to her. ''Wait! Wait! We're leaving, too! Do you have room for us, too?''

Zoe knelt, and Noah came flying into her arms. ''Not today, my precious darling.'' She stroked his straight hair and stared into his eyes, trying to memorize everything about him. Big teeth. Bright blue eyes. Spiky yellow hair. Freckles.

''Oh, Noah.'' She hugged him closer.

He put his head on her shoulder and clung. ''Are you leaving because Dad made that new friend?''

She swallowed a deep breath.

Gently he pushed away so he could see her. ''Is that why?''

Intense longing filled her as she studied him. He was wearing overlarge beige shorts and a white T-shirt and his tattered sandals. A half-eaten edible necklace of brightly colored candies hung from his neck. In one hand he gripped two small stuffed animals and a yellow paper.

"What do you have in your hand?"

"Beanie Babies and a paper I found in your trash can. Were you writing a story?"

"Oh, dear." He had that awful note when she'd spilled out her heart last night. "That's my paper. Could I have it?"

His eyes danced with mischief as he wadded the paper tighter and hid it behind his back. She was about to plead with Noah to hand it over, when Anthony stepped out of the resort with their suitcases.

Instantly she forgot all about her crazy scribbling. She had to get out of here—fast.

"Goodbye, Noah." She hugged him.

When she stood up, Anthony yelled for her to wait. She pressed Noah's fingers and then touched his cheek. "Goodbye," she repeated. "I won't ever forget you."

Noah's eyes glistened. "Hey! You can have one of my lucky rocks." His cheeks paled as he slipped a perfect round rock into her hand.

"Thank you," she whispered.

Quite suddenly he began to cry.

"Oh, darling, darling, don't." She knelt again. "I wish I could stay, but I can't."

"You could. You can do anything you want to do. That's what Nana says."

"No, Noah."

Then she got in the cab and told the driver she was in a hurry to make her plane. She clutched Noah's rock tightly against her heart as her cab sped away just as Anthony raced out to the curb and yelled at her to wait.

* * *

Zoe had a window seat on her return flight to Athens. A plump little old lady with blue hair had the aisle seat. The middle seat was empty.

Suddenly a little boy in beige squirmed across the old lady's knees and threw himself into the middle seat.

"Looks like we've got the same seat assignment problem again," said a deep male voice bristling with tension.

"We can play a game together as soon as I finish this one," Noah said to Zoe.

Zoe barely glanced up at Anthony. "Go away and leave me alone," she whispered. Then she tugged at the twin halves of her seat belt and snapped them together.

"Not until you let me explain."

"I can fill in the dots, thank you very much. Veronica was riding around half-naked in your car. Her thong panties and bra were in your pocket."

The blue-haired lady sucked in a deep breath. "Thong—" Her head bobbed as she turned from Anthony to Zoe.

Noah's head was bent low over his game. Thank goodness, he was totally absorbed.

"Veronica's idea," said Anthony in a low voice. "Not mine."

"And you loved every minute of it."

"What the hell was I supposed to do with her? She was *your* important writer."

"Not anymore!"

"Oh, blame me for that, why don't you?"

"You tempted her to betray me again."

"Again?"

"Never mind."

"You introduced us. You could have told me what she was like the night before."

"I didn't trust you. And with good reason. You followed us. Then you fell for her like a ton of bricks."

"This is ridiculous."

"Right. So go!"

Passengers and luggage stacked up fast behind Anthony. When the flight attendant shoved her way through the throng to settle the dispute between Anthony and Zoe, she took their boarding assignments and counted passengers and seats. Then she recounted and then recounted a third time.

When she returned with their boarding passes, she was white with tension.

"Sir," she said, handing Anthony his boarding passes. "I'm very sorry, but we don't have enough seats."

"But I have two valid passes."

"But we only have one seat left on the plane. You and your son need two seats."

"I'll sit with Aunt Zoe," Noah volunteered cheerily, looking up from his game. "Dad, you can take the next plane."

"But I'm going to New York, darling," Zoe said.

"So are we," Noah countered.

"What?" Zoe glanced at Anthony warily. "Don't you dare follow me to New York."

"If you won't listen to me here, you leave me no choice. We have to talk."

"There's nothing to say. I won't see you. Understand? We've been through all this. It's finished."

"Sir...sir," the flight attendant said. "You really must get off the plane."

"All right. I'm getting off, and you're getting off too, young man." Anthony placed a hand on Noah's lap and undid his seatbelt. "Have it your way, Zoe. You win this round."

"You could get off, too, Aunt Zoe, and come with us—"

"I'm afraid I can't—"

"Aunt Zoe—"

"Quit calling her that," Anthony snapped. "She's not really your aunt, damn it."

"You said she was!"

"I just said it to make her mad."

"If you'd be nice and say you're sorry, maybe she'd get off, too."

"Noah! We've got to go!"

With a broad hand still on Noah's shoulder, Anthony herded Noah, whose blond head kept whipping around to see if Zoe would change her mind at the last minute and follow them down the aisle.

She didn't.

The last thing Zoe saw as the plane taxied down the runway was Noah clinging to a chain-link fence waving at the plane.

She put her hands on the glass. Condensation dripped across the little window like tears.

Father and son blurred.

"Cute kid," the old lady said. "Precious."

"Yes!"

"And the man's as handsome as the devil."

"Great analogy." Zoe opened her paperback and pretended to read. But the words ran together. Her mind was too muddled to read. All she could do was sit there.

It was a long flight home.

Zoe stepped into her apartment and Super Cat appeared and began rubbing against her legs. She went to her bedroom and flung her backpack down on the bed and unzipped it. Super Cat hopped inside and began sniffing the bag and her clothes in an attempt to fathom where she'd been.

Liking the scent of her green sundress, he lay down on top of it, slitted his eyes at Zoe and began flicking his tail, daring her to disturb him by trying to slide something out from underneath him.

"I guess I'd better go open your tuna or I'll never get unpacked."

Jade-green eyes blinked at her. Then Super Cat yawned and laid his head on his two front paws.

"Stubborn!"

She was staring out her window at her view of multitiered rooftops when her doorbell rang.

"Now, who could that be?" Her heart racing, she dashed down the hall. When she stared through the peephole, Abdul was squaring his shoulders and adjusting his tie. When she threw the first bolt, he thrust out his chin. He looked wonderful. He had on that single-breasted suit made of worsted blue wool he'd had custom made in London last fall. He only wore it for the most special occasions.

When she opened the door, he stepped inside carrying a bouquet of red roses and a black velvet jewelry box.

"What's the occasion?" she asked.

"No occasion. I just remember you had those pictures in your hall that needed hanging. Your apartment's old. High ceilings. And I'm tall.'' He smiled sweetly at her.

Men were so hopeful.

He handed her the bouquet.

"Thank you. Roses. My favorite," she said.

If you don't count bluebonnets.

She lifted the flowers to her nose and inhaled their fragrance. "They're beautiful. I'll find a vase. And how very helpful of you to remember about the pictures.''

"It's the least I could do. I promised I'd do it, didn't I.''

"Months ago.''

She got out a stool and held the hammer and nails while he hung the photographs, which were all of Super Cat in cute poses. When Abdul secured the last three over her bookshelf, she made them jasmine tea.

"So, how was Rhodes?'' he asked, squeezing lemon into his cup.

She sipped, but her tea was too hot. So she set her cup down before she burned herself. "I found out I belong here.''

"Bad vacation?''

"Rhodes was lovely, but I don't really want to talk about it.''

The doorbell rang before they'd finished their tea. She looked up, startled.

"You expecting someone?''

"No. I'm home an hour, and suddenly it's like Grand Central Station.''

"Everybody missed you. At least, I did.''

Suddenly it was a relief not to face Abdul and that

little black box, a relief to have an excuse to answer the door.

She got up. Once again she glanced through her peephole.

"Noah! Anthony!" she said, opening the door.

Noah raced inside, but Anthony stopped abruptly when he saw Abdul and Abdul's flowers and the black velvet box on the table beside their empty teacups.

"Who's this?" Abdul demanded, rising as if he still had the right to ask.

"Who's he?" Anthony's dark voice held equal, proprietary displeasure.

"I'm her boyfriend, that's who," Abdul said. "Who are you?"

"Her boyfriend? Since when?"

"Since a year ago."

Anthony's eyes locked on Zoe's pale face, willing her to say Abdul was lying.

But she nodded. "I did tell you not to follow me here."

"What was I?" Anthony ground out. "What was Rhodes?"

"What was Veronica to you?" Zoe asked.

"Nothing! That's what I keep trying to tell you!"

"There! What was Rhodes, you ask. I'll give you the same answer you gave me—nothing." She moved toward the door and pushed it wider. "Please go."

"Okay. I get it. Noah, come here—"

"But we just got here, Dad, and she's got this cool, fat cat." He broke off sneezing.

"Leave the cat alone. You're allergic. He might bite—"

"He won't bite," Zoe retorted touchily, defending Super Cat. "He has a wonderful disposition."

Anthony turned from Noah to her. "One last thing," he said as Noah knelt to pet Super Cat, "before I go..."

"Just leave."

Before Zoe knew what happened, Anthony took a long step toward her and spun her around roughly in his arms. For an eternity his mouth hovered an inch above hers. Then he pushed her against the wall.

"Don't," she pleaded, even as her heart pounded wildly and quite eagerly against her rib cage.

"I love you, you little fool," he whispered. "Doesn't that matter?"

Stubbornly she shook her head back and forth. "Not if you lie and cheat."

"Damn you. You're always assuming the worst about me. About yourself, too. You didn't ever believe we belonged together when we were kids. You thought you were this geek. You were a doll—precious, smart, sweet. I loved you, but you wouldn't let yourself believe it."

"You went from me to Rene."

"No, I didn't. You thought I did, so you married my uncle. Then I was an idiot to marry her so impulsively. I made her miserable because I loved you. But what's the use? You're so insecure, you probably prefer to believe the bad stuff." He snugged her closer. Then he lowered his mouth and rained hard kisses on her face and her cheek and the lush curve of her ivory throat with a desperate passion.

She fought him, pushing at his shoulders even as his arms tightened around her rigid body. His urgent kisses aroused feelings she didn't want, feelings and truths that wouldn't stop until he let her go.

"You humiliated me in Rhodes and you'll do it again," she said. "So you can't be here! And you can't do this! We can't do this!"

"*Please,* Zoe. I came here to ask you to marry me. The three of us could hop a plane to Vegas and be married today."

"I don't want to marry you."

His tongue slid against her lips, and Zoe let out a breathy moan. "I'm getting over you if it's the last thing I do."

"That so?" The pain in his eyes tore a hole in her heart even before he kissed her again, tenderly this time and with so much love, she melted utterly.

Only she didn't tell him she loved him nor did she even kiss him back. She'd never be able to hold on to him. She knew that now. There'd always be a Rene or a Veronica.

When he released her, she stood still against the wall, her head turned away from him.

"Marry me," he whispered.

"No." She kept her eyes downcast until he and Noah trooped outside.

"Who the hell was that?" Abdul demanded in a surly tone from his chair when they had gone.

She sighed. She'd totally forgotten Abdul was there. "You, too, Abdul."

"What?"

"Just go."

"Me?"

"You. And take that little black jewelry box."

"But you don't even know what's inside it."

She lifted it and placed it in his hand. "I know

enough. I know we don't belong together. I…I think I only dated you because you looked like him.''

''The caveman who was just here with the kid?''

She sighed. ''You're a nice man. Find some nice girl. Have a nice life.''

''What are you going to do?''

''I haven't a clue. I need some time alone…to think.''

''But…''

''Veronica wasn't the first girl, was she?''

''You and I weren't married. You were always so busy.''

''Always reading,'' she agreed. ''Always so upset about things that went on at work.''

''And that crazy writer. You didn't pay nearly enough attention to me.''

''Then go find that nice girl who will.'' Zoe's voice was gentle.

''The caveman had a point about you not believing in yourself. You should listen to him. I used to tell you the same thing.''

''The last thing I need is advice from you.''

''You should try listening.''

She touched his arm. ''Goodbye.''

They hugged one last time. Then he left, and she was alone.

Her mouth burned from Anthony's kisses. Her heart ached for more, but the intense longing she felt just made her more determined than ever to forget Anthony Duke.

Vegas? He'd asked her to marry him. He'd said he loved her.

She touched her bruised lips. ''I love you, too,'' she whispered, and then, determined not to cry, she brushed at the hot tears that stung her eyes.

Twelve

Sweat dripped off the end of Anthony's straight brown nose as he stubbornly eyed the wild-eyed palomino in the center of the round corral.

"You're not getting up on that horse again," Henrietta said. "I won't stand here and watch my only son commit suicide."

"Then go inside." Anthony wiped his brow and then leaned back against the wooden fencing.

"Don't you be sassing me."

Anthony bit his tongue to keep from saying anything. Ever since he'd come home from Rhodes, he'd been madder than hell at his mother for setting him up with Zoe.

"How come you can't ride 'im, Dad?" Noah wanted to know. "You said you could ride anything."

"Damn it, I can."

The palomino laid both ears back at the sound of Anthony's voice.

"You ain't been yourself, boss, since you got back." Frank, his top hand, spit a wad of tobacco onto the ground near Anthony's boots. "Your timin's off."

Going through the motions. That's all Anthony had been doing since he'd come home from New York. Without Zoe, his whole damn life was off, and there wasn't a damn thing he could do about it but go on living and hoping, making it through the days and the hellish nights.

"You've got better things to do than ride that bronc," Henrietta said. "You should be in the breeding barns or revising those new hunting leases."

She was right, of course. Besides running cattle, Anthony was a scientific deer breeder. He used stud stock to improve the breed and sold the progeny to high-fence ranchers in Texas, who could charge more for their deer leases if hunters walked away with trophy kills.

But the wild ride on the bronc in the corral resulting in aches and pains took his mind off losing Zoe. Not that Anthony could admit his heartbreak or how bleak his future seemed. Not to anybody. The trick to life was to ignore pain and go on.

He jammed his Stetson onto his brow and made a beeline for the thick braided-cotton reins trailing beside the palomino. To his surprise, the beast stood still when Anthony came up to him and eased his pointed black toe into the stirrup. Then Anthony grabbed hold of the horn and quickly swung himself up in the saddle. In another minute he had his other boot in the stirrup.

The palomino just stood there.

"Don't just sit there like a damn sissy, boss!"

"You shut your mouth, Frank," Henrietta warned.

"Ride him, Dad!"

Anthony turned his boot toes out and nudged the palomino gently. That set him off. The palomino went wild. He began to buck, lunging upward, crashing down. Again and again, the palomino hit the ground with bone-rattling thuds.

"You got 'im," Frank yelled.

The trouble with Frank was he was too damned optimistic, and his optimism always jinxed things. Sure enough, in the next second the palomino threw his damn head down.

"Pull his head up, boss."

"Easier said than done," Anthony fumed.

Anthony pulled with both hands on those reins, but the horse was powerful in his brute strength. He jumped high, kicking all the way down again and again until Anthony hurt all over. Which was good because only then could he forget *her*.

Then Frank started cussing up a storm, and Anthony flew out of the saddle, flying higher than the tops of the stunted mesquite trees and swearing even louder than Frank.

Then Anthony hit the ground hard, scraping his chin and jaw on a rock. But the pain almost felt good 'cause it hurt so bad he stopped thinking about her.

It was raining lightly outside the offices of Field and Curtis. There was no wind, and the black wall of buildings across the street seemed to be holding up the heavy, dark sky.

Zoe hated these steamy, spring days.

"You've got to talk to Veronica," Ursula said.

"I'm not her editor."

When Ursula arched her brows, Zoe crossed her arms and hoped Ursula couldn't feel her panic slipping out around the edges.

Ursula was always so suave, so sure of herself. Today her black bob was as glossy as ink, and, as usual, not a single hair was out of place. She was wearing high-heeled navy pumps and a navy silk suit.

Zoe felt very unattractive by comparison in her rumpled slacks and a cotton sweater. She had stuck a red pencil into the messy knot at her nape when she'd been editing a manuscript and forgotten it was there.

"Believe me, I wouldn't ask you to do this if I had any other options. We've all tried to work with Veronica. She's..."

"Impossible," Zoe supplied.

"You and she have a special chemistry."

"I used to think so."

Zoe stared past Ursula at the skyscraper cliffs and the park in the misty, dreary distance. Why had working in New York seemed so glamorous? It felt empty and wrong, not the right life for her at all somehow.

"What really happened in Rhodes?" Ursula asked, her voice softening.

The red pencil fell out of Zoe's hair, and she stooped to retrieve it. "I-it's complicated."

"The work you and Veronica did there is wonderful. She has three-fourths of a book—"

"The rest will come."

"Why can't you just talk to her?"

"Because I...I..."

There was a brisk knock at the door.

"I have a little confession," Ursula began hastily.

A slim, blond woman dressed in a sedate black silk suit stepped inside.

"Did you ta-a-lk her into it yet?" came that all-too-familiar Texas drawl.

"Veronica!" Zoe whirled on Ursula and met her boss's stern, chocolate dark eyes.

Ursula raised her brows again. "She begged me to talk to you. I have a better idea. Since she's come all this way, why don't you two just use my office to talk and get this little disagreement settled?"

"Little disagreement?" Zoe whispered, putting a shaky hand on the swivel chair behind Ursula's desk to steady herself.

"You'll both feel better, and I have a meet-ing—"

"Ursula, don't you dare leave me with her," Zoe pleaded.

Ursula picked up her purse and briefcase and glided out of her office.

"Do you like it?" Veronica patted her blond hair that was secured in a demure knot at her nape. "The new...subdued me?"

"You may look subdued. But you're faking it."

"Why aren't you with him and Noah?" Veronica asked.

"Who, Anthony? You know the answer better than I do."

"But we didn't— We didn't do anything— He wouldn't—"

"He wouldn't? I don't believe you."

"You don't believe in yourself any more than I

believe in me. Maybe that's why I can work with you so well and we somehow stumble into our little literary miracles.''

"He didn't?"

"And I was bad, too."

"Those thong panties—"

"I don't remember taking them off. I swear. That ouzo stuff… No more drinking, my therapist said. No more men, either, until I get myself together. And I've stuck to that…ever since Rhodes. I'm really sorry, Zoe. Sorry I messed things up between you two. I met Noah. He's darling. He needs you. I'm sorry about Noah, too. And sorry I messed things up between us.''

"Do you understand that saying you're sorry doesn't mean anything when you keep doing the same thing?''

"I passed out in the restaurant right after you left. All your Anthony did was try to drive me home so I wouldn't get into real trouble, but I wouldn't tell him where the villa was. Not that I'm sure I could have found it anyway. When I tried to seduce him, he told me he loved you, that he always had…even when he was married—''

"He really wouldn't do anything…?"

"How many times do I have to tell you that. He was a perfect gentleman. He was protecting me because I was your writer. He was loyal to you.''

Zoe raced past her.

"Where are you going? What about my book?"

"Put that cute tail of yours in your chair and write it. Write anything. Believe in yourself. It'll come.''

"But—"

"Just do it. You've written four bestsellers.''

"Not without you! Stop! Where are you go-ing—"

"I have a phone call to make and a plane to catch."

"Where—"

"Vegas. I'm getting married."

"Does Anthony know?"

"I'm fixing to call him and propose. Right now."

"Oh, great! This is great!"

"What?"

"My ending! All this passion! It's coming! I can feel it!" Veronica threw herself into Zoe's arms.

"It's called self-confidence. I didn't do anything to help you find your ending. You just got your mind off your fears. Which is what you just caused me to do. I was afraid to believe him. Afraid to believe in me. Afraid to love."

"You're really something," Veronica whispered, squeezing her tightly.

"So are you."

"I will never ever make a fool of myself and hurt you over a man again."

Zoe hugged her back. "Okay. I forgive you. But you'd better get your act together—you hear. Next time, you'll be toast."

"One question—can I be in the wedding?"

"Now, that's pushing it. That's definitely pushing it."

"Remember—believe in you."

The rain had just about stopped outside as Zoe sat down at her desk and pressed her cordless telephone against her ear.

"Vegas?" Anthony murmured slowly, not really

comprehending. "Why in the world would I meet you in Vegas?"

"You proposed."

"You said no."

"I wish I hadn't."

His end of the line went quiet. "I was just reading something you wrote about me in Greece and threw away," he finally said. "Noah dug it out of your trash can."

Suddenly she could barely breathe.

"I thought you hated me until I read this."

Oh, dear. Now he knew how desperately she loved him. "Yes or no, Anthony?" she whispered. "Will you marry me?"

"Are you serious? You're talking forever? You were pretty upset in Greece and determined never to see me again…even if you loved me. You said love made you too vulnerable to hurt. You went into how much you'd loved your parents and how devastated and lost you felt when they died and that you never wanted to be hurt like that again. That if you didn't let yourself get really close to somebody, you couldn't hurt like that. Then in New York, you turned me down again. What changed your mind?"

"Because I love you. I always have and I always will. I just have to start believing in me and in us, that's all. I let my insecurities get the best of me. Maybe we'll be lucky. Maybe I won't ever have to face losing you."

"I'm glad you called. I damn near killed myself on a bronc awhile ago. My life isn't worth much to me without you."

"I know the feeling."

"What about being an editor?"

"I can freelance from Texas. Maybe I'll even write something other than…personal drivel."

"Hey! That stuff was good."

"Just because now you see how out of control I am about you."

"I like knowing that. So, you're really serious about us?"

"You're all that matters. You're everything. Oh…and Noah. I can't wait to talk to Noah."

"He's right here."

As Zoe held the receiver and waited for him to find Noah, she felt so completely loved. They weren't even married, but she already felt as if Anthony and Noah were her family.

Love. Magic lived in that simple word.

Noah's voice burst against her ear. "Oh, boy! Are you really going to be my new mommy?"

Her heart swelled. She nodded as tears of happiness streamed down her cheeks.

"You know what? Nana said that sometimes fortunes come true."

"Fortunes?"

"Fortunes in fortune cookies."

"And ours did come true," he said. "I got a new mommy and Daddy got you."

"Oh, Noah, I can't wait to see you!"

"Daddy wants to talk to you again."

"There's something I want to know," Anthony said when he got back on the phone.

"Anything."

"Did you and Uncle Duncan… Was he able to consummate the marriage?"

"I don't know. He wouldn't tell me."

"How…"

"I have absolutely no memory of our wedding night."

"I swear on all that's sacred, our wedding night will be a night you'll remember."

"Then, no ouzo," she teased.

Epilogue

The newlyweds' penthouse suite had gilt walls, red carpet and stunning views of Las Vegas. The king-size bed was surrounded by lavish floral arrangements.

Zoe snuggled closer to her new husband. Moving her body against him lazily, she trailed a fingertip down his nose.

"You are so handsome. I still can't believe you're all mine," she said.

"Believe it."

"Just like I can't believe you made love to me all night," she whispered.

"You were counting…"

"To make it last. I still feel tingly."

"I did all the work."

"Don't complain. It was fun."

"Boy, was it." He fingered a tendril of her auburn hair.

"I can't believe every single citizen of Shady Lomas sent us flowers."

Anthony's dark face broke into a grin. "The shady lady of Shady Lomas isn't shady any longer. She's married to the right man, and she's a new mom to boot."

"I wonder where Noah is right now."

"Veronica had better be minding him around those damn slot machines."

Aunt Peggy and Henrietta had rented a huge suite of their own. Along with Veronica, they were supposed to be taking turns keeping tabs on Noah. The plan was that one of them would baby-sit while the others went downstairs to play the slots. Only, Noah was fascinated by the bright, noisy casino, especially the slot machines that spit silver dollars, and he kept following whoever went down to the casino.

"I still can't believe you let Veronica fly in and be your maid of honor," Anthony said.

"She explained everything. She said you were the most incredible gentleman."

"How come you believed her and not me?"

"Maybe I was so miserable without you, I was ready to listen. Being stubborn wasn't paying off too well, you know."

"I couldn't believe how restrained and ladylike she was during the ceremony. Her suit came all the way up to her neck. And she's so good with Noah."

"It's the new her. And no ouzo. She says she adores children. Plus, she's in therapy."

"Good. Deep down she's probably a wonderful person."

"Oh, she is."

"You're the one who's really wonderful." Anthony kissed his wife's mouth and then her cheek.

Passion burst inside her. "No," she whispered playfully.

"What?"

Zoe wrapped her arms around his broad shoulders and climbed on top of him. "This time I'm going to do all the, er, work."

He didn't complain when she deftly brushed her lips down his throat and then moved her head lower, much lower.

"You know I dreamed of making it big in New York, of proving myself to you," she said. "Funny, how being married to you and kissing you makes me feel that all my dreams have finally come true."

"Mine, too," he whispered huskily.

"I believe in you and me."

"It's about time." He pulled her into his arms and rolled on top of her.

"I thought you didn't want to do all the work," she murmured.

"I changed my mind. I love you. Oh, I love you so much."

She grinned. "I love you, too."

"We're going to have a wonderful life," he promised.

"I know," she agreed. "I can't wait."

"So, who's waiting?" he whispered.

They kissed each other and clung as if to make this special moment last forever.

Then he let her go and stared into her eyes and smiled.

* * * * *

*Look out for more from Ann Major
later in the year.*

BECKETT'S CINDERELLA
by
Dixie Browning

DIXIE BROWNING

is an award-winning painter and writer, mother and grandmother. Her father was a big-league baseball player, her grandfather a sea captain. In addition to her nearly 80 contemporary romances, Dixie and her sister, Mary Williams, have written more than a dozen historical romances under the name Bronwyn Williams. Contact Dixie at www.dixiebrowning.com or at PO Box 1389, Buxton, NC 27920, USA.

SILHOUETTE®

DESIRE™

proudly presents

a brand new trilogy from bestselling author

Dixie Browning

Beckett's Fortune

How one family's fortune leads them to love!

BECKETT'S CINDERELLA

Silhouette Desire

January 2004

BECKETT'S BIRTHRIGHT

Mills & Boon Historical

February 2004

BECKETT'S CONVENIENT BRIDE

Silhouette Desire

March 2004

To the wonderful and caring staff
at Britthaven Nursing Home in Kitty Hawk, N.C.
You're the best!

One

Just before his descent into Norfolk International Airport, Lancelot Beckett opened his briefcase, took out a thin sheaf of paper and scanned a genealogical chart. In the beginning, all they'd had to go on was a name, an approximate birthplace and a rough time line. Now, after God knows how many generations, the job was finally going to get done.

"What the hell do I know about tracking down the descendents of an Oklahoma cowboy born roughly a hundred and fifty years ago?" he'd demanded the last time he'd stopped by his cousin Carson's restored shotgun-style house outside Charleston. "When it comes to tracking down pirates, I'm your man, but cowboys? Come on, Car, give me a break."

"Hey, if you can't handle it, I'll take over once

I'm out of this.'' Carson, a police detective, was pretty well immobilized for the time being in a fiberglass cast. Now and then, even the Beckett luck ran out. About two months earlier, his had. ''Looks like something you can do on your way home anyhow, so it's not like you'd have to detour too far off the beaten track.''

''You know where I was when Mom tracked me down? I was in Dublin, for crying out loud,'' Beckett had explained. They were both Becketts, but Lancelot had laid down the law regarding his name when he was eleven. Since then, he'd been called by his last name. Occasionally, tongue-in-cheek, he was referred to as ''The Beckett.''

''I had to cancel a couple of appointments in London, not to mention a date. Besides, I'm not headed home anytime soon.''

What was the point? Officially, home was a two-room office with second-floor living quarters in Wilmington, Delaware. It served well enough as a mailing address and a place to put his feet up for a few days when he happened to be back in the States.

As it turned out, the place where the Chandler woman was thought to be hiding out was roughly halfway between Wilmington and his parents' home in Charleston.

Hiding out was probably the wrong term; relocated might be closer. Whatever her reasons for being in North Carolina instead of Texas, she'd been hard as the devil to track down. It had taken the combined efforts of Carson's police computers, a few unofficial sources and a certified genealogist to locate the woman.

And with all that, it had been a random sighting— something totally off-the-wall—that had finally pinned her down. Grant's Produce and Free Ice Water, located on a peninsula between the North River and the Currituck Sound, somewhere near a place named Bertha, North Carolina. Hell, they didn't even have a street address for her, just a sign along the highway.

Beckett tried to deal with his impatience. He was used to being on the move while his partner stayed in the office handling the paperwork, but this particular job had to do with family matters. It couldn't be delegated. The buck had been passed as far as it would go.

He'd allowed himself a couple of hours after leaving the airport to find the place and another half hour to wind things up. After that, he could go back to Charleston and tell PawPaw the deed was done. Any debt his family owed one Eliza Chandler Edwards, direct descendant of old Elias Matthew Chandler of Crow Fly, in what had then been Oklahoma Territory, was finally settled.

The genealogist had done a great job in record time, running into a snag only at the point where Miss Chandler had married one James G. Edwards, born July 1, 1962, died September 7, 2001. It had been police research—in particular, the Financial Crimes Unit—that had dug up the fact that the lady and her husband had been involved a couple of years ago in a high-stakes investment scam. Edwards had gone down alone for that one—literally. Shot by one of his victims while out jogging, but before he died he had cleared his wife of any involvement. She'd never been linked directly to any illegal activities. Once cleared, she had hung around Dallas only long enough to liquidate her assets before dropping out of sight.

Beckett didn't know if she was guilty as sin or totally innocent. Didn't much care. He was doing this for PawPaw's sake, not hers.

In the end, it had been pure luck. Luck in the form of a reporter with an excellent visual memory who spent summer vacations on North Carolina's Outer Banks and who had happened to stop at a certain roadside stand on his drive south.

He'd called Carson from Nags Head. "Hey, man, weren't you checking out this Edwards woman a few weeks ago? The one that was mixed up in that scam out in Texas where all these old geezers got ripped off?"

And just like that, they'd had her. She'd holed up in the middle of nowhere with a gentleman named Frederick Grant, a great-uncle on her mother's side. Check and double-check. If it hadn't been for that one lucky break, it might've taken months. Beckett would've been tempted to pass the buck to the next generation, the way the men in his family had evidently been doing ever since the great-grandfather for whom he'd been named had cheated a business partner named Chandler out of his rightful share of Beckett money. Or so the story went.

At this point there was no next generation. Carson wasn't currently involved with anyone, and Beckett had taken one shot at it, missed by a mile, and been too gun-shy to try again.

Although he preferred to think of it as too busy.

"Money, the root of all evils,." Beckett had mused when he'd checked in with his cousin Carson just before leaving Charleston that morning.

"Ain't that the truth? Wonder which side of the law old Lance would've been on if he'd lived in today's society."

"Hard to say. Mom dug up some old records, but they got soaked, pretty much ruined, during Hurricane Hugo." He'd politely suggested to his mother that a bank deposit box might be a better place to store valuable papers than a hot, leaky attic.

She'd responded, "It's not like they were family photographs. Besides, how was I to know they'd get wet and clump together? Now stop whining and taste this soup. I know butter's not supposed to be good for you, but I can hardly make Mama's crab bisque with margarine."

"Mom, I'm nearly forty years old, for cripes' sake. While I might occasionally comment on certain difficulties, I never whine. Hmm, a little more salt— maybe a tad more sherry?"

"That's what I thought, too. I know you don't, darling. Just look at you, you're turning grayer every time I see you."

According to his father, Beckett's mother's hair had turned white before she was even out of her teens.

All the girls in her high-school class had wanted gray hair. "It's one thing to turn gray when you're young enough to pass it off as a fashion statement. It's another thing when you're so old nobody gives it a second thought," she'd said more than once.

For the past fifteen or so years, her hair had been every shade of blond and red imaginable. At nearly sixty, she scarcely looked more than forty—forty-five, at the most.

"Honey, it's up to you how to handle it," she said as he helped himself to another spoonful of her famous soup, which contained shrimp as well as crab, plus enough cream and butter to clog every artery between Moncks Corner and Edisto Island. "PawPaw tried his best to find these people, but then he got sick."

Right. Beckett's grandfather, called PawPaw by family and friends alike, was as charming an old rascal as ever lived, but at the age of one hundred plus, he was still putting things off. Cheating the devil, he called it. When it came to buck passing, the Beckett men took a back seat to none.

Which is why some four generations after the "crime" had been committed, Beckett was trying to get the job done once and for all.

"What's the latest on the new tropical depression? You heard anything this morning?" Carson had asked.

"Pretty much stalled, last I heard. I hope to God it doesn't strengthen—I've got half a dozen ships in the North Atlantic using the new tracking device. They all start dodging hurricanes, I'm going to be pretty busy trying to find out if any of them are being hijacked.''

''Yeah, well…take a break. Go play fairy godfather for a change.''

''Easy for you to say.''

When his mother had called to say that PawPaw had had another stroke, Beckett had been in the middle of negotiations with an Irish chemical tanker company that had been hijacked often enough for the owners to feel compelled to contact his firm, Beckett Marine Risk Management, Inc. ''Just a teeny-weeny stroke this time, but he really would like to see you and Carson.'' She'd gone on to say she didn't know how long he could hang on, but seeing his two grandsons would mean the world to him.

Beckett came home. And, as Carson was still out of commission, it was Beckett who'd gotten stuck with the assignment.

So now here he was, chasing an elusive lady who had recently been spotted selling produce and God knows what else at a roadside stand in the northeast corner of North Carolina.

''PawPaw, you owe me big-time for this.'' Beckett loved his grandfather. Hadn't seen much of him recently, but he intended to rectify that if the old guy would just pull through this latest setback. Family, he was belatedly coming to realize, was one part anchor, one part compass. In rough weather, he'd hate to be caught at sea without either one.

So, maybe in a year or so, he thought as he crossed

the state line between North Carolina and Virginia, he might consider relocating. He'd incorporated in Delaware because of its favorable laws, but that didn't mean he had to stay there. After a while, a man got tired of zigzagging across too many time zones.

Pulling up at a stoplight, he yawned, rubbed his bristly jaw and wished he had a street address. He'd called ahead to rent a four-wheel-drive vehicle in case the chase involved more than the five-lane highway that ran from Virginia to North Carolina's Outer Banks. Having experienced back roads of all descriptions from Zaire to Kuala Lumpur, he knew better than to take anything for granted. So far it looked like a pretty straight shot, but he'd learned to be prepared for almost anything.

"We're out of prunes," came a wavering lament from the back of the house.

"Look in the pantry," Liza called. "They've changed the name—they're called dried plums now, but they're still the same thing." She smiled as she snapped her cash box shut and tied a calico apron over her T-shirt and tan linen pants. Uncle Fred—her great-uncle, really—was still sharp as a tack at the age of eighty-six, but he didn't like it when things changed.

And things inevitably changed. In her case it had been a change for the better, she thought, looking around at the shabby-comfortable old room with its mail-order furniture and hand-crocheted antimacassars. A wobbly smoking stand, complete with humidor and pipe rack—although her uncle no longer smoked on orders from his physician—was now weighted down with all the farming and sports magazines he'd collected and never discarded. There was an air-conditioning unit in one of the windows, an ugly thing that blocked the view of the vacant lot on the other side, where someone evidently planned to build something. But until they could afford central air—which would be after the kitchen floor was replaced and the house reroofed—it served well enough. Both bedrooms had electric fans on the dressers, which made the humid August heat almost bearable.

Liza hadn't changed a thing when she'd moved in, other than to scrub the walls, floors and windows, wash all the linens and replace a few dry-rotted curtains when they'd fallen apart in her hands. Discount stores were marvelous places, she'd quickly discovered.

Shortly after she'd arrived, Liza had broken down and cried for the first time in months. She'd been cleaning the dead bugs from a closet shelf and had found a shoe box full of old letters and Christmas cards, including those she'd sent to Uncle Fred. Liza and her mother had always done the cards together, with Liza choosing them and her mother addressing the envelopes. Liza had continued to send Uncle Fred a card each year after her mother had died, never knowing whether or not they'd been received.

Dear, lonely Uncle Fred. She had taken a monumental chance, not even calling ahead to ask if she

could come for a visit. She hadn't know anything
about him, not really—just that he was her only living
relative except for a cousin she hadn't seen in several
years. She'd driven all the way across the country for
a few days' visit, hoping—praying—she could stay
until she could get her feet on the ground and plan
her next step.

What was that old song about people who needed
people?

They'd both been needy, not that either of them
had ever expressed it in words. *We're out of prunes.*
That was one of Uncle Fred's ways of letting her
know he needed her. *Danged eyeglasses keep moving
from where I put 'em.* That was another.

Life in this particular slow lane might lack a few
of the amenities she'd once taken for granted, but she
would willingly trade all the hot tubs and country
clubs in the world for the quiet predictability she'd
found here.

Not to mention the ability to see where every penny
came from and where and how it was spent. She
might once have been negligent—criminally negligent, some would say—but after the lessons she'd
been forced to learn, she'd become a fanatic about
documenting every cent they took in. Her books, such
as they were, balanced to the penny.

When she'd arrived in May of last year, Uncle Fred
had been barely hanging on, relying on friends and
neighbors to supply him with surplus produce. People
would stop by occasionally to buy a few vegetables,
leaving the money in a bowl on the counter. They

made their own change, and she seriously doubted if it ever occurred to him to count and see if he was being cheated. What would he have done about it? Threaten them with his cane?

Gradually, as her visit stretched out over weeks and then months, she had instigated small changes. By the end of the year, it was taken for granted that she would stay. No words were necessary. He'd needed her and she'd needed him—needed even more desperately to be needed, although her self-esteem had been so badly damaged she hadn't realized it at the time.

Uncle Fred still insisted on being present every day, even though he seldom got out of his rocking chair anymore. She encouraged his presence because she thought it was good for him. The socializing. He'd said once that all his friends had moved to a nursing home or gone to live with relatives.

She'd said something to the effect that in his case, the relative had come to live with him. He'd chuckled. He had a nice laugh, his face going all crinkly, his eyes hidden behind layers of wrinkles under his bushy white brows.

For the most part, the people who stopped for the free ice water and lingered to buy produce were pleasant. Maybe it was the fact that they were on vacation, or maybe it was simply because when Uncle Fred was holding court, he managed to strike up a conversation with almost everyone who stopped by. Seated in his ancient green porch rocker, in bib overalls, his Romeo slippers and Braves baseball cap, with his cane hidden behind the cooler, he greeted them all with a big smile and a drawled, "How-de-do, where y'all from?"

Now and then, after the stand closed down for the day, she would drive him to Bay View to visit his friends while she went on to do the grocery shopping. Usually he was waiting for her when she got back, grumbling about computers. "All they talk about— them computer things. Good baseball game right there on the TV set and all they want to talk about is going on some kind of a web. Second childhood, if you ask me."

So they hadn't visited as much lately. He seemed content at home, and that pleased her enormously. Granted, Liza thought as she broke open a roll of pennies, they would never get rich. But then, getting rich had been the last thing on her mind when she'd fled across country from the chaos her life had become. All she asked was that they sell enough to stay in business, more for Uncle Fred's sake than her own. She could always get a job; the classified ads were full of help-wanted ads in the summertime. But Fred Grant was another matter. She would never forget how he'd welcomed her that day last May when she'd turned up on his doorstep.

"Salina's daughter, you say? All the way from Texas? Lord bless ye, young'un, you've got the family look, all right. Set your suitcase in the front room, it's got a brand-new mattress."

The mattress might have been brand-new at one time, but that didn't mean it was comfortable. Still, beggars couldn't be choosers, and at that point in her life, she'd been a beggar. Now, she was proud to say, she earned her own way. Slowly, one step at a time, but every step was straightforward, documented and scrupulously honest.

"I'll be outside if you need me," she called now as she headed out the front door. Fred Grant had his pride. It would take him at least five minutes to negotiate the uneven flagstone path between the house and the tin-roofed stand he'd established nearly forty years ago when he'd hurt his back and was no longer able to farm.

Gradually he and his wife had sold off all the land, hanging on to the house and the half acre it sat on. Fred ruefully admitted they had wasted the money on a trip to the Grand Ole Opry in Nashville and a fur coat for his wife. He had buried her in it a few years later.

Now he and Liza had each other. Gradually she had settled into this quiet place, far from the ruins of the glamorous, fast-paced life that had suited James far more than it had ever suited her.

By liquidating practically everything she possessed before she'd headed here—the art, her jewelry and the outrageously expensive clothes she would never again wear—she had managed to pay off a few of James's victims and their lawyers. She'd given her maid, Patty Ann Garrett, a Waterford potpourri jar she'd always admired. She would have given her more, for she genuinely liked the girl, but she'd felt honor bound to pay back as much of what James had stolen as she could.

Besides, her clothes would never fit Patty Ann, who was five foot four, with a truly amazing bust size. In contrast, Liza was tall, skinny and practically flat. James had called her figure classy, which she'd found wildly amusing at the time.

For a woman with a perfectly good college degree, never mind that it wasn't particularly marketable, she'd been incredibly ignorant. She was learning, though. Slowly, steadily, she was learning how to take care of herself and someone who was even needier than she was.

"Good morning…yes, those are grown right here in Currituck County." She would probably say the same words at least a hundred times on a good day. Someone—the Tourist Bureau, probably—had estimated that traffic passing through on summer Saturdays alone would be roughly 45,000 people. People on their way to and from the beach usually stopped at the larger markets, but Uncle Fred had his share of regulars, some of whom said they'd first stopped by as children with their parents.

After Labor Day, the people who stopped seemed to take more time to look around. A few even offered suggestions on how to improve her business. It was partly those suggestions and partly Liza's own creativity she credited for helping revitalize her uncle's small roadside stand, which had been all but defunct when she'd shown up. First she'd bought the second-hand cooler and put up a sign advertising free ice water, counting on the word *free* to bring in a few customers. Then she'd found a source of rag dolls, hand-woven scatter rugs and appliquéd canvas tote bags. She'd labeled them shell bags, and they sold as fast as she could get in a new supply. Last fall she'd added a few locally grown cured hams. By the time they'd closed for the winter, business had more than doubled.

Now, catching a whiff of Old Spice mingled with the earthy smell of freshly dug potatoes and sweet onions, she glanced up as Uncle Fred settled into his rocker. "You should have worn your straw hat today—that cap won't protect your ears or the back of your neck."

The morning sun still slanted under the big water oaks. "Put on your own bonnet, woman. I'm tougher'n stroppin' leather, but skin like yours weren't meant to fry."

"Bonnets. Hmm. I wonder if we could get one of the women to make us a few old-fashioned sunbonnets. What do you bet they'd catch on?" Mark of a good businesswoman, she thought proudly. Always thinking ahead.

She sold three cabbages, half a dozen cantaloupes and a hand-loomed scatter rug the first hour, then perched on her stool and watched the traffic flow past. When a dark green SUV pulled onto the graveled parking area, she stood, saying quietly to her uncle, "What do you think, country ham?" When business was slow they sometimes played the game of trying to guess in advance who would buy what.

Together they watched the tall, tanned man approach. His easy way of moving belied the silver-gray of his thick hair. He couldn't be much past forty, she decided. Dye his hair and he could pass for thirty. "Maybe just a glass of ice water," she murmured. He didn't strike her as a typical vacationer, much less one who was interested in produce.

"That 'un's selling, not buying. Got that look in his eye."

Beckett took his time approaching the tall, thin woman with the wraparound calico apron, the sun-struck auburn hair and the fashion model's face. If this was the same woman who'd been involved in a high-stakes con game that covered three states and involved a few offshore banking institutions, what the hell was she doing in a place like this?

And if this wasn't Eliza Chandler Edwards, then what the devil was a woman with her looks doing sitting behind a bin of onions, with Grandpaw Cranket or Crocket or whatever the guy's name was, rocking and grinning behind her.

"How-de-do? Where ye from, son?"

"Beg pardon?" He paused between a display of green stuff and potatoes.

"We get a lot of reg'lars stopping by, but I don't believe I've seen you before. You from up in Virginia?"

"It's a rental car, Uncle Fred," the woman said quietly.

Beckett tried to place her accent and found he couldn't quite pin it down. Cultured Southern was about as close as he could come. She was tall, at least five-nine or -ten. Her bone structure alone would have made her a world-class model if she could manage to walk without tripping over her feet. He was something of a connoisseur when it came to women; he'd admired any number of them from a safe distance. If this was the woman he'd worked so damned hard to track down, the question still applied—what the devil was she doing here selling produce?

He nodded to the old man and concentrated on the woman. ''Ms. Edwards?''

Liza felt a gaping hole open up in her chest. Did she know him? She managed to catch her breath, but she couldn't stop staring. There was something about him that riveted her attention. His eyes, his hands—even his voice. If she'd ever met him before, she would have remembered. ''I'm afraid you've made a mistake.''

''You're not Eliza Chandler Edwards?''

Uncle Fred was frowning now, fumbling behind the cooler for his cane. Oh, Lord, Liza thought, if he tried to come to her rescue, they'd both end up in trouble. She had told him a little about her past when she'd first arrived, but nothing about the recent hang-up calls, much less the letter that had come last month.

''I believe you have the advantage,'' she murmured, stalling for time. How could he possibly know who she was? She was legally Eliza Jackson Chandler again, wiping out the last traces of her disastrous marriage.

''Could I have a glass of that free ice water you're advertising?''

On a morning when both the temperature and the humidity hovered in the low nineties, this man looked cool as the proverbial cucumber. Not a drop of sweat dampened that high, tanned brow. "Of course. Right over there." Indicating the container of plastic cups, Liza fought to maintain her composure.

When he tipped back his head to swallow, her gaze followed the movement of his throat. His brand of fitness hadn't come from any gym, she'd be willing to bet on it. Nor had that tan been acquired over a single weekend at the beach. The contrast of bronzed skin with pewter hair, ice-gray eyes and winged black eyebrows was startling, not to mention strikingly attractive.

The word *sexy* came to mind, and she immediately pushed it away. Sex was the very last thing that concerned her now. Getting rid of this man overshadowed everything.

But first she needed to know if he was the one who'd been stalking her—if not literally, then figuratively, by calling her in the middle of the night and hanging up. Just last month she'd received a letter addressed to her by name at Uncle Fred's rural route box number. The return address was a post office box in South Dallas. Inside the plain white envelope had been a blank sheet of paper.

"I don't believe you answered my question," he said, his voice deep, slightly rough edged, but not actually threatening. At least, not yet.

"First, I'd like to know who's asking." She would see his demand and raise him one.

"Beckett. L. Jones Beckett."

"That still doesn't explain why you're here asking questions, Mr. Beckett." If that really is your name.

"The name doesn't ring any bells?"

Liza turned away to stare down at a display of summer squash. Had any of James's victims been named Beckett? She honestly couldn't recall, there had been so many. With the help of her lawyer, she'd done the best she could to make amends, but even after liquidating everything there still hadn't been enough to go around. Of course the lawyers, including her divorce lawyer, whom she'd no longer needed at that point, had taken a large cut of all she'd been able to raise.

He was still waiting for an answer. "No, I'm sorry. Should it?"

"My grandfather was Lancelot Elias Beckett."

"He has my sympathy." Her arms were crossed over her breasts, but they failed to warm her inside, where it counted. Uncle Fred, bless his valorous heart, had stopped rocking and stopped smiling. His cane was at the ready, across his bony knees.

Two

This was the one. Beckett was certain of it. Other-wise, why was she so skittish? A simple farmer's daughter selling her wares on a country road, no mat-ter how stunning she might be, would hardly slam the door shut on a potential customer.

And she'd slammed it shut, all right. Battened down the hatches and all but thrown open the gun ports. *Guarded* didn't begin to describe the look in those whiskey-brown eyes. *Frightened* came closer.

But frightened of what? Being brought in for questioning again?

So far as he knew, that particular case had been closed when her husband had taken the fall. She'd been a material witness, but they'd never been able to tie anything directly to her—even though she'd still been legally married to Edwards when he'd been shot in the throat by a man who'd been bled dry by one of his shell games. The victim, poor devil, had returned the favor.

"Not from Virginia, are ye?" the old man asked, causing them both to turn and stare. His smile was as bland as the summer sky. The brass-headed cane was nowhere in sight.

"Uh...South Carolina. Mostly," Beckett admitted. He'd lived in the state of his birth for exactly eighteen years. He still kept his school yearbooks, his athletic trophies and fishing gear at his parents' home, for lack of space in his own apartment.

The old man nodded. "I figgered South C'lina or Georgia. Got a good ear for placing where folks is from."

"What do you want?" It was the woman this time. Her eyes couldn't have looked more wary if he'd been a snake she'd found in one of her fancy canvas bags.

Under other circumstances, he might have been interested in following up on her question. Her looks were an intriguing blend of Come Hither and Back Off. "Nothing," he told her. "I have something for you, though." What he had was a worthless, mostly illegible bundle of paper. He'd left the money in his briefcase in the truck. If she wasn't the right one, the papers wouldn't mean anything to her, and if she was...

She was. He'd lay odds on it.

But she wasn't ready to drop her guard. "Something you want me to sell for you? Sorry, we deal only with locals.''

Irritated, he snapped back, ''Just some papers for now. Look, if you'll give me a minute to explain—''

She jammed her fists in her apron pockets and stepped back against the counter. ''No. You can keep your papers. I refuse to accept them. You're a…a process server, aren't you?'' She had a face that could be described as beautiful, elegant—even patrician. That didn't keep her from squaring up that delicate jaw of hers like an amateur boxer bracing for a round-house punch.

For some reason it got to him. ''I am not a process server. I am not a deputy, nor am I a bounty hunter. I'm not a reporter, either, in case you were worried.'' In his line of work, patience was a requisite. Occa-sionally his ran short. ''I was asked to locate you in order to give you something that's rightfully yours. At least, it belonged to a relative of yours.'' Might as well set her curiosity to working for him. ''I might add that I've had one devil of a time tracking you down.''

If anything, she looked even more suspicious. Con-sidering what her husband had been involved in, maybe she had just cause. But dammit, if he was will-ing to fork over ten grand from his own personal bank account, the least she could do was accept it. A gra-cious thank-you wouldn't be too far out of line, either.

''Why don't I just leave this packet with you and you can glance through it at your leisure.'' He held out an oversize manila envelope.

Liza jammed her fists deeper into the pockets of her apron. At her *leisure?* No way. He might not be a process server—she'd never heard of one of those who suggested anyone examine their papers at her leisure—but that didn't make him any less of a threat. Lawsuits were a dime a dozen these days, and there were plenty of aggrieved parties who might think they had a case against her, just because she'd been married to James and had benefited from the money he'd swindled.

Benefited in the short run, at least.

Before she could get rid of him—politely or otherwise—a car pulled up and two couples and three kids piled out.

"Mama, can I have—"

"I've got to go to the bathroom, Aunt Ruth."

"My, would you look at them onions. Are they as sweet as Videlias, Miss?"

Forcing a smile, Liza stepped behind the homemade counter, with its ancient manual cash register surrounded by the carefully arranged displays of whatever needed moving before it passed its prime.

"Those are from the Lake Mattamuskeet area." She gestured in the general direction of neighboring Hyde County. "They're so sweet and mild you could almost eat them like apples."

She explained to the round-faced woman wearing blue jeans, faux diamond earrings and rubber flip-flops that there were no bathroom facilities, but there were rest rooms at the service station less than a mile down the road. Uncle Fred still referred to the five-lane highway as "the road."

While she was adding up purchases, two more customers stopped by. Uncle Fred engaged one of the men in a conversation about his favorite baseball team. Finding a fellow baseball fan always made his day.

"Does that thing really work?" One of the women nodded to her cash register.

"Works just fine, plus it helps keep my utility bills down." It was her stock answer whenever anyone commented on her low-tech equipment. Although what they expected of a roadside stand, she couldn't imagine. She weighed a sack of shelled butter beans on the hanging scales.

"I saw something like that once on the *Antiques Roadshow*," the woman marveled.

From the corner of her eye, Liza watched the stranger leave. Actually caught herself admiring his lean backside as he sauntered toward his SUV. Curiosity nudged her, but only momentarily. Attractive men—even unattractive men—who knew her name or anything at all about her, she could well do without.

He started the engine, but didn't drive off. Through the tinted windshield, he appeared to be talking on a cell phone.

Who was he? What did he want from her? *Just leave me alone, damn you! I don't have anything more to give!*

After James had been indicted, one distraught woman had actually tracked her down to show her a picture of the home she had lost when her husband had invested every cent they had saved in one of James's real-estate scams. She'd been crying. Liza had ended up crying, too. She'd given the woman a diamond-and-sapphire bracelet, which certainly wouldn't buy her a new home, but it was all she could do at the time.

To her heartfelt relief, the dark green SUV pulled out and drove off. For a few blessed moments she and Uncle Fred were alone. The midday heat brought a bloom of moisture to her face despite the fact that she still felt cold and shaky inside. She opened two diet colas and handed one to her uncle. She was wondering idly if she should bring one of the electric fans from the house when she spotted the manila envelope.

Well, shoot. She was tempted to leave it where it was, on the far corner of the counter, weighted down with a rutabaga.

Uncle Fred hitched his chair deeper into the shade and resumed rocking. "Funny, that fellow wanting to give you something. What you reckon it was?"

"Some kind of papers, he said." She nodded to the envelope that was easily visible from where she sat, but not from the other side of the counter.

"Maybe we won the lottery." It was a standing joke. Every now and then her uncle would mention driving up into Virginia and buying lottery tickets. They never had. Uncle Fred had surrendered his driver's license a decade ago after his pickup had died, and Liza didn't want anything she hadn't earned. If someone told her where a pot of gold was buried, she'd hand over a shovel and wish them luck.

"I guess I'd better start stringing beans while things are quiet. I'll freeze another batch tonight." She froze whatever didn't sell before it passed its prime. Her uncle called it laying by for the winter. It had a solid, comfortable sound.

"Aren't you going to see what's in the envelope?"

"Ta-dah! The envelope, please." She tried to turn it into a joke, but she had that sick feeling again—the same feeling that had started the day James's so-called investment business had begun to unravel. At first she'd thought—actually hoped—that the feeling of nausea meant she was pregnant.

Thank God it hadn't.

"Here comes another car." She handed her uncle the envelope and moved behind the counter. "Help yourself if you're curious."

There wasn't much choice when it came to a place to stay. He could've driven on to the beach, but common sense told Beckett that on a Saturday in late August, his chances of finding a vacancy weren't great. Besides, he wasn't finished with Queen Eliza. By now she would have looked over the papers and realized he was on the level, even if she didn't yet understand what it was all about. The name Chandler was easy enough to read, even in century-old faded ink. Add to that the letter from his grandfather, Elias Beckett—funny, the coincidence of the names. Elias Chandler and Elias Beckett. Two different generations, though, if the genealogist had the straight goods.

At any rate, he would go back after she'd closed up shop for the day to answer any questions she might have and hand over the money. Meanwhile, he could arrange to see a couple of potential clients at Newport News Shipyard. Things had clamped down so tight after September 11 that it practically took an act of Congress to get through security.

Fortunately, he had clearance there. He'd make a few calls and, with any luck, be on his way back to Charleston by tomorrow afternoon. He would spend a few days with his parents before heading back to Dublin to wind up negotiations with the tanker firm.

The important thing was to set PawPaw's mind at ease. If, as he'd been given to understand, the Becketts owed the Chandlers money, he would willingly pay it back. In exchange, however, he wanted a signed receipt and the understanding that any future heirs would be notified that the debt had been settled. A gentleman's agreement might have served in PawPaw's day—not that it had served the original Chandler very well. But in today's litigious society, he preferred something more tangible.

After that, he didn't care what she did with the money. She could buy herself a decent cooler and a cash register that didn't date back to the thirties or get herself a grind organ and a monkey for all he cared. He'd been given a mission, and he'd come too far not to carry it out. But he could hardly ask for a signed receipt for ten thousand dollars while she was busy weighing out sixty-nine cents' worth of butter beans.

"Over to you, lady," he said softly, setting up his laptop on the fake mahogany table in his motel room. He placed his cell phone beside it, tossed his briefcase on the bed, set the air-conditioning for Arctic blast and peeled off his sweat-damp shirt. He'd stayed in far better places; he'd stayed in far worse. At least the room was clean and there was a decent-size shower and reasonably comfortable bed. Slipping off his shoes, he waited for the phone call to go through.

"Car? Beckett. Yeah, I found her right where your friend said she'd be. Tell him I owe him a steak dinner, will you?" He went on to describe the place, including the old man she was apparently living with. "Great-uncle on her mother's side, according to the genealogist's chart. Looks like he could use a few bucks. The house is listing about five degrees to the northeast."

Carson congratulated him. "When you headed back this way?"

"Tomorrow, probably. I'd like to handle some business in the Norfolk area as long as I'm this close. Maybe stop off in Morehead City on the way and be back in Charleston by tomorrow night."

"Want me to call Aunt Becky and let her know?"

"Wait until I know for sure when I'll be heading back again. I ran into a small snag."

"Don't tell me she's the wrong Chandler."

"She's the right Chandler, I'm pretty sure of that. Trouble is, she doesn't want to accept the papers."

"Doesn't want to accept *ten grand?*"

"We never got that far. I gave her the papers, but she needs to look 'em over before I hand over the money. Or at least as much as she can decipher."

"Didn't you explain what it was about?"

"I was going to, but she got tied up with customers before I had a chance to do any explaining. I didn't feel like hanging around all day. I'll go back later on, after the place closes down and explain what it's all about. Listen, did it ever occur to you that if she starts figuring out the rate of inflation over the past hundred or so years, we might have a problem on our hands?"

"Nope, never occurred to me. Sorry you mentioned it, but look—we don't really know how much money was involved originally, do we?"

Beckett idly scratched a mosquito bite. "Good point. I'm going to ask for a receipt, though. You think that's going too far?"

"Hey, you're the guy who deals with government regulations and red tape. Me, I'm just a lowly cop."

He was a bit more than that, but Beckett knew what he meant. He didn't want the next generation of Beck-etts to trip on any legal loopholes. Before he handed over the money, he would definitely get her signature on a release.

"You know, Bucket," Carson mused, "it occurs to me that the way we're doing this, we could end up in trouble if old man Chandler scattered too many seeds. Just because we were only able to locate two heirs, that doesn't necessarily mean there aren't any more."

"Don't remind me. That's one of the reasons I want things sewed up with lawyer-proof thread. You can handle the next contender however you want to. If any more turn up after that, we'll flash our receipt and send them to Ms. Edwards and what's-her-name—the other one. They can share the spoils…or not."

After answering a few questions about various family members, Beckett stripped down and headed for the shower. He started out with a hot deluge and let it run cold. The hot water eased the ache caused by too many hours strapped into a bucket seat, while the cool water helped clear his mind. As he slathered soap from the postage-stamp-size bar onto his flat midriff and let the suds trickle down his torso, the image of Eliza Chandler Edwards arose in his mind.

Lancelot Beckett had known his share of beautiful women—maybe more than his share; although, ever since he'd been left at the altar at the impressionable age of twenty-two, he'd made it a policy never to invite a repetition. At this point in his life he figured it was too late, anyhow. Any man who wasn't married by his midthirties probably wasn't a viable candidate.

All the same, it had been a long time since he'd met a more intriguing woman than Ms. Edwards. Skilled at reading people, he hadn't missed the flash of interest that had flickered in those golden-brown eyes just before wariness had shut it off. Pit that against the physical barriers she'd erected and, yeah…*intriguing* wasn't too strong a word. Her hair was not quite brown, not quite red. Thick and wavy, with a scattering of golden strands that had a tendency to curl, she wore it twisted up on her head and anchored down with some kind of a tortoiseshell gadget. Her clothes were the kind deliberately designed to conceal rather than reveal. He wondered if she realized that on the right woman, concealment was a hell of a lot more exciting than full exposure.

Oh, yeah, she was something all right. Everything about her shouted, "Look but don't touch."

In fact, don't even bother to look. Which had the reverse effect. Did she know that? Was it deliberate?

Somehow he didn't think so.

He adjusted the water temperature again, trying for ice-cold, but only getting tepid. Not for the first time he told himself he should have waited and let Carson do the honors. Car was two years younger and didn't have quite as much rough mileage on him as Beckett did.

But he'd promised. As his mother had stated flatly, time was running out, and it was time to lay this business to rest once and for all. "PawPaw's worried sick, and Coley doesn't need that kind of aggravation."

Ever since Beckett's father had been diagnosed with emphysema, his mother's main purpose in life had been to spare him anything more stressful than choosing which pair of socks to wear with his madras Bermudas when he got up in the morning.

She'd been waiting at the airport when Beckett had flown in more than a week ago. She'd hugged him fiercely, then stepped back to give him her patented Inspector Mother's once-over. Nodding in approval, she said, "You do this one thing for me, honey, then you come back here and tell PawPaw it's finished. Just find somebody named Chandler and hand over that mess of old papers and whatever else you think the Becketts owe them, then you can go back to chasing your pirates. Honestly, of all things for a grown man to be doing." She'd tsk-tsked him and slid in under the wheel.

Beckett had tried several times to explain to his mother that piracy on the high seas was as prevalent now as it had been in the days when Blackbeard had plied his trade off the Carolina coast. No matter. To her, it was still a kid's game. She'd wanted him to go into politics like his state senator father, Coley Jefferson Beckett. Or into investment banking like his grandfather, Elias Lancelot Beckett, and his great-grandfather, L. Frederick Beckett—the man who had started this whole bloody mess.

A few years ago he had fallen hard for a sexy marine biologist named Carolyn. Fallen hard but, as usual, not quite hard enough. After about six months he'd been the one to call it quits. He'd done it as graciously as he knew how, but Carolyn had been hurt. Beckett had readily accepted his guilt. Fortunately—or perhaps not—his work made it easy to run from commitment.

The payback had come a year later when he'd run into a glowing and very pregnant Carolyn and her professor husband at a jazz festival. He'd had a few bad moments as a result, wondering if he might have made a mistake. Family had always been important to him. Even seeing that old man today, rocking away the last years of his life at a roadside produce stand, had reminded him a little too much of his own mortality.

True, the Beckett men were generally long-lived, but what would it be like to grow old completely alone, with no wife to warm his bed—no kids to drive him nuts? No grandkids to crawl up on his arthritic knees?

His only legacy was a healthy portfolio and a small, modestly successful firm he'd built from practically nothing—one that included a two-room office in Delaware, a partner and a part-time secretary. His will left whatever worldly goods he possessed at the time of his death to his parents. Who else was there? Carson? A few distant cousins he'd never even met?

Cripes, now he really was getting depressed. Maybe it was all this humidity—he was coming down with a bad case of mildew of the brain, he told himself, only half joking as he crossed the bedroom buck stark naked to dig out a change of clothes.

On the other hand, it could be due to the fact that he hadn't eaten anything since the lousy chili dog he'd bought at the airport. One cup of free ice water didn't do the job.

Liza washed her hair and towel dried it before fixing supper. Then she did something she hadn't done in a long, long time. She stood in front of the fogged and age-speckled mirror on her dresser and studied her naked body. James had called her classy. Any man in his right mind would call her clinically emaciated. Her hipbones poked out, her ribs were clearly visible, and as for her breasts…

Tentatively she covered the slight swells with her hands. Her nipples, still sensitive from the rough toweling, nudged her palms, and she cursed under her breath and turned away.

That part of her life was over. Fortunately, sex had never played that large a role. After the first year or so, she had done her wifely duty once a week, sometimes twice, and then even that had ended. They'd gone out almost every night, entertaining or being entertained, and by the time they got home, they'd both been ready to fall into bed. To sleep, not to play. After a few drinks James hadn't been up to it, and she'd felt more relief than anything else.

Dressing hastily, she hurried into the kitchen. There was a Braves game tonight; they were playing the Mets. Next to the Yankees, the Mets were her uncle's favorite team to hate. Once the dishes were washed she could retire to her room and look through those blasted papers. It wouldn't hurt. The envelope wasn't sealed, just fastened with a metal clasp. If it had anything to do with James, she would simply toss it, because that part of her life was over and done with. She had repaid as much as she was able, although she hadn't been obligated to do even that much. She'd been cleared of all responsibility after James had made it quite clear before he'd died that she'd never even known what was going on, much less been involved.

His last act had been one of surprising generosity, but that didn't mean she hadn't been brought in for questioning. Nor did the fact that she hadn't known what was going on mean she'd escaped feeling guilty once she'd found out. She'd lived high on the hog, as Uncle Fred would say, for almost eleven years on the proceeds of James's financial shell games. The beautiful house in North Dallas, the trips to all those island resorts that James always claimed were for networking. Like a blind fool, she'd gone along whenever he'd asked her to; although, for the most part, she hadn't particularly liked the people he'd met there.

When the dishes were done, she turned out the light. Uncle Fred called from the living room. "Game time. You want to bet on the spread?"

"A quarter says the Mets win by five points." She knew little about baseball and wasn't particularly interested, but he enjoyed the games so much that she tried to share his enthusiasm.

"You're on! I know you, gal—you like that Piazza feller that catches for 'em." His teasing was a part of the ritual.

Liza leaned against the door frame and watched him prepare for the night's entertainment: fruit bowl nearby, recliner in position and a bag of potato chips hidden under the smoking stand. She was turning to go to her room when headlights sprayed across the front window. Traffic out on the highway didn't do that, not unless a car turned in.

"Uncle Fred, did you invite anyone over to watch the game?"

But her uncle had turned up the volume. Either he didn't hear or was pretending not to, so it was left to Liza to see who'd come calling. Occasionally one of the women who supplied the soft goods would drop off work on the way to evening prayer meeting. But this was Saturday, not Wednesday.

She knew who it was, even before he climbed out of the SUV parked under one of the giant oaks. She checked to be sure the screen was hooked, then waited for him to reach the front porch. He'd instructed her to look over the papers and said he'd see her later. She'd thought later meant tomorrow—or, better yet, never.

Doing nothing more threatening than sauntering up the buckled flagstone walk, the man looked dangerous. Something about the way he moved. Not like an athlete, exactly—more like a predator. Dark, deceptively attractive, moving silently through the deepening shadows.

Get a grip, woman.

"Let me guess," she said when he came up onto the porch. She made no move to unhook the screen door. "You came to tell me I won the Publisher's Sweepstakes."

"Have you had chance to look over what I left you?"

"Not yet." She refused to turn on the porch light because it attracted moths and mosquitoes. Besides, it wasn't quite dark yet. But it didn't take much light to delineate those angular cheekbones, that arrogant blade of a nose and the mouth that managed to be firm and sexy at the same time.

Listen to you, Eliza, would you just stop it?

"Then how about reading them now? It shouldn't take long. Unfortunately, most of the pages have stuck together, but once you've skimmed the top layer or so, I'll explain anything you don't understand and hand over the money. Then you can sign a release and I'll leave."

"I'm not signing anything, I'm not buying anything, I'm not—" She frowned. "What money?"

"Give me three minutes, I'll try to talk fast. Are you or are you not the great-granddaughter of Elias Matthew Chandler, of…uh, Crow Fly, in Oklahoma Territory?"

Her jaw fell. Her eyes narrowed. "Are you crazy?"

Beckett slapped a mosquito on his neck. "Man, they're bloodthirsty little devils, aren't they? Any reports of West Nile virus around these parts?"

She shoved the screen door open, deliberately bumping it against his foot. "Oh, for goodness' sake, come inside. You've got two minutes left to tell me why you're harassing me."

He took a deep breath. Liza couldn't help noticing the size and breadth of his chest under shoulders that were equally impressive. Not that she was impressed. Still, a woman couldn't help but notice any man who looked as good and smelled as good and—

Well, shoot! "One minute and thirty seconds," she warned.

"Time out. You still haven't answered my question."

"You haven't answered mine, either. All right then, yes, I might be related to someone who might originally have been from Oklahoma. However, I don't happen to have a copy of my pedigree, so if whatever you're trying to prove involves my lineage, you'd better peddle your papers somewhere else. One minute and counting."

"I have." His smile packed a wallop, even if she didn't trust him.

"You have what? Tried peddling your papers somewhere else?" And then, unable to slam the door on her curiosity, she said, "What money? Is this a sweepstakes thing?"

"You might say that." The smile was gone, but the effect of those cool gray eyes was undiminished. "Would you by any chance have a cousin named Kathryn, uh—Dixon?"

Some of the wind went out of her sails. From the living room, her uncle cackled and called out, "Better get in here, missy—your team just struck out again."

"Look, would you please just say whatever you have to say and leave? I don't know much about my family history, so if you're trying to prove we're related, you'd do better to check with someone else who knows more about it than I do. And if you're after anything else, I'm not interested." Never mind the money. She knew better than anyone not to fall for the old "something for nothing" dodge.

The man who called himself L. Jones Beckett

edged past her until he could look into the living room. "Is that the Braves-Mets game? What's the score?"

"So you're back, are ye? Thought ye might be. General Sherman's not going to be taking Atlanta tonight, no siree. Score's one to one, the South's winning."

Liza closed her eyes and groaned. If he could talk baseball, she would never get rid of him. Uncle Fred would see to that. She might as well read his damned papers and be done with it.

Three

"**B**ring Mr. Beckett a glass of iced tea, Liza-girl. Have some potato chips, son." Suddenly Uncle Fred leaned forward, glaring at the screen. "What do you mean, strike? That pitch was outside by a gol-darn mile!"

Liza left them to their game and headed down the hall to her bedroom. She would skim whatever it was he insisted she read, hand it back to him and show him the door, and that would be the end of that. If he did happen to be peddling some kind of get-rich-quick scheme, he'd come knocking on the wrong door this time. Any junk mail that even hinted that she was a big winner got tossed without ever getting opened. She didn't want one red cent unless she knew exactly where it had come from.

The papers slid out in a clump. For a moment she only stared at them lying there on her white cotton bedspread. They looked as if they'd been soaked in tea. The top sheet appeared to be a letter, so she started with that.

"My Dear Eli…"

Liza made out that much before the ink faded. The ornate script was difficult to read, even without the faded ink and the work of generations of silverfish. She squinted at the date on the barely legible heading. September…was that *1900?* Mercy! Someone should have taken better care of it, whether or not it was valuable. Maybe the writer was someone important. If it had been a baseball card from that era—if they'd even had baseball cards back then—her uncle would have done backflips, arthritis or not.

She gave up halfway down the page after making out a word here, a few words there. Whoever had written the letter more than a hundred years ago appeared to be bragging about making loads of money on something or other, but the script was too ornate, the ink too faded, the insect damage too great, to make out more than a few random lines.

Judging by the fancy borders, the rest of the papers appeared to be certificates of some sort. They were so fragile she didn't dare risk prying them apart. In a separate clump were a few sheets that looked as if they might have been torn from a ledger. The only words she could make out were "Merchants Bank" and "deposit to the…" Amount of? Account of? Something that looked like shorehavers.

Shorehavers? Shaveholders?

"Shareholders," she murmured aloud, "500 shares of…"

Whatever the name of the company, whatever the value of the stock, an army of silverfish had successfully obliterated the record.

And then she caught her breath. That creep! That slow-talking, smooth-walking creep!

Oh, sure. He'd found these valuable-looking certificates, but before they could go up for sale they needed to be authenticated by an expert. Wasn't that the way it was supposed to go? Only poor Mr. Beckett, if that really was his name, couldn't quite swing it alone. He was willing to cut her in, however, for the small sum of, say five hundred dollars—a thousand would be even better if she could scrape it up—to have the certificates authenticated. As earnest money, he would toss in an equal amount.

How many suckers had he talked into investing in his scheme? It was a classic street con. The found wallet. The pocketbook left in a phone booth.

What she ought to do was turn this jerk over to the sheriff.

From the front of the house she heard a roar. Baseball fans were an excitable lot. Her uncle shouted, "Go it, son! Show them fellers how it's done!"

Evidently one of the Braves had hit a home run. She only hoped L. J. Beckett enjoyed the baseball game, because his other game wasn't going to play. Not tonight. Not with her.

Before leaving her room, she shook down her hair,

gave it a few swipes with the hairbrush and then fastened it back up again, tighter than ever. It was more a security thing than a matter of style or even comfort. James used to call her a throwback to a time when women over a certain age wore their hair pinned up. Only their husbands had the privilege of seeing them with their hair hanging down their backs. Now, every Tom, Dick and Harry had the privilege of seeing any woman of any age with her hair down.

Okay, so maybe she was a throwback. Or maybe she was instinctively searching for a safer time.

Fat chance.

She'd put on a clean pair of jeans after her bath, along with a T-shirt that was now damp where she'd splashed it washing dishes. Hardly her most flattering outfit, but then, she wasn't out to impress anyone. Especially not some silver-haired devil who thought he had her number.

"Are we still winning?" She addressed her uncle, but handed the envelope back to the visitor.

He ignored her outstretched hand. He'd stood when she'd come back into the room, but turned back to the screen when several players huddled on the mound, their words screened behind gloves, mitts and face masks.

"Interesting," she said calmly, placing the envelope on top of the *Coastland Times* on the coffee table when he failed to take it from her. If he left it behind again she would simply trash it. Let him find himself a relic from someone else's attic to use as bait.

"You read the letter?" He was still watching the game, but there was no mistaking who he was talking to.

"As much as I needed to."

"Then you understand what this is all about?"

"Oh, I understand. Don't let us keep you, Mr. Beckett, I'm sure you're a busy man."

Picking up on her skepticism, Beckett raised his dark eyebrows. In other words, go peddle your papers somewhere else, he interpreted, half amused, half irritated. If she'd understood only half of what she'd read, and been able to read just a fraction of what he'd given her, she'd done better than he had. Of course, he had the advantage of knowing what it was all about. The legend had been handed down in his family for generations. Once upon a time, someone named Beckett had cheated or stolen a sum of money from someone named Chandler. His mission was to make restitution so that the remaining Becketts could quit fighting their collective guilty conscience and concentrate on more important matters. Such as dealing with strokes, broken bones, Alzheimer's and emphysema.

The old man was watching them curiously instead of the action on the small-screen TV. Beckett would just as soon not have to try and explain over two sports announcers and a mob of cheering fans. "Look, could we go somewhere quiet where we can talk?"

"We've talked. I've read your papers, and I'm not interested." As if to prove it, she crossed her arms.

His stomach growled, protesting its emptiness.

Dammit, he needed to wind up this business and get back to his own life. He made the mistake of reaching out to lead her into the hall. The brief brush of his fingers on her arm created a force field powerful enough to set off mental alarms. If the startled look on her face was anything to go by, she'd felt it, too. Jerking her arm free, she led the way to the front door, held it open and stood at attention, waiting for him to leave.

Reaching past her, he closed the screen door. "Mosquitoes," he reminded her.

"Will you please just go?" Crossed arms again. The lady was at full battle stations. "Whatever it is you're doing, you're not doing it with me."

Oh, but lady, I'd like to. The thought came out of nowhere, catching him off guard. And dammit, he didn't need that particular distraction. He made it a policy never to mix sex with business.

"I'm not interested," she said flatly.

"You're not interested in ten thousand dollars?"

Her jaw fell, revealing a tiny chip in an otherwise perfect set of china-white teeth. Beckett found the small imperfection immensely satisfying for reasons he didn't care to explore. He was growing a bit irritated by her refusal to hear him out.

"No. Absolutely not. I told you, I don't play that kind of game."

"You think this is some kind of *game?*"

Her eyes flashed. "Isn't it?"

"No, ma'am, it is not!" He'd figured he'd be in, out and gone by now. Game or not, the lady wasn't playing by the rules, which made him feel better about leaving the envelope containing the money with the old man while she was in another room going over the documents. "This belongs to Ms. Edwards," he'd said to Uncle Fred.

"She goes by Chandler now. Maiden name. Don't want nothing to do with that rascal she married."

Beckett could understand why, if the police reports and press coverage had been accurate. "Would you mind giving her this after I've left? She'll know what it's for."

The old farmer had looked as if he'd like to know more, but just then, Chipper had hit a two-run homer. Then Queen Eliza had stalked into the room and tried to hand off the papers.

Now she did it again. He'd given the money to the old man, who had absently stashed the envelope under a half-empty potato chip bag. The papers had been left in plain sight. "Here, take these with you." She said. "Don't trip over that big oak root on your way out. It's buckled some of the flagstones."

Beckett stared her down. He was tempted to—

No, he wasn't. The only reason his glands were in an uproar was because he hadn't had a decent meal since he'd left his parents' home before daybreak that morning. Just because the woman was attractive didn't mean he'd lost his lost his mildewed mind—it only meant he hadn't lost his powers of observation.

He left, nearly tripping on the gator-size root. He quickly strode out to his rental, rationalizing that while he might not have a signed receipt, at least he had a witness. Tomorrow, on his way to the airport, he'd stop by and get the old man's signature on a statement saying that Ms. Chandler-Edwards had received the money. He'd be a fool not to. No telling how many heirs might come crawling out of the woodwork once word spread that someone was making reparations by paying off a generations-old debt.

In a certain fourth-floor apartment in South Dallas, Charles "Cammy" Camshaw hunched over a table, munching French fries and concentrating on the list he was making. "Look, we know for sure where she's at now. It's been a week and the letter hasn't come back, right? And it was her that answered the phone?"

"I don't know, Cammy, she was always real nice to me. I mean, like, what if we go to all this trouble for nothing? Driving all that way costs money, and like, we'll have to eat and sleep and all."

"I got it covered. We can write it off on our income taxes once we're up and running."

"I don't know," the shapely, freckle-faced blonde said again. She was sitting on the foot of the bed in a fourth-floor, two-room apartment painting her toenails a deep metallic blue. "You're so sure this is gonna work, but me, I'm not so sure. I mean, the police cleared her and all."

"Hey, that's what makes this so great. Can't you just see it? Cops clear suspect. Security guard—make that private investigator Charles Camshaw—digs deeper and solves the crime of the year."

"Huh. I wouldn't hardly call it that. He stole a whole bunch of stuff, but they caught him. Anyway, the guy was creepy, always smiling when people were looking and trying to cop a feel whenever his wife went out. But she was okay. I mean, she gave me stuff and all. She didn't act all stuck-up like some women I worked for."

"Yeah, well, once we get our business off the ground, you won't have to go nosing up to no society types. It'll be you and me, babe. Camshaw and Camshaw, Private Investigations at Bargain Rates. How's that grab ya?"

Patty Ann capped the bottle and wiggled her toes. "What if it's a bust? She sold off all her stuff—pictures and jewelry and some old furniture. Even her designer gowns. I was there when the lawyer showed up and she gave him the money so he could pay back what her husband stole. That don't strike me as being so bad."

"Hey, we're not going to do anything to hurt her, but you said yourself she was a smart lady. The way I see it, a smart lady would stash enough away until the stink blew over, then move to a brand-new location and start over, right? So she had a bunch of stuff and sold some of it—that was for show."

"You don't know that."

"Trust me, honey, in my business, you get to know how far people will go to survive. Now, I'm not saying she's done anything wrong, I'm just saying she's got plenty stashed away, waiting for things to cool down. You don't think folks might like to know where their money is?''

''They weren't even living together when he got caught. He was staying at a hotel, and she'd just rented this cheesy apartment—I helped her move, even after she told me she wouldn't be able to afford me no more.''

''I still say she was in on it. Maybe not all the way, but she had to know something. Way I see it, she copped a plea, and they let her off easy.''

''That's not what the papers said.''

''Don't trust everything you read in the papers. They can be bought off just like everybody else. Look, she's living it up out there on the beach, right?''

''It didn't look like a beach on the map.''

''Close enough. We've got her spooked now, so once we turn up she'll break and then we can get us a story and sell it to the highest bidder. I'm thinking *National Enquirer*, but I'll settle for the *Star*.''

''I guess,'' Patty Ann said doubtfully. ''I'm startin' to wish I hadn't stole her address book. It makes me feel kind of…I don't know. Bad, I guess.''

''I know, babe. But look at it this way—she had her big chance. She blew it. That's tough, but hey, that's the breaks. Now it's our turn. Once we get the goods on her, we write our own story. If she's dirty, we go to the cops. If she's really innocent like you say, we go to the papers with a story about how this society woman is repenting her sins, living in the sticks and all. Papers pay big money for human-interest stuff, and the good part is, either way, we get our name out there. First thing you know we'll be going on all the talk shows, telling about how we tracked her down using no more than an address book, a few phone calls and a first-class stamp. That's real brainpower. Best kind of publicity in the world. Hey, we might even write a book.''

''Ha! Now I know you're crazy.''

''Look, all I'm asking is, trust me on this. Either way it turns out, we get enough publicity to launch our business, and like they say in the movies, the rest is history.''

Patty Ann Garrett, currently employed by an old cow who called her Betty Jean half the time, idly scratched the back of her ankle with a freshly polished toenail. It was one thing to be in love with a brilliant, ambitious man. It was another thing to try and keep up with the way his mind worked. What if he thought she was too dumb and started looking around for another partner? She loved him, she really did. She'd loved him ever since they were in high school together.

''I guess it won't hurt to show up, like we just happened to be in the neighborhord and all.''

''I promise, we'll just show up accidental-like and talk to her.''

''Won't she wonder how we knew where she was?''

''I'll figure out something on the way. But listen, six years as a security guard is five years too much. The uniform's okay, but the pay's rotten and the benefits are worse. I been planning this thing for years, just waiting for the right opportunity to connect—something that'll get me some free publicity. You're my connection, babe. I won't forget it. From now on, we've got it made.''

It was too early to go to bed. Liza knew she'd never be able to fall asleep. Wouldn't be able to concentrate on the book she'd thought was so wonderful just yesterday, either. The writer was clever—she had a great ear for dialogue, but the hero was only in his twenties and had baby-blue eyes and boyish dimples. In Liza's opinion men didn't even begin to ripen until they were in their midthirties.

L. J. Beckett was probably nearing forty, maybe even a year or so on the other side. If he had a dimple, it was in a place that didn't show. Which brought on a whole new line of thought, one that was strictly off-limits.

"What's the score now?" she asked, dropping into the vacant chair, shucking off her clogs and sighing.

"Tied at three, but our guys is red-hot tonight."

"Ever the optimist." She smiled fondly at the relative she had never met until little over a year ago. He had saved—well, if not her life, at least her sanity.

There hadn't been any more hang-up calls for more than a week now, and the single letter could have been a fluke. Probably one of those automated envelope stuffers that couldn't tell when the ink ran out on the printer.

Oh, sure. The hang-up calls were wrong numbers,

and the blank letter was a computer glitch. And L. J. Beckett was a friendly IRS agent, trying to find out if she had stashed away any unreported ill-gotten gains.

"Storm looks like it's headed this way. Too far out to tell yet."

"Lord, not a rainy Labor Day weekend, that would be awful for everybody's business."

"Feet don't hurt, leastways no more'n usual. Maybe she'll sheer off. Feller said to give you this." Without looking away from the screen, her uncle fished out an envelope and handed it over.

Liza stared at it as if it were a copperhead poised to strike. "Do you know what it is?"

"Said he owed you some money."

"He doesn't owe me a darned thing. I've never even met the man before today."

"Seen a lot of folks in my life. This one don't strike me as a fool or a crook. He says he owes you money, it's 'cause he does. Or thinks he does. Any rate, you might's well open it, long's he left it here."

Liza could tell her uncle was burning with curiosity. Another batter struck out, and he didn't even turn to watch. "All right, I'll open it, but that doesn't mean…" The bills fell out in her lap. Ten of them, each featuring a portrait of Grover Cleveland. Nausea clenched like a fist in her belly.

"Cash money, huh? Know what that means? Means we don't have to report it."

When she could catch her breath again, she said,

"Uncle Fred, stop joking. I can't take this money. The man's out of his mind."

"Who says I'm joking? I've not got many more miles left in me, but I wouldn't mind seeing me a ball game at Turner Field. Might even take in a race or two while we're down that way."

Liza stared down at the Federal Reserve notes scattered on her lap. Ten thousand dollars. Nobody owed her so much as a single dollar, much less ten thousand of them.

"I've got to find him and give it back. Did he say where he was going?"

"Back to the motel, I reckon. Not much else he could do around these parts."

"He's staying at the beach?" She didn't look forward to driving all the way to Kitty Hawk at this time of night, but if he got away, she would never be able to put an end to this stupid charade.

"Fin and Feather, right up the road. Asked me this morning if there was a place, and I told him it was clean as any and cheaper'n most."

Liza continued to stare down at the bills scattered across her lap. She was so tired she could cry. Why couldn't people just leave her alone? She hadn't done anything wrong. She might have been stupid for not realizing where James's money was coming from all those years, but she'd paid for her stupidity. Paid for it dearly.

"I'll be back in half an hour," she said, gathering up the thousand-dollar bills and cramming them back into the plain brown business-size envelope.

He was good. Oh, he was good, all right, but whatever he was up to, she wasn't falling for it. Even stupid people could learn from their mistakes.

Beckett wasn't too surprised when lights flashed across the window of his unit, which was one of only five. He'd parked off to one side to avoid a pothole. Whoever had just driven up—he'd lay odds it was Queen Eliza—didn't care about potholes. Ten-to-one she was steaming. Back stiff as a poker, fire blazing in those whiskey-brown eyes. Oh, yeah, she'd be something to see, all right. Move over, Old Faithful, get ready to see a real eruption.

He opened the door before she could knock. Grinning, he asked, ''What took you so long?''

Stabbing him in the chest with the envelope, she said, ''You can take your blasted money and—and shove it!'' She stepped back, but he caught her arm.

''Whoa...hold on a minute, how do I know it's all here?''

Her eyes alone could be classified as lethal weapons. Tossing the envelope onto the table beside the remains of his take-out meal, he led her gently into the room, careful not to exert any undue pressure. He had a feeling she would bruise easily.

Had a feeling she could also inflict a few bruises of her own, given the opportunity.

''Look, I think you've got the wrong idea about me—about what this is all about.''

''I don't think so.'' Her arms were crossed again. If she had any idea what it could do to a man's libido to see a pair of small, soft breasts under thin white cotton, squished together and propped up on a shelf of tanned forearms, she'd be running for cover instead of glaring at him that way.

"I guess the papers have spent too much time in various attics over the past century or so. Charleston's gone through a few major hurricanes over the years—what with leaky roofs, hungry bugs and fading ink, it's a wonder we were able to resurrect even that much. The thing is, the Beckett men—" He broke off, wondering how to explain it in the simplest terms.

"The Beckett men *what?*"

He tried a smile on her, then shrugged and said, "They have a tendency to procrastinate. Look, could we sit down? It'll take a few minutes, but I'll try to sum it up. My father is Coley Jefferson Beckett. You might've heard of him, he was a state senator for three terms."

"Not my problem."

"Fine. The thing is, he was supposed to have located any Chandler heirs and paid them off years ago, only he was too busy campaigning. Now he's suffering from emphysema, so it's pretty much out of the question. Dad's brother, my uncle Lance, might've done it. Trouble is, he's got his hands full at the moment with—well, that's beside the point. That leaves me and my cousin Carson, who's currently laid up with a few broken bones."

Her eyes had gradually grown round with disbelief, so he hurried to finish before she got up and walked out on him. "But now that PawPaw's had this stroke—"

"*PawPaw?*"

"My grandfather. At any rate, it was PawPaw who originally promised *his* father to find these people and make good on the old family debt, only he never got around to it. I told you the Beckett men were good at procrastinating."

Liza stared at him for a full count. "Am I supposed to understand all that gibberish?"

"Yeah, I know what you mean. It's pretty hard to keep score. I've got a genealogical chart in my brief-case, but it's yours, not mine."

Frowning, Liza nibbled on her lower lip. She was half tempted to believe him, if only because the whole mess sounded so utterly absurd that nobody in his right mind could make it up. The con artists she'd read about usually went for simpler setups. The more complicated the lies, the easier it was to trip over them.

Actually, James was the only con she'd known per-sonally. When his palatial house of cards first began to collapse, he claimed it was all a mistake. Liza had tried to believe him. She'd lived with the man for nearly eleven years, after all. And although he was far from perfect—far, *far* from perfect—she'd once loved him enough to marry him. The initial passion had quickly faded, but she'd never had an inkling of what kind of man he really was until shortly before the end.

He'd always been something of a charmer—it was

one thing she'd come to despise about him. Teasing her and calling her his trophy wife, he'd spend a fortune on her clothes and jewelry, far more than she would ever have spent on herself. In the early years, he'd taken her with him to entertain potential clients. But then he began going on trips without her, which suited her just fine. By the time she'd learned about his mistresses, their marriage had essentially been over. She'd been more sad than angry. At that point, James had moved to a hotel and she had started divorce proceedings.

And then things had started getting crazy. First the police—two men from something called the Financial Crimes Unit. Then James's lawyer, her own lawyer, and then the victims' lawyers and, finally, the IRS.

Months later, after James had been shot and killed and she'd done everything she knew how to make amends to the people he had cheated, she started reading about all the ways unscrupulous people could trick gullible ones out of everything they possessed. What hurt the most was the fact that James's victims had usually been people who had saved all their lives for a decent retirement. On being told that they could live in relative luxury rather than eke out an existence in some low-rent retirement community, some had borrowed even more money to buy into whatever it was her bastard of a husband had been peddling. Offshore oil leases that never existed. IPOs for nonexistent companies that were guaranteed to double in value within the first three months. Promissory notes…

Oh, yes. James George Edwards had been smooth, all right.

And so was this man. "Do you have any identification?"

He pulled out a worn ostrich-skin wallet. Flipping it open to reveal a driver's license, he handed it to her. "Pilot's license? Credit cards? You want to see my business card?"

Liza shoved it back at him, trying not to notice the shape of his mouth, the way it moved when he spoke. "Business cards are a dime a dozen," she said flatly. "Same goes for fake licenses. I suppose next you're going to tell me you're a card-carrying member of the Screen Actor's Guild, right?"

He did a slow double take. "Beg pardon?"

All right, so he reminded her of a cross between Mel Gibson and George Clooney. "Look, can we just let this whole thing drop? I'm tired. I've obviously interrupted your supper. I'm not interested in accepting money from a stranger, so why don't we just leave it—"

A soft buzzing sound had him reaching for a cell phone. "Yeah? What's up, you find out anything new about the other one?"

And then he frowned. Liza couldn't help but stare. Even frowning, the man was strikingly attractive. He might even be on the level—she supposed most con games were built on a logical, legitimate premise. The missing heir or heiress. The forgotten deposit box. Did she dare trust him enough to explore any further? It might be…interesting.

Stop it. Just stop it right now. And stop what you're thinking about, too. Good Lord, you don't even like sex.

"Thanks, Car. If I leave now I can make it to the airport in about an hour, give or take. Meanwhile, keep me posted on any further developments."

Liza rose, thinking to escape while he was distracted. Something in his expression held her there. "Is anything wrong?"

He looked up, blinking as though he'd forgotten she was in the room. "PawPaw just had another stroke, a big one this time. He's in the hospital."

Four

He was gone. Out of her life for good. So why, Liza wondered, did she feel this nagging sense of disappointment? She didn't want his money. Even if what he said was true—that, way back in the dark ages, someone in his family had cheated someone in hers— what difference did it make now? L. J. Beckett hadn't cheated Eliza Chandler. Might've tried to, but he'd picked the wrong victim this time.

Still, she wished she knew. It would be nice to be able to dismiss him as a crook. That way she wouldn't waste any time mooning about him. Not that she intended to. Moon about him, that was. So he was good-looking; she'd seen far better-looking men. James, with his almost-too-perfect features, his carefully gym-contoured body and his impeccable wardrobe, had looked like a cover model for a men's fashion magazine…and look how he'd turned out. She was beginning to believe that handsome men were not only vain but they also relied too often on their looks alone to get them through life.

Oh, yes, she had definitely learned her lesson. The fact that she'd had no trouble resisting a ruggedly handsome man with a wild tale about wanting to make her rich…that just proved it, didn't it?

Sure it did. So why didn't she feel relief instead of this nagging sense of having missed out on something special?

It wasn't the money she was thinking about. It was L. J. Beckett.

PawPaw—Elias Lancelot Beckett—gazed up at his two grandsons, marveling silently that he'd been born in the nineteenth century, lived through the entire twentieth century, and would die in the twenty-first. How many men's lives had covered a span of three centuries?

Unable to participate actively for the past few years, he'd still made a point of keeping up with what was happening in the world around him. And what was happening, he thought, was that history kept right on repeating itself, with the same old lessons having to be learned over and over. At least the soldiers no longer wore red coats with a white *X* marking the spot.

Of course, that had been a few years before even his time….

He'd been watching the news last night when he'd had that little dizzy spell. Whole body had gone numb on him. Couldn't move. Couldn't talk. No point in watching the news if you couldn't talk back. By the time they got him to the hospital, some of the feeling had come back to one arm. But now he couldn't even shake a fist for all the dratted tubes they had hooked up to his body. He could've told 'em, if he could've got his tongue to work right, that all the potions Florence Nightingale and her friends kept pumping into his frail old carcass weren't going to do one dagnab bit of good. What he needed was a stiff shot of good bourbon.

Pain in the ass, that's what it was. Might's well die and be done with it, with all these wires and tubes and blinking black boxes hooked up to his body.

What are you two young nippers whispering about over there in the corner? You think just because I can't move, I don't know what's going on?

Eli saw the looks that passed between his two grandsons. He knew what they were thinking. Why'n hell don't this old buzzard pull the plug, head on upstairs and let us go home? He's taken up space down here long enough.

That tall, good-looking pair of fellers staring down at him like they wanted to cry but had forgotten how— they were his own begats, once removed. Big gray-headed boy looked just like him. Other one—Lance's boy—he had his mama's eyes. Blue as the fire off'n a stick o' lightwood. Young Lance had picked himself a real good-looking woman, that he had.

Elias Lancelot Beckett struggled internally to make wasted muscles respond to the command of his still-sharp brain. Silently, he shouted at his grandsons, telling them to quite wasting time hanging around here, to get on with doing what he should've done while he was still up and kicking.

Dagnab it, he'd promised his papa to find the man who'd delivered him, a man named Elias Chandler. Find him and pay back the money Papa owed him. Trouble was, he'd been having so much fun begetting and piling up worldly riches on top of what his papa had piled up before him that he'd put it off too long.

Of his five young'uns, only two had survived childhood. Whooping cough had taken the twins. Little Emaline had drowned in the creek. That had left Lance and poor Coley.

Lance couldn't do it. Coley, he couldn't do it, either. Nice enough fellow—smart for a politician, but sickly. It was up to these two, Lance's son Carson and Coley's son, Lancelot.

Good-looking boys, if he did say so. Both of 'em. Took after him in that respect. Likely had to beat the women off with a stick.

The years fell away, and Eli was once more a young man. Those were the days, oh my, yes. Smiling inwardly, although it never showed on his face, the old man closed his eyes.

"Should I call the nurse?" Carson whispered.

"He's sleeping. Mom says he sleeps most of the time. No pain involved—at least we can be thankful for that. Ever stop to think there could be a downside to the family longevity gene?''

"Tell you one thing—in case I live that long, I'm going to start practicing how to use my eyes the way PawPaw does. You ever get the feeling he's telling us to quit hanging around here and get on with paying off his debt?''

"It was actually his father's debt, the way I heard it.''

"Yeah…I guess.''

"Any luck yet? If you can get your woman to spread the wealth to the rest of her kinfolks, I'll ante up my share and we can wind this thing up PDQ.'' The men had agreed to put in ten thousand each of their own, without telling their grandfather. It wouldn't do PawPaw any good now to know that the stock he'd been supposed to deliver more than half a century ago was worthless—that while they'd all been fiddling away their time, Rome had burned.

The two men stepped outside in the hall, where they could speak above a whisper. Carson was hobbling around on crutches now. One of his arms was still in a sling, which made maneuvering tricky, but he got around pretty well for a guy who'd been targeted by a drug dealer armed with a two-ton truck. Beckett told himself it was a good thing his cousin was a fast healer, else he'd be ripe for a psychiatric ward by the time he finally shed the last of his fiberglass shell. Patience wasn't one of Car's virtues.

Nor his own, Beckett acknowledged.

"Mom's coming over this afternoon," he said. "Miss Dora will spell her for a couple of hours later on." He held the elevator door open, then waited until they were outside the hospital before bringing his cousin up-to-date. Standing in the shade of a big magnolia tree, he said, "You were asking if I'd located the Edwards woman? No trouble, I told you that on the phone. You want to know if I handed over the money? Yeah, I did that, too. Trouble is, she handed it right back."

"What do you mean, she handed it back? She crazy, or what?"

"Spooked, I guess. You read her record, at least what there was of it."

"Which wasn't all that much," Carson said thoughtfully. "Mostly, it covered the husband. If I remember correctly, no charges were ever brought against her."

"Yeah, well whatever happened, she's still gun-shy. I don't know—could be a guilty conscience for living high at the expense of all those poor suckers her husband conned. Maybe she's doing penance, living in a rundown house out in the middle of corn country, selling stuff in a roadside stand."

"Hey—whatever works. But she can use the money, right?"

"Oh, she could use the money, all right. The problem is getting her to accept it. I don't know if it's pride or what. I played it safe and gave her the papers to read first, figuring once she understood, we could wind things up. But, hell, you know the condition they were in, and when I tried to explain…."

Beckett shoved his sunglasses up on top of his head, sighed and mentally retraced his steps. "At least, I think I did. The old guy—the one she's living with? Baseball nut. There was a game going on with the volume turned up full blast, and to tell the truth, I'm not sure who said what, now that I think back. Once we got to my motel—"

"She went with you to your *motel?* Oh, brother."

"Hold on, it wasn't like that. I left the money with her uncle. Once she discovered it, she came after me, loaded for bear. Matter of fact, she was there in the room when you called last night."

"Okay, so you handed over the money. Then what? She gave it back? So where does that leave us?"

Beckett flexed his shoulders, trying to ease the stiffness in his back. Seemed as if he'd been sleeping in a different bed every night for the past year. Some nights he never even made it to bed. "Bottom line, I'll have to go back and hog-tie the lady long enough to make her listen, then stuff the money in her apron pocket and get out of Dodge—or whatever the name of the place is—before she can throw it back at me."

"Apron pocket? You trying to tell me the woman I saw on CNN wearing a hot-looking designer gown— the woman who owned a fancy house in Dallas and a condo in Vegas—she's wearing an *apron* these days? Man, that's taking penance pretty damned far."

Beckett nodded. He was dog tired from too many sleepless nights.

"Yeah, she wears an apron. But if you're thinking hausfrau, think again. Think like, diamond tiara wrapped up in brown paper sack. Any way you wrap it, it's still a diamond tiara."

"Classy, huh?"

"And then some." That was one way to describe her. Skinny women had never been a real big turn-on for him, but then, he'd never before met a woman like Eliza Chandler. "Funny thing, though—maybe I'm overcaffeinated, but I get this feeling there's something going on in her life that's got her spooked."

"So maybe she wasn't as clean as she was made out to be." Carson readjusted his crutch to a more comfortable position. "Maybe she copped a plea when her husband went down. According to my sources in Dallas, they didn't spend too much time together the last few years. He traveled a lot, usually with a female companion, but they put in joint appearances at a few fancy social functions. Art openings, charity bashes—things like that. Enough to get their names and faces in the social columns. According to one of the reports I read, she's not even on the books as a witness in New York, where a lot of this stuff went down."

"Yeah, well…that's their take. Big-city cops probably figured you bubbas down here wouldn't know what to do with the information if they handed it over, so why bother."

"Could be, Bucket…could be. Anyhow, this bubba

still has some work to do. I've got this physical therapist jerking me around three days a week. She looks like one of Charlie's Angels, but I'm pretty sure she was a drill sergeant in a former life.''

Beckett chuckled. ''You're the only guy I ever knew who flunked phys ed in high school.''

''Hey, it was boring, what can I say? I'm more the cerebral type. Look, how about asking your lady if she'll contact her cousin so I won't have to go through what you've been going through. This old body can't take too much more punishment.''

His lady. A vision of Eliza Chandler formed in Beckett's mind, complete with long, lean, calico-clad body, snapping light brown eyes and masses of auburn hair that refused to be confined. For a mouth that was clearly made for passion, hers could clamp shut quicker than any snapping turtle he'd ever taunted with a broom handle as a kid. ''You got it, but look—don't count on too much. First I've got to get her to sit still long enough to hear what it's all about. Evidently she's got her mind all made up that I'm some kind of creep trying to con her into playing games.''

''Now, why would she think that?'' Carson asked, all innocence.

''Dammit, not *that* kind of game!''

''Famous last words,'' Carson said with a smirk.

Liza threw her book across the room and asked herself why she'd ever wasted her money buying it in the first place. She knew the answer, of course. Because there was a baseball game almost every night, which meant that she could either watch with her uncle or go to her room and read. And because she didn't have a social life.

She'd declined several invitations—graciously, she hoped—from the women who supplied the stand, to join them at Wednesday night prayer meeting. By the end of the day, she was usually too tired to go out, anyway. Besides, she'd always been a reader. She had favorite authors she could rely on, knowing that no matter how frustrating her days were, she had a good, safe place to disappear for a few hours.

What she hadn't counted on was having the aggravating image of a man who might or might not be a crook come between her and the printed page. "Well, shoot," she muttered. Obviously, she'd been reading too many romances.

From the living room came the drone of the postgame analysis. Uncle Fred was snoring. She'd have to wake him up to go to bed, but that was all a part of the unspoken bargain they'd struck that day last spring when she'd shown up on his doorstep.

One of these days, she reminded herself, he wouldn't be here. She would miss him more than she would have thought possible only a year ago. The house would have to be sold, rotted eaves, sagging floors and all, and she'd have to move on. Again. She didn't want to think of it now, so, mostly, she didn't.

He was family, after all. The only family she had left except for a cousin she hadn't seen in years. And dammit, since she'd lost her address book, she didn't even have Kit's last address. She could write to the publisher, of course. Kit wrote children's books. She'd called over a year ago to say that her latest creation, *Claire the Loon*, was being optioned by a TV producer. Liza had been out, and Kit had left a message, but no clue as to how to get in touch with her. At the time, Liza had been putting the Dallas house up for sale and liquidating every possible asset. Evidently, Kit hadn't heard about the scandal. At least she hadn't mentioned it.

Liza bent to retrieve the book she'd flung across the room in disgust, mostly at herself for not being able to concentrate. She reached behind the door for her nightgown just as the phone rang in the kitchen.

It was too early for her creepy caller. On the other hand, it was too late for any of her suppliers. Uncle Fred's friends usually called during the day.

She reached for the phone on the fourth ring, then waited until the fifth to lift the receiver. "Hello?"

"Eliza?"

Air left her lungs in a whoosh. She felt behind her for a chair. "What do you want?"

"Would you please just set aside your suspicions and think about what I said? Ask your uncle if he knows anything about your family's history." Before she could respond, he said, "But I guess he's the wrong side, isn't he? He's your mother's brother, not your father's."

She hooked a chair with her foot and sat, willing her heart to slow down. "Actually, he's my maternal grandfather's brother, but that's none of your business.'' The silence lasted for three beats. Then, in a quieter tone, she said, "How about your grandfather, uh, PawPaw? Is he all right?''

"Thanks. Yeah, he's still hanging in there. Waiting for you to come to your senses and let me square things so he can die in peace.''

She took instant offense, as if his grandfather's health were somehow dependent on her. "You're waiting for him to die? What kind of creep are you, anyway?''

Too tired to try to justify himself, Beckett cut her off. "Eliza, PawPaw's over a hundred years old. We're not quite sure how old he really is, but I don't think he'll be around too much longer. And, yeah, before you ask, I'm sorry. I'll miss him—we all will. Now, how about it, can we talk again? This time will you just listen while I explain and then take the damned money?''

"I'll think about it,'' she said after a long pause. Great. She'd think about it. "Fine. You do that.''

Beckett decided to hold back on asking about her cousin Kathryn and any other cousins they hadn't been able to confirm until he'd solidified his position. After that, with any luck, he would be able to concentrate on business long enough to meet with a couple of ship owners in Newport News, maybe another one in Morehead City, and get back to Charleston in time to help deal with whatever came next, be it a nursing home or a funeral home.

God, he was tired.

Had he or had he not told her to expect him to show up in the next day or so?

Dammit, PawPaw, hang in there. I'm not ready yet to let you go!

After hanging up the phone, he sat in the semi-darkness of the east room of the elegant old house where the distinguished old man had once read him stories about Blackbeard's exploits off the Carolinas. Oddly enough, he could easily picture Eliza here in the same room, maybe arranging flowers or talking over the day's events with his parents, his friends.

The room no longer smelled of cigar and pipe tobacco, but of leather, wood polish and the eucalyptus oil his mother used to refresh her bowls of potpourri. It was a familiar smell, one he hadn't realized he'd missed until lately. Lavender in the linen closet, cedar in the coat closet, eucalyptus in the potpourri. Funny the way different scents could arouse different emotions, different memories. A whiff of cinnamon always made him homesick, no matter where he happened to be. His mother's cinnamon-raisin bread, fresh from the oven...

Rebecca Jones Beckett was a terrific cook. She and Miss Dora, the housekeeper, fought for kitchen dominance. Miss Dora usually won because of his mother's many social and charitable obligations.

Now she was spending most of her time at the hospital, taking benne seed wafers or whiskey cookies to the nurses, driving his father and his breathing apparatus back and forth and helping his uncle Lance interview companions for his aunt Kate, who was in the early stages of Alzheimer's.

Close family ties, Beckett thought with a deepened sense of his own mortality, were both a blessing and a burden. He couldn't imagine being without them. All the same, in these uncertain times he couldn't imagine a man's deliberately taking on the responsibility of a wife and kids. Not that there had ever been any guarantees.

Unlike premature graying, the commitment gene was one that had skipped his generation. Carson showed no more inclination to settle down than he did. Which probably meant the end of this particular branch of Becketts, he admitted with an unexpected shaft of regret. His mother would be disappointed. Already was, for that matter. She'd had her grandkids' names picked out and waiting for years.

Idly he wondered if it was family feeling alone that had brought Eliza Chandler from the high-rent district of a big Western city to the boondocks of rural North Carolina. Could be she was trying to outdistance her past, if she'd been a part of her husband's scams after all. Maybe she'd skated clear by using her looks and that touch-me-not attitude she projected so well. Wouldn't be the first time something like that had happened. On the other hand, she might simply have come to the rescue of an elderly relative.

He yawned, stretched and thought about replacing the mattress in his old bedroom with a king-size model. But that would mean getting rid of the old mahogany sleigh bed, and his mother would be unhappy. He'd sleep on the carriage-house floor before he'd add to her woes.

Not that he'd spent all that much time here over the past few years, anyway. If he ever did decide to move his headquarters from Delaware to Charleston, he would definitely need to get a place of his own, else his mother would be running his business instead of just trying to run his life. For all he loved her more than anyone in the world, Becky Beckett was one managing woman. The proverbial steel magnolia.

Five

It was two days later when Beckett pulled into the Grants' driveway. Queen Eliza's modest chariot was parked close to the house. Beyond that, between the house and a half-grown holly tree, what appeared to be an old Packard was permanently enshrined on four cement blocks. The fact that he even recognized the make made him feel older than his thirty-nine and a quarter years.

"Must be the life I lead," he muttered as he skirted a ladder propped against the roof, dodged a pot of pink and purple flowers and knocked on the screen door.

Funny, he mused as he waited for her to answer the door, the way the dilapidated old house looked so familiar. He'd been here, what? Twice? Even that crazy old fruit-and-vegetable stand out front, with its homemade counters and bins and its rusted tin roof, looked welcoming. He couldn't say much for her security system—a flimsy wraparound wall made of hinged lattice panels with a single padlock. But then, maybe fresh produce wasn't that much of a draw to shoplifters.

Beckett heard her muttering from somewhere inside the house. He'd tried unsuccessfully to call from New Bern and again from Elizabeth City. She needed an answering machine, if her old rotary dial phone could be retrofitted to support such an accessory.

"Ready or not, here I come," he muttered. He had a twinge in the small of his back from too many hours of driving and he was working on a pressure headache. Both complaints fell off the radar screen the minute he saw her.

What *was* it about this particular woman that riveted the attention of every male cell in his body? She was beautiful, sure, but he'd seen beautiful women before. Feature by feature, there was nothing particularly outstanding about her. Yet, even in the middle of a family crisis, he couldn't seem to pry her from his mind.

Which was plain crazy. Because despite the hasty research into her background and a few nonproductive conversations, he scarcely knew the woman.

She greeted him with a dry "I might've known." But then, he could hardly expect her to welcome him with open arms. He tried to picture her welcoming her late ex-spouse at the end of a workday. *Hello, honey, how was your day? Rip off any more senior citizens?*

Somehow, it didn't ring true.

She'd screwed her hair into a shaggy knot and anchored it with that tortoiseshell gadget again. She was barefoot, wearing pants that were a few inches too short—or maybe they were meant to show off her world-class calves. No makeup. Wouldn't want anyone to get the wrong idea, now would we? He wondered if she realized how sexy she looked with her naked mouth looking rebellious and just a little bit pouty.

"Am I interrupting a ball game?" he asked when she opened the screen to let him inside. Did it reluctantly, he noted with something akin to amusement. She wasn't going to give an inch, oh, no.

"The game was this afternoon."

"Right. I actually forgot this was a holiday weekend until I got out on the highway. Is your uncle…?" Raising a questioning brow, he nodded to the living room.

"Gone to bed. His arthritis bothers him when the weather forecast calls for rain—sometimes even when it doesn't."

"Old bones are a better barometer than any computer model NOAA uses, at least that's what PawPaw says."

Liza led him into the living room. It was smaller than his boyhood bedroom back in Charleston, its furnishings undistinguished—a few of them downright ugly—but it was a comfortable room. A small pile of orange peelings and a scattered newspaper indicated what she'd been doing when he'd arrived. He waited until she took her seat before settling onto the faux leather recliner.

"Would you like to have another go at the documents, such as they are, or would you rather I just cut to the chase and tell you what I know about how it all started?"

"Tonight?"

"I'm here. You're here." Granted, it was later than he'd planned. What with the way both clock and calendar had lost all meaning during the process of traveling between Delaware and Dublin, his parents' home and the hospital, then back and forth to this place, he hadn't realized until after he'd left Charleston what day of the week it was, much less that it was the start of Labor Day weekend. Once he'd hit the highway, traffic had been pretty much bumper-to-bumper in both directions.

"I'm listening," she said.

Yeah, sure you are, he thought. Her arms weren't crossed over her breasts yet, but that didn't mean she'd lowered the drawbridge. "There's really not much to tell. You looked over the packet. I've already given you a rough outline—at least, as much as I know about it. Evidently, our great-grandfathers were in business together around the turn of the century. Some kind of investment business, I believe."

The first shield snapped into place: she crossed her arms. He waited for her to comment, and when she didn't he went on. "I don't know what went wrong, but sometime after they split up, mine evidently got to worrying about some kind of debt he owed yours. Before he died, he asked his son—that's PawPaw— to make good on it. Incidentally, that's where the letter and the stock certificates came from.''

''Stock certificates,'' she repeated.

''Well, yeah…you saw it. Stuff's worthless now. I had it checked out with a broker. It might've had some value back in PawPaw's day—enough to cover whatever my family owed yours, at any rate. Now it's worth whatever a collector might offer. My guess— not even pennies on the dollar. It's yours if you want it, but to settle the debt, the Becketts—''

''Wait a minute, back up. If your—if the stock's worthless, where did the ten thousand dollars come from?''

Beckett frowned at a framed photograph on the mantel above the boarded-up fireplace. He could just make out a couple standing in front of a field of corn that was taller than they were. ''Well, you see—''

''Just tell me the truth, that's all I ask. Because, quite frankly, when some stranger tracks me down and offers to give me something I've neither earned nor want, alarm bells start going off.''

''Right. Sure. I mean, I can understand that.'' *Under the circumstances* was implied. He was tactful enough not to mention it aloud. ''But this is on the level. It started out with some old stock and a few promissory notes, but—'' Oops. Hadn't Car said that one of the charges the Financial Crimes Unit had nailed her husband on was selling fake promissory notes? "What I mean is—"

"What you meant was that since my husband was a crook, I must be one, too. Either that or incredibly naive. That I'll grant, but did you actually expect me to grab the bait and not even bother looking for a hook?" Patches of color bloomed on both her cheeks. "Or wait—I get it now. This is one of those pyramid schemes, isn't it? You hook me, then I'm supposed to talk all my friends into buying your worthless stock or notes or whatever, right? I'm supposed to get a big commission for every sucker I bring in. They drag in their friends, and they're promised commissions, too, only the commissions never happen. If that's the way it works, I already know the routine, so thanks but no thanks."

In other words, been there, read the book, bought the T-shirt. Beckett couldn't much blame her for being skittish, but dammit! "Look, I know what you must be thinking and I'm sorry, but I'm not your husband. This is on the level." He'd made the mistake of activating the recliner when he first sat down. Now he clicked the leg rest back into place, sat up and glared at her. "If you'd just listen to what I'm saying and stop—"

"I listened."

"—stop interrupting, maybe we could wind things up here and I could get on with my own business."

"Oh? You mean this isn't your real business?"

He looked at her.

"Would you like some coffee?" Her smile was utterly guileless.

"That's it. Try to throw me off balance so I'll forget where I was. Coffee? Yes, thank you very much, I would like a cup of coffee! Black, no sugar." And no arsenic, please.

That smile of hers would have one-upped the *Mona Lisa*, chipped front tooth and all. "Black, no sugar," she repeated. "Right. Now, why am I not surprised?"

She left, and a few moments later he got up and stalked after her. If she had any thought of slipping out through the back door, she was in for a surprise. It wasn't that he didn't trust her; surprisingly enough, he did. But Beckett had no intention of letting her off the hook, now that he was so close to winding things up. He had a feeling PawPaw might not be around much longer, and if he could do this one thing to put his mind at rest he would damned well do it. Even if he had to hold her down and force her to accept the money.

Five minutes—make that ten. Five for a cup of whatever brew she was concocting, five more to wind up this crazy business. Then he'd be on his way.

She hadn't escaped out the back door, after all. With a mutinous look on her face, she was measuring coffee, spilling almost as much as she poured into the filter basket.

"What's with the ladder I saw propped up against the roof? Getting ready to put up a bigger sign?" Two could play the game of diversion.

"Hardly. Roof rot. A section of gutter fell off this

morning, and Uncle Fred wanted to know if the roof was going to cave in.''

"Is it?" Leaning against a counter, he crossed his legs at the ankles. God, he was tired.

"Probably. Sooner or later. Nothing lasts forever."

"I'm surprised you could find anyone to check it out on a holiday weekend." Absently, he reached for a peach from the bowl on the kitchen table. Miss Dora always kept a fruit bowl filled in the kitchen of his mother's house. She used to swat his hand whenever he reached for a cookie before meals, but she never minded his sneaking fruit.

Now, without even thinking, he took out his handkerchief and rubbed the fuzz off before biting into the soft, ripe fruit.

"You might try washing it first."

"Sorry. What you mean is, I might try asking first."

"That, too," she said dryly, setting the coffee to brew. With any luck, he told himself, they'd have wound up their business by the time it was done. He could gulp and run. He needed the caffeine.

Wrong. Caffeine was the last thing he needed. He'd refueled his nervous system at every pit stop along the way. Maybe what he was looking for was an excuse to prolong his exposure to this maddening woman until he could figure out what it was about her that kept drawing him back here. He had an unsettling feeling it was no longer entirely PawPaw's unfinished business.

"What's the word on the gutter—eaves, whatever?'' If he could keep her off guard, maybe he could sneak in with a flank attack.

''I told you I don't know yet. I got out the ladder and set it up first thing this morning, but so far I haven't had a minute all day to go up and look.''

God, she was something else. Up close, her skin was even more remarkable. Pale to the point of translucency. She smelled like soap and oranges. Probably rushed off her feet all day selling her cabbages and peaches and whatnot. On her, even exhaustion looked good. ''You know, you really should hire some help. Has it occurred to you that while you're busy trying to operate that antique gizmo of yours, a lot of stuff probably walks out without stopping by the checkout counter first? Not all the pirates are on the high seas.''

''You know, you really should mind your own business.'' She threw his words back at him. ''Has it occurred to you that if I could afford to hire help, I'd have done it long before now? And for your information, I know—better than most, probably—that not all pirates are on the high seas.'' She speared him with a look from her clear, whiskey-colored eyes.

''Ouch,'' he said softly. ''Eliza, I'm sorry. I didn't mean anything personal, I was just making an observation.''

He expected her to tell him to take his observations and hit the road. Wouldn't much blame her if she did. Instead, she did the last thing he'd ever have expected. ''Have you eaten supper yet?''

Like a bear coming out of hibernation, his stomach growled. Well, hell. ''Not yet. I was hoping to wind things up early enough to head back to Charleston tonight. Figured I'd get something to eat on the road.''

''You shouldn't drive when you're this tired.'' It was a quarter past nine.

''I'll need to go back at least as far as Elizabeth City to find a vacancy. The place where I stayed last time I was in this area is booked up, all five units. I called ahead once I saw all the traffic and realized what was going on.''

She got out a frying pan. Beckett bit into the peach, afraid to say more for fear of rocking the boat. Obviously exhausted, she was moving like a sleepwalker, and hungry as he was, he'd almost rather see her go to bed than stand there and cook whatever she had in mind to cook.

His imagination, hyped by too much caffeine over the long day's drive, created moving images of her elegant body stepping out of those rumpled pants, pulling the chambray top over her head and reaching behind to unfasten her bra. Women's arms were a remarkable feat of engineering, the way they could reach back and then so far up. Men's arms were different—at least his were. But even as tired as he was, he'd have made it easy for her if she'd asked. Pulled her closer, supporting her while he reached around and unhooked her bra, then eased the straps off her shoulders, following them with his lips until—

''One egg or two? I'm scrambling.''

''Uh...two?'' *Wake up, man, you're dreaming!* ''I can make toast if you'll show me where—''

"Bread box." She pointed it out, then indicated the toaster before dropping three slices of bacon into a skillet. Dare he hope one of them was for him?

"About the ladder—Eliza, you shouldn't—"

"Most people call me Liza."

"Thanks…Liza. Some people call me Bucket, but I'd appreciate it if you didn't." That earned him a reluctant smile. "You mentioned setting up the ladder. You didn't do it yourself, did you?"

"You think I'd let Uncle Fred lift something that heavy? I'm perfectly capable of carrying and setting up a ladder, but thanks for your concern. We don't have butter—we use that healthy kind of margarine. Uncle Fred's cholesterol isn't anything to brag about."

"Neither is mine."

She was trying not to smile again, but the corners of her mouth were twitching. Her eyes were sparkling again, too, this time not with anger. "Funny, the things men find to brag about, isn't it? Uncle Fred brags that his blood pressure is lower than his doctor's." Small talk. He could handle that. "Of course, that doesn't keep him from getting all hot and bothered and yelling at the TV."

"Any particular targets?"

"Politicians and baseball teams who aren't the Braves."

Grinning, Beckett accepted a plate with a mound of golden eggs and two slices of bacon just as the coffeemaker uttered its last gurgle. He dropped a slice of toast onto each plate while Liza set out a jar of fig preserves. "He and PawPaw would hit it off. PawPaw used to watch the news every night just so he could trace the ancestry of every politician even mentioned. You'd be surprised at how many unmarried mothers had sons who grew up and went into politics. Excluding my own father, of course. I've seen the marriage records inside the family bible."

She actually laughed aloud. Beckett wondered if sleep deprivation had finally done him in. He'd never before realized what a turn-on a woman's laughter could be. He said, "Nobody ever took offense. I guess it was just PawPaw's way of blowing off steam once he got too old to do much else."

"He lives with you?"

"With my folks. Uncle Lance and Aunt Kate would have been glad to have him, but our house is bigger. Dad and I used to watch Mom and PawPaw going at it over some issue or another and place bets on who would win the argument."

"I wish I'd gotten to know my family that well," she said wistfully.

She picked up a slice of crisp bacon, and he admired her hands. They were long, slender and looked surprisingly capable. In fact, he admired them all the way up to her shoulders. And beyond.

"My mother died when I was eleven," she went on. "My father remarried less than a year later, and he and his new bride moved to New Mexico while I was in boarding school in Austin. I visited during vacations, but somehow—you know." She shrugged. "It just wasn't the same. It was her house, not my home. Daddy was more her husband than he was my father.''

It was a perfect opening to ask about her cousin, the only other Chandler heir they'd been able to find. He hoped to God her father hadn't started a second family out in New Mexico, because as far as Beckett was concerned, the buck stopped right here.

She rose and topped off their cups and he murmured his thanks. At the rate he was drinking the stuff, he wouldn't have to worry about finding a room tonight. What was that old poem about having ''miles to go before I sleep'' or words to that effect?

They ate silently and efficiently. They weren't the best scrambled eggs he'd ever tasted—Miss Dora put cheese and sour cream in hers—but they did the job. He could have eaten half a dozen slices of bacon.

''You wanted to explain something,'' she reminded him.

Back to business. Beckett rose, scraped off his plate. Seeing no sign of a dishwasher, he rinsed it, left it in the sink and sat down again. As long as she was in the mood to listen, he'd better start talking. ''To start with, this is something that's carried over for—what, four generations now? Like I said, we Becketts are notorious procrastinators.''

''Oh, I don't know…you're here, aren't you?'' Even when she was tired, her smile got to him. There was something about her….

Or maybe it was just that his resistance was low. Lack of sleep, worry about his father and PawPaw— throw in irregular hours and too much junk food on the road and it was no wonder his mind kept straying from the business at hand.

Nah, it was the woman. Something about her seemed to resonate in a way that was…disconcerting, to say the least. He had a feeling that if they hadn't met here and now, they'd have met some other time, some other place.

Which was downright spooky.

"You do understand, then? You're not still thinking this is some kind of a con?"

Bedraggled and visibly tired, she blotted her lips with the grace and finesse of a grand duchess. "Let's just say I'm willing to listen with an open mind and this time I'll try not to prejudge. I won't promise to take whatever it is you want to give me—the money, I mean. It's not mine, no matter how much your family wants to clear its conscience, but if you can make your case before I fall asleep, I promise to listen."

"Point taken. Liza, did it ever occur to you that you could simply accept the money and hand it over to your favorite charity? Or buy your uncle a new roof?"

"I haven't—" But before she could say more, the phone rang. And rang again. Beckett glanced at the old-fashioned instrument and waited for her to reach for it.

On the third ring, he said, "Aren't you going to get it?"

"It's probably a wrong number. I get a lot of those."

"Dammit, it might be for me!" Before common

sense could kick in to remind him that anyone calling him would have called him on his cell phone, he snatched up the receiver. "Grant residence, Beckett speaking."

Silence. He heard what sounded like a muffled whisper somewhere in the background and the connection was broken. "What the hell?" he muttered, glaring at the receiver.

"I told you so."

"Yeah, you did. Probably a wrong number."

When she shrugged and looked away, he said, "Liza?" Reaching across the table, he covered her hands with his. Hers were ice-cold. "You want to tell me what's going on here?"

She shook her head dismissively. "Oh, you know—kids' games. Call someone in the middle of the night and then hang up." It was hardly the middle of the night, but he got the point. "I'll probably go out some morning and find the stand's been decorated with toilet tissue."

His thumb continued to stroke the back of her hand. "Have you reported it?"

She raked back her hair with her free hand, causing the tortoiseshell clip at the back of her head to lose its grip. A length of wavy, auburn hair fell across her shoulder. Steeling himself, Beckett resisted the urge to touch it.

"It's only happened four times," she went on. "This makes five. And who would I report it to? What could the sheriff do? I doubt if even the phone company could do anything about it. Besides, it's just a wrong number.''

"Was it? Maybe not. Have you considered getting caller ID, or having your number changed?''

"It's not my phone, it's Uncle Fred's. Besides, I don't know if the phone company would even let me do it.''

"Who knows your number here?''

She shrugged again, a subtle movement involving no more than the lift of one delicate shoulder. He'd seen mimes that were more expressive. "Nobody, I guess. Uncle Fred has a nephew-in-law who calls occasionally. He works on a boat—one of those big container ships, I think. I meant to let my maid know where to get in touch in case anything came up later, but in all the confusion of putting the house on the market and packing up and—and everything, I forgot.''

"Can you think of anyone else?''

She shook her head.

He said, "Close friends? Not so close friends?''

Boyfriends? It had been over two years since her husband had been murdered. If she'd been celibate ever since, it was a hell of a waste.

"Actually, I was busy for several months before I left Dallas—I sort of lost touch with my friends there.'' She smiled, and he wanted to tell her that it was okay. That he understood. But he couldn't tell her that without disclosing how much he knew about her past. He wasn't ready to do that.

"If it's someone from the IRS,'' she said, making

a feeble attempt to laugh, "then they're out of luck. My income is a joke. If it's one of Uncle Fred's friends from Bay View—that's a retirement home over on the river—they'd be calling during the day. So, you see, it has to be kids. School starts in a couple of days, though, so it'll probably stop."

"And if it doesn't?"

"If it doesn't…" She bit her lip and looked away. Did she have any idea how tempted he was to gather her into his arms, find the nearest bed and curl up with her for the next few hours? No talking. No sex, just sleep.

Although, all bets would be off once they woke up together, rested and refreshed.

Six

Patty Ann lay curled up on the bed, watching the Weather Channel. Cam was in the bathroom shaving. She'd been the one to insist on sleeping in a real bed instead of in the car, but he'd been quick to take advantage of the facilities.

All she wanted was to stop moving, to get finished with this half-baked scheme, and go back home. She was beginning to think it was a bad idea even though Cammy said it was their big chance to get some free publicity.

"They say it's turning more northwest," she yelled through the half-closed bathroom door. "They show this yellow shape on the Weather Channel that's supposed to be where it's going. Are we headed anywhere near a place called Outer Banks?"

"Close, but quit worrying, hon, those guys always guess wrong. Anyhow, the place we're going, it's not right on the ocean. All we'll see is a bunch of rain. Trust me, would I put you in any danger?"

Patty Ann closed her eyes and sighed. She did trust him, she really did. Trusted his heart, at least, because that was just as honest as the day was long. His judgment was something else. It wouldn't be the first time he'd taken hold of some brilliant idea and not bothered to work out all the kinks before barging into action.

"Keep thinking about Camshaw and Camshaw, Private Investigations at Bargain Prices," Cam called. "Hey, you want in here before I grab a shower?"

"Uh-uh, I'm going to sleep." She fumbled with the controls to tune out a noisy commercial. "Rambo Camshaw, Harebrained Ideas, Two For a Nickel," she muttered under her breath.

After a brief argument—brief because neither he nor Liza had the energy to do more—Beckett ended up spending the night on Fred Grant's sofa. Lumpy didn't begin to describe the cushions. Now he knew where Liza stored her stock of root vegetables.

Still, it was better than trying to drive after about forty hours of sleep deprivation. He'd left a message, letting Pete know where he was in case anything came up at the office. Not that he expected anything to crop up over a holiday weekend. His partner was good at dealing with rules, regulations and red tape— better than Beckett was, at any rate. Which was why he'd hired him. As a negotiator, the guy had all the skills of a disgruntled cottonmouth, but he was a wizard with paperwork.

Good thing he'd driven instead of flying this time, he thought the next morning, yawning. Looked like they might be in for some heavy-duty weather. Lying on his back, Beckett squinted up at the ceiling for several minutes, trying to focus on how much more he needed to explain before he handed over the money, got a signed receipt and headed back to Charleston. He made a mental note to check on the storm situation. The last thing he needed was to get caught in an evacuation situation. Everything up and down the Eastern Seaboard was subject to that, if Tropical Storm Greta took a notion to upgrade and move inshore.

He yawned again as his eyes gradually shifted to the front windows. When the view registered on his brain, he sat up abruptly, grabbed the small of his back and groaned, staring at a pair of women's shoes planted on the top visible rung of the ladder.

What in God's name was that crazy fool trying to do? Avoid confrontation by breaking her neck? That ladder was a homemade job, the rungs roughly eighteen inches apart. It hadn't been designed for a woman, even a long-stemmed woman like Liza.

Beckett had slept in his clothes, removing only his belt, his shoes and his socks. He had about a two-days' growth of beard on his face, and his back felt as if it were broken in at least three places.

And now he had to go drag a crazy woman down from a roof?

Yeah, now he had to do that.

Barefoot, he let himself out the front door, wondering how he could get her attention without startling her into losing her balance.

She was humming. Either that or she'd disturbed a nest of yellow jackets. With his luck, it would be the latter. "Liza?" he called softly, trying to sound as nonthreatening as possible when what he wanted to do was grab her, haul her down and shake some sense into her stubborn head.

She stopped humming.

"What are you doing up there? If the eaves are rotten that ladder could shift any minute. Dammit, woman, it's dangerous!"

"Shall I rent a helicopter to check out the roof? Sorry, my budget doesn't run to aerial inspections." She started down, first one foot then the other, feeling for the rungs while he held his breath and stared up at her long white thighs. She was wearing shorts today. Not the kind cut up to the creases, thank God. His heart couldn't have survived that.

"Easy, easy—just two more rungs," he cautioned, moving into position to catch her if she stumbled.

"Get out of the way, in case I fall. I don't want to mash you."

"Go ahead, mash me," he said with a shaky laugh. By the time she was one rung off the ground, his arms were around her. Breathless, she turned, placed her hands on his shoulder, and he lifted her down. "Judas

Priest, woman, don't do this to me. With PawPaw in the hospital, my dad hooked up to a breathing machine, my cousin in a cast and my favorite aunt forgetting where she lives, I don't need any more problems.''

''Well, it's going to rain and the roof leaks,'' she said, looking at him as if she thought he'd lost his mind. Funny thing, though…she didn't move out of his arms. Just went on staring up at him while his senses absorbed her soap-and-shampoo smell, the heat of her skin and the birdlike delicacy of her bones.

At six-one, 182 pounds, he was not a huge man by today's steroid standards, yet she felt fragile in comparison. For one fleeting moment, before other impulses kicked in, she reminded him of a stunned dove he'd once briefly held in his hands after it had flown into a window.

Reminded him, too, of just how long it had been since he'd made love to a woman. She was staring up at him, her eyes wide with…shock?

Yeah, well, he was feeling his share of that, too.

When it came to women, Beckett's record was less than impressive. A generous man might describe him as cautious. He'd come close to falling in love a couple of times, but since his first disastrous affair, he'd made it a policy to steer clear of anything resembling commitment. Bad case of Once Bitten, Twice Shy.

So far as he knew, bachelorhood didn't run in his family. Just the opposite, in fact. His parents had fallen in love on their first blind date, married three months later to the day and never looked back, as his mother made a point of reminding him each time she launched into one of her latent-grandmother talks. Even PawPaw, when he used to talk about his Emaline, would get a certain look in his eyes.

Oh, yeah, Beckett thought wryly. The marriage gene was one family trait that had passed him by.

Not that what he was feeling had anything to do with marriage.

He'd held the woman's hand, eaten her scrambled eggs and tried to give her some money. He'd gone a lot further than that with dozens of women.

During his second year at Clemson he'd been involved with an art teacher who was really into New Age stuff. Claimed she'd recognized him from a former life. At the time, he'd been more interested in sports than philosophy, which had pretty much ended that affair.

But maybe there was something to the karmic theory. Why else would a woman he barely knew affect him the way this one did? Lust, he could understand, but this feeling of…of something else, that was harder to explain.

Karma. Sure. Like maybe you ripped her off in a past life, and now you're trying to make amends.

He'd been standing there for what suddenly seemed like hours, holding her—staring at the way her mouth looked up close, full and gleaming with moisture after she'd run a nervous tongue over it once or twice.

It would've been nice if one of them had a functioning brain. What the hell did a man say at a time like this, when he was visibly aroused with no chance of doing anything about it?

She was wearing a thin cotton top again, and it was pretty obvious she wasn't wearing a bra underneath. Or if she was, it was no match for those nipples of hers. They were standing at attention. Which sure as hell didn't help his condition. Here it was, broad daylight; they were standing out in the front yard, and he had no more control over his urges than a teenager.

He was about to make some inane remark about the weather when she reached up, brushed the hair off the back of her neck and said, "I wish it would hurry up and rain, leaks or no leaks. We need some relief from this heat."

Lady, you don't know the half of it. "You're not worried about the storm?"

She frowned up at the sky, which had taken on a nacreous tint as the first wave of clouds moved in. "Not worried exactly. It's awful for business, of course. Mine and everyone else's if they call for an evacuation, but I don't think it'll come to that. Uncle Fred says it's going to veer offshore."

Liza willed her heart to slow down. She'd never been afraid of storms, anymore than she'd been afraid of heights. It was neither the storm nor the ladder that had her gasping for breath, trying to slow down a runaway pulse. If she had to fall, she'd rather fall off the roof than fall in love again. It would be far less painful.

The first time it had happened she'd been eleven years old. Kermit Bryant—she'd never forgotten his name—had edged his seat closer to hers, leaned over and sniffed loudly. He'd told her she smelled good. Thrilled and embarrassed, she'd blushed and scowled down at her paper. Then he told her she sure could run good for a girl. She'd been thinking of asking if he wanted half of her devil's food cupcake when she'd caught him copying answers off her test paper.

Tall and skinny, she'd never been wildly popular with the opposite sex, but she'd dated some in high school and college. The next time she'd fallen mindlessly in love, however, she'd been a sensible, mature and independent twenty-seven-year-old gallery assistant. They'd been introduced at a charity fund-raising concert and James Edwards had literally swept her off her feet when someone in front of her had spilled a drink. She'd known him all of five days before ending up in his bed.

God help her if she ever did anything so stupid again.

Now she caught herself staring at Beckett's bristly jaw and wondering if it would grow out as black as his eyebrows. Embarrassed, she blurted, "Do you want coffee before you go?"

Oh, God. She had all the savoir faire of a week-old gosling. His smile was so gentle she had to wonder if he'd read her mind.

"I've already put you to enough trouble."

His khakis were wrinkled, the tail of his black knit shirt hanging out; his hair was standing on end, he needed a shave and he was barefoot. And at this moment if he'd asked her to undress and follow him into the nearest bedroom, she wasn't entirely sure she'd say no. Even rumpled, there was something remarkably appealing about him. He smelled warm and clean and real, the way a man should smell. James had adored cologne and used it with a lavish hand.

Whatever it was with Lancelot Beckett that affected her the way it did, it was 100 percent natural. Pheromones. She hadn't a clue about their chemical components, but they were clearly potent. That much she did know.

"We're out of prunes again," came a disgruntled complaint from the doorway.

Liza closed her eyes, torn between laughter and tears. They went through this every morning. It took Uncle Fred awhile to assimilate new developments. At this particular moment, she could certainly empathize.

"They're in the cereal cabinet, Uncle Fred. I'll come show you."

"Young man here for breakfast? That's nice. Game starts at one. That new feller's pitching. Reminds me of Maddux in the old days."

"Thanks, but I can't stay," Beckett said. "As soon as I have a few words with Liza, I'll be on my way."

Already hurrying into the house, Liza glanced over her shoulder, "I can't talk now—I have to find Uncle Fred's prunes, and then I have to dress and get ready to open up in case any stragglers stop by." She paused long enough to say, "Look, do we really need to talk anymore? I think we've both said everything that needs saying."

"One thing I learned a long time ago—when it comes to negotiations, you're not finished until both sides agree that you're finished, even if it's only an agreement to disagree. So far we haven't even reached that point."

"Sure we have, don't you remember?"

"Look, I'll drop by later, all right? I've got a few calls to make—I might even run up to Newport News, but I'll be back this afternoon. Have dinner with me and we'll wind things up." He turned away before she could reject the invitation. Halfway to his car, he realized he'd forgotten his shoes, his belt, his wallet and cell phone.

Well, hell. Wincing at every other step, he avoided the buckled flagstone walk as he made his way back to the house.

"Forget something?" she said a little too cheerfully from the open doorway.

He glared at her. "Go ahead, gloat," he muttered under his breath.

"It's the holly leaves. They're almost as bad as cockleburs." She was grinning broadly by the time he reached the front steps. "I never would have taken you for a tenderfoot."

His dignity already in sad repair, he tried to glare at her, but ended up chuckling. "I'd forgotten how long it's been since I went barefoot."

Still smiling—he refused to call it smirking—she led the way past the living room where he'd left his personal effects. She nodded toward the bathroom and suggested he might want to wash up before he left.

Splashing cold water over his face and throat, Beckett considered telling her that there'd been a time when he could grind out a cigarette butt with his bare heel. Back in his reckless, hard-drinking, sports-fishing, womanizing days.

Aware that he was in danger of regressing, he combed his hair, examined his stubble and decided it could wait another few hours before reaching the itchy stage. By the time he returned to the kitchen, she had his breakfast on the table. The electric moment they'd shared out in the yard might never have happened.

Or maybe they hadn't shared anything at all—maybe he'd been the only one stunned by the unexpected current that passed between them when he'd lifted her down from the ladder. Sure, she'd been breathing hard. The pulse at the side of her throat had been fluttering like a captured wild bird. It could have been from exertion.

But dammit, exertion couldn't account for the fact that her nipples had been standing up like a pair of tiny thumbs poking through her soft cotton shirt. And it sure as hell wasn't the temperature, because today promised to be another steam bath. There was only one explanation: she'd been as aroused as he was.

Smiling, Beckett slipped into a chair and inhaled the fragrance of freshly brewed coffee. The kitchen was about a third of the size of his mother's kitchen back in Charleston, yet there were enough similarities to make him feel right at home. It was a…a family feeling, for lack of a better word.

Liza shoved the fig preserves across the table. Uncle Fred smacked his lips and said, "What did you say you did for a living, young man?"

He didn't recall saying, but maybe he had. "I sell insurance." It was the simplest way to put it. He sold security systems that could be installed on ships to help track them and alert the owners if one of them strayed off the charted course.

"Got anything that covers rotten roofs?"

"No, I'm afraid not." So then he had to add a little more, explaining the growing threat of piracy that had bankrupted more than a few small-ship owners. While the two men talked, Liza listened, her expression telling him she wasn't buying it. Not the whole package, at any rate. But then, she'd probably earned the right to be suspicious.

"Pirates? You're kidding, right?" They were sharing cleanup tasks while her uncle read the morning paper in the living room. Liza had gone out to open the stand and returned a few minutes later. When business was slow, she explained, she could keep an eye on it from the house. Today she'd be lucky to sell much of anything.

"Yeah, I know—it sounds crazy, but it happens more than most people think, if they think about it at all. Just like in the old days, it's usually a matter of profit. Occasionally it's desperation—a handful of poor thugs feel like they have nothing left to lose, so they hijack a ship, planning to sell the cargo to help feed their families. Mostly, though, it's a calculated risk. Like bank robbery, only on a slightly larger scale. My business is to cut the risks for ship owners and insurance companies as much as possible.''

''With what, armed guards?'' She raked a few strands of hair from her brow, leaving a blob of soap-suds behind. Beckett turned her to face him, tilted her chin with one hand and blotted the suds with the dish towel.

Without releasing her, he said gruffly, ''Mostly tracking. Monitored GPS systems. If a ship goes off course, certain steps are taken and then—''

He sighed. ''Liza, I think I'm going to have to kiss you. Consider this fair warning.''

She didn't move. If anything, her mouth softened, those full, naked lips parting on the whisper of a sigh.

One touch was all it took. What started out as a gentle exploration quickly escalated into a full-scale assault. His hands moved from her shoulders down her back, pressing her against him as he angled his face for better access. Scented heat seemed to rise and swirl around them. Her lips trembled and conformed to his as if they'd been made to fit together.

Beckett groaned. His tongue engaged hers in a dance as old as time. Tasting mostly of coffee, with a deeper, more personal note that affected him pro-foundly, she felt incredibly right in his arms. Almost familiar—as if they'd done this a thousand times be-fore, yet each time it happened it was a brand-new experience.

Man, you're losing it.

Then consider it lost, the last reasoning cell in his brain shot back. She couldn't have fitted him more perfectly if they'd been adjoining pieces of a puzzle, her pelvis nestled against his throbbing groin, her breasts flattened against his chest. It was like coming home. Forcing himself to hold back, he used the tip of his tongue to trace a line between her lips and her ear, nibbling little kisses along the way, grazing her with his teeth, then soothing her with his tongue.

She was trembling, her breath coming in irregular little gasps. Her fists were bunched in his shirt—he imagined them clasping him the same way.

Finally, painfully aroused, with no relief possible, he forced himself to begin easing away. He'd already put on his belt, but his shoes, wallet and cell phone were still in the next room, along with Uncle Fred.

From outside came the abrasive blare of a car horn. Liza groaned softly and buried her face in his throat. Beckett wanted nothing more at that moment than to back her up to the table, spread her legs and move between them. But it wasn't going to happen. Not now—probably never.

Sounding flustered and embarrassed, she said, "I'd better go out and—oh, shoot! I'm not even dressed." She was still wearing the shorts, clogs and faded shirt instead of her uniform of slacks and calico apron.

Beckett caught her when she would have slipped past him to dart into her bedroom. "Liza…don't." He wanted to tell her not to be embarrassed. He settled for, "Don't change, you look fine. Let me go out and see what they want. I'll hold 'em until you get whatever you need and get out there, okay?"

"My apron...the till," she said breathlessly.

And so he went outside, still barefoot, hoping his arousal would take care of itself before he had to discuss the price of turnips with a bunch of tourists.

Seven

"**I** want to go home." Patty Ann's face was pale under her freckles. Her conscience was bothering her. "Cammy, she hasn't done anything wrong. Maybe we shouldn't do this."

"Head still hurtin' you? Swallow another one of them pills." She'd had a headache earlier. "Honey, you said yourself she was smart. Now I ask you, would a rich lady that was smart give away everything she's got and walk off, not knowing where her next steak dinner was coming from? Trust me, in my line of work, you have to get to know people."

In his line of work, he had to know how to punch a clock, Patty Ann thought, and was instantly awash in guilt.

Absently, Cammy patted her on the knee. "Look,

the old man she's living with, he's not going to let her starve, right? He's got a house and all—probably some rich old coot—maybe he's kin, maybe not. But if she's as smart as you say she is, she'll stay put until she gets ready to make her next move.''

"I think he's her uncle. She said something once…'' Patty Ann's voice trailed off as she thought of how well she'd been treated over the five and a half years she'd worked for Ms. Edwards. If she hadn't already hired herself another maid, maybe Cammy could find a job at this place they were going, and she could go back to work for Ms. Edwards, and they could forget all about starting a private investigating agency. Cammy had been studying for months, but he still had to get a license. And even as brilliant as he was, Patty Ann wasn't sure how good he was at taking tests. She would still love him. She always had, but in some ways men never did grow up.

"Listen, the letter didn't bounce. She's still there—you found that out when she answered the phone.''

"Yeah, well a man answered once.''

"Sure. The old guy. Look, hon, chances like this don't come along twice. 'Member that guy down in Atlanta when some creep set off a bomb at that Olympic place? He was a security guard, just like me. Once it was over, everybody in the country knew his name.''

Patty Ann hauled off and whopped him on the shoulder, causing the old Chevy to veer toward the centerline. "Cam-my! Everybody thought he was a crook! We're not crooks!''

"Neither was he. See, that's what I'm getting at, babe. Publicity's the name of the game. You get it any old way you can."

He flashed her a quick grin, and Patty Ann was reminded all over again of why she loved this man. Most handsome guys were full of it, but Cammy had never been stuck on himself.

"Like I said, once you get enough publicity, people remember your name, but they forget where they heard it."

"Yeah, sure they do," Patty Ann grumbled half-heartedly. He was not only handsome, he was sweet and way smarter than people gave him credit for being. Sometimes she wished he wasn't so smart. Truth was, it didn't seem so smart to her to quit a good steady job to gamble on some crazy scheme that might even land them both in jail. For all she knew, calling somebody on the phone and then hanging up could be against the law. Cammy said it wasn't, but he hadn't graduated from his correspondence course yet. Maybe that was in one of the last lessons.

"Look, we'll stop off in the next town we come to and get something to eat, that'll make you feel better."

"Starting my period'll make me feel better," she mumbled.

"Jeez, you don't think you're pregnant, do you? Honey, I told you, we can't afford kids until we get our business up and running. I figger a couple of years ought to do it if we can get us some publicity. Then we start with a blast and the sky's the limit."

"Uh-huh." The Edwards case had been big in Texas, but maybe not anywhere else.

"Whatcha want for lunch, burgers and fries?"

"I don't want anything, I already told you. Maybe hot cocoa. Not the kind from a mix or a machine, either—the kind you make on the stove with cocoa and milk and all."

"Ba-abe, come on, we're in this together, remember? Another few hours, we ought to be in the neighborhood, then I'll spring for another motel room and we can shower and all before we show up at her place."

"I don't know…"

"Hey, maybe she'll invite us to stay. Ocean beach just a few miles away? Probably got a swimming pool and all?" Catching her skeptical look, he said, "No? Okay, but just keep saying it over in your mind… Camshaw and Camshaw, Private Investigations at Bargain Rates. Maybe something on the next line about discreet and all. Think about it, okay? I'm going to stop in the next town for food and gas."

Liza sprayed a whiff of her favorite fragrance. The bottle was practically empty, and once it was gone she would do without. If Beckett thought she was wearing it for him, then that was just too bad. She was wearing it for herself, along with one of the few decent outfits she'd kept when she'd sold practically her entire wardrobe. For a while she'd felt guilty about keeping back anything at all, but now she was glad she had. It helped to remind her, in case she was in danger of forgetting, that there was more to life than a produce stand, a house that was gradually sinking into the ground and a dear old man who was totally dependant on her to look after him.

"Just a few hours of my own, that's all I want," she told her mirror image as she arranged her hair in a softer style.

Liar.

She had just finished putting on her earrings—a pair of simple, inexpensive onyx studs, when Beckett arrived, his head and shoulders covered with a limp newspaper. "Hey, I hope you have a raincoat. It's really starting to come down."

She had a cheap plastic raincoat. No way was she going to wear that. Instead, she reached into the coat closet for her uncle's big umbrella. It was so old the black had turned green in streaks, but it didn't leak. Uncle Fred was watching an Andy Griffith rerun, waiting out a rain delay before the game could get started. He would stay up for hours if there was the slightest chance of resuming play.

Liza had cooked him a squash casserole with cheese and made apple pie for dessert.

Before coming to North Carolina she'd done very little cooking. They'd always had a live-in cook while she was growing up, and James had preferred eating out. Actually, he'd preferred being seen in all the best restaurants among all the best people, only his idea of best and Liza's had gradually diverged.

After seeing the way her uncle ate, mostly junk food and things that came out of a can, she had quickly learned her way around the kitchen. In fact, she might even write a cookbook one of these days— 101 ways to use up leftover produce.

Beckett stepped inside, looked her over and whistled silently.

"Too much?" She shouldn't have dressed up, especially as it was starting to rain really hard. Now he'd think he had to take her somewhere special.

"Too much," he echoed admiringly, giving the words an altogether different meaning.

She looked in on her uncle to be sure his chair was tipped back so that he wouldn't topple out if he fell asleep. Gently she removed the remote from his hand so that he wouldn't drop it when he dozed off, and then touched him on the shoulder. "Uncle Fred, I'm leaving now."

"Wha—what's that? Who's this? Who let you in?"

"It's Liza, Uncle Fred. I told you, I'm going out for a little while, but I'll be back soon. You go on to bed whenever you're ready, I'll look in on you when I get back."

The old man smacked his mouth few times, mumbled something about possums and was snoring softly by the time she reached the front door. "I don't know if I should go or not. I feel guilty about leaving him, even for a few hours."

"How long had he lived here alone before you came?"

"You're right. I guess I'm trying to make myself

feel indispensable. He lived here alone for years before I arrived on the scene.''

Beckett took the umbrella from her, opened it on
the porch and held it so that it covered them both as
they passed by the ladder that was still propped
against the eaves. ''Notice I didn't open the umbrella
in the house, and we walked beside the ladder, not
under it.''

She slanted him a quick smile that made even the
soles of his feet tingle, ''Duly noted.''

To shield them both from the blowing rain, he had
to wrap his free arm around her waist. Feeling her
hip pressed against his as they hurried out to the car,
he found himself almost regretting his impulsive dinner invitation. Liza in calico and wrinkled linen was
enough to make a man forget his own name. Liza in
a flowing black skirt with a silky shirt was enough to
make him forget to breathe. He finally remembered,
only to be sucker punched by the tantalizing whiff of
some cool fragrance that mingled enticingly with her
own subtle scent.

''You did something to your hair,'' he accused,
steering her carefully over the uneven flagstones. It
was looser than usual, a few wisps left to trail down
her nape and over her temples. Tempting as the devil.

He hurried her out to where he'd parked his car, a
few feet away from where the tin roof of the produce
stand was being hammered noisily by the rain. Even
for a guy who knew his way around most of the large
port cities on three continents, it was surprising how

quickly this particular wide spot in the road had come to feel so personal.

Beckett held the passenger door open, shielding her with the umbrella as she swung her long legs inside. If he got any wetter he'd be sending off steam.

Once inside, he started the car and backed out, unable to think of a single intelligent thing to say. Delayed adolescence overlapping premature senility. Hell of a thing.

"You probably know more about the restaurants around these parts than I do. Any recommendations?"

"Beckett, we can get something from a drive-in if you want to. I just needed to get away for a little while. You don't have to feel obliged to entertain me."

They were on a straight stretch of highway, which helped, because he found it impossible to devote his full attention to driving. "Look, let's get one thing straight. No, let's get several things straight. I came here with a purpose, we both know that—not that we ever reached an agreement, but at least you know why I tracked you down in the first place." He waited for a response.

Then, a direct man by nature, he figured he might as well lay his cards on the table. "What happened next was as big a surprise to me as it is to you. I don't know what to call it. I do know—at least I hope— that it's not entirely one-sided. You want to tell me I'm wrong?" he challenged.

Passing cars and the occasional neon sign only served to emphasize the premature darkness. Rain continued to fall, creating an odd sense of intimacy. By the time they reached the Currituck Sound Bridge on the way out to the beach area, traffic had noticeably increased. It was all headed inland, a steady stream of oncoming headlights.

"What was the name of that man?" she said.

"You mean Wrong Way Corrigan?" Beckett picked up on it immediately. For every three cars headed to the beach, at least a dozen were headed the other way. "Turn on the radio, see if you can find a weather broadcast. I have a feeling we're missing some information." Come to think of it, he'd stopped following the storm news once he'd got here. Too many other things on his mind.

She scanned past blurbs of music, past several commercials, and stopped on a news break. "...not expected to run for another term. Meanwhile, Greta is now a full-fledged hurricane. She's expected to strengthen by the time she reaches land. Hurricane warnings are posted for—" a burst of static interrupted "—South Carolina. If she stays on her present course—" More static. Before he could switch to an FM station, the cheerful voice came back. "...or possibly head inland. Stay tuned for the next update."

He turned the sound down. Neither of them spoke. As Beckett continued to drive, the only sound was the *slap-slap* of the windshield wipers and the rhythmic *bump-bump* of expansion joints as they crossed the long bridge. Nearing the beach, the unbroken line of oncoming headlights had Beckett swearing under his breath.

Suddenly he turned sharply, pulling into a visitors' center perched high on a dune. Parking so that they had a clear view of the intersection where north and south beach traffic merged to head inland, he switched off the engine and said quietly, "Well, hell."

For several moments the only sounds were the *tick-tick* of cooling metal, the steady drumming of rain and the occasional sound of screeching brakes and blaring horns. Even so, as evacuations went, it was surprisingly orderly.

"He said something about South Carolina. How far is your family from the coast?"

"Not right on the beach, but close enough to catch hell if it comes ashore anywhere in that area." Beckett shifted in his seat so that he faced her. "About the same distance as you and Fred are, but at least our roof doesn't leak. Dad replaced the whole thing after Hugo."

"Know what I think? I think we should just forget about this family debt business. If it's waited this long, another generation or so won't matter. Whatever Greta does, you need to be there for your family and I need to be there for Uncle Fred. In fact, I think we'd better head back and get started right now."

"Get started doing what?"

She appeared to consider the idea. He waited, aware of her warmth and the faint scent of a very good perfume. He didn't know what it was, but it lacked the shrill edge of some of the more modern scents. Just as Liza lacked the hard edge of too many women he'd met, including a few he'd been briefly involved with.

"Well, actually, I'm not sure. In Dallas we don't get too many hurricanes. Uncle Fred will know, though. At any rate, you don't need to waste any more time here. If you start back right now…" Her smile was a little too quick, a little too bright.

"I'll get bogged down in traffic. If this really is an official evacuation, every room within miles is going to be booked up. People who've rented cottages for a week aren't going to miss out on any more beach time than they have to."

"You can't drive all the way back to Charleston tonight."

"I don't intend to."

"But what about your family?"

"I'd say South Carolina's pretty much in the clear by now, if they're starting to evacuate this area." He turned to her then, both his features and hers illuminated by the security lights surrounding the sprawling rest area. "Liza, things aren't turning out the way I'd planned. Under the circumstances, I guess dinner at a restaurant is out. They're probably busy right now boarding up windows. So why don't we find a grocery store and stock up on the basics, then go back to Uncle Fred's, light a few hurricane candles for a festive touch, and open a few cans? What do you say, corned beef hash or roast beef hash? Fried up with onions and tomato sauce, they taste pretty much the same to me."

"You mean ketchup." She laughed.

Beckett thought, another woman would have whined about having her evening spoiled and sulked all the way home, but not Liza. Sitting there in a deserted parking lot in her silk finery, with her hair all soft and sexy, smelling like three hundred bucks an ounce, she was laughing.

You had to love a woman like that, you really did. *Oh, no.* No way!

"Where's the nearest supermarket?" he asked gruffly, scowling as he started the engine and circled the dune to pause at the intersection. Better keep his hands occupied, else he might reach out to her. One touch and all bets would be off as to which way this evening would end up. He could tell by a certain uneven quality of her voice that he wasn't the only one affected by the unnatural tension.

"There's one a few miles ahead on the beach, and another one back in Grandy. We passed it on the way."

"I vote for Grandy. Here's hoping it's still open." After several minutes he got a green light and merged with the traffic flow. Thank God there were signal lights at the intersection or they'd have been stuck here for the duration. A couple of decades ago he might have welcomed the opportunity. But Liza wasn't the kind of woman you made it with in the back seat of a car.

The tension mounted even higher as they were forced to maintain the bumper-to-bumper pace. Liza found a classical music station. Sebelius helped. If he'd been alone, Beckett might've pulled over and waited it out. With Liza beside him, that wasn't an option. Patience, as he'd been reminded more than once recently, was not his strong suit.

They bought the last two loaves of bread on the shelves and one of the few remaining gallons of milk. Liza added an assortment of canned soups and cookies, while Beckett raided the meat counter.

"What if we lose power?" she asked, on seeing all the perishables in his basket.

"We cook it all and pig out."

"Who's this *we?* You're going back to Charleston, aren't you?"

"Depends," he said, not bothering to elaborate.

"Beckett, they're already evacuating the beaches. That means it's headed this way real soon."

"Not necessarily. A lot of people will clear out, even before an evacuation is called for."

"Yes, well…" Liza leaned forward, trying to see the now-familiar landmarks. Everything looked different at night. She could count on one hand the number of times she'd been out after dark. The rain only made it worse. Neon signs, taillights, the occasional streetlight, all reflected on wet pavement.

Slowing, Beckett made a right turn. "Here we are," he said.

Liza hadn't even realized they'd arrived. She felt a thread of resentment that her evening out had already ended, accepting the guilt that followed hard on its heels.

And then she noticed that all the lights in the house

were on. "Omigod," she whispered, and without waiting for the umbrella, she opened the door, slid down to the ground and started running.

Beckett was two steps behind her. He yelled for her to watch her step just as the heel of one of her flimsy sandals skidded on a wet stone. Arms flailing, she was trying to save herself when she tripped.

He was beside her in an instant, kneeling, touching…running his hands down her legs. "Jeez, don't move, okay? Let me—"

"I'm all right! Dammit, just give me a minute." His hands were getting tangled in her wet skirt as he felt to see if she'd broken any bones. She hadn't. She was fairly certain of that. All the same, when an adult fell, it wasn't quite the same as when a child took a tumble. "My hands and knees burn like the devil, but I'm all right," she said through clenched teeth. "Go see what's happened to Uncle Fred."

She was furious. What an utterly humiliating way to end her big evening, sprawled out in the pouring rain on her hands and knees. Or, rather, her knees and chest. Her hands had skidded out from under her when she'd tried to save herself. They hurt almost as much as her knees.

"I'm going to pick you up. If anything hurts, speak up."

Everything hurts, dammit! She thought it, but didn't say it. Walls of wind-driven rain flew at them as, ever so carefully, he eased her over onto her bottom and lifted her off the ground. "Okay so far?"

"I can walk, just give me a minute," she growled,

making no attempt to free herself. Aside from hurting, she was badly shaken. "What I need to know is why all the lights in the house are on."

With her head tucked up under his chin, her long legs dangling, Beckett carried her carefully up the front steps and onto the wet porch. The door opened almost immediately. Fred Grant said calmly, "Saw the lights turn in. Thought it was you." He was standing there in his best bib overalls, his blue-and-white striped Sunday shirt and his Braves baseball cap. On the floor beside him was Liza's Hartmann suitcase and the latest copy of *Choptalk*, the Braves monthly publication.

"She took a tumble out on the front walk."

Liza lifted her head. "Uncle Fred, are you all right? Beckett, put me down."

He lowered her to the floor, and she held on to his arm until she was certain she was steady on her feet. Poor Uncle Fred, he looked so worried. They were both drenched, rainwater trickling off their hair.

It was Beckett, eyeing the suitcase, who asked, "Mr. Grant, what gives?"

Eight

"Lady on the TV said they had this hurricane shelter set up at Bay View. Thought I'd go visit for a spell."

Beckett looked at Liza. She shrugged. She was holding her hands up in front of her chest, as if she'd just finished scrubbing for surgery.

"Liza?" It was her call to make. Actually, it was Uncle Fred's call, and evidently he'd already made it. Beckett preferred to trust Liza's judgment. Her uncle showed every sign of being fairly sharp, but then his aunt Kate had been sharp, too, right up until she'd gone shopping one day and forgotten to come home. Forgotten where she lived. Someone who knew the family had seen her sitting on a bench outside a hardware store and noticed she was still there a couple of hours later. He'd called Uncle Lance, who had been frantically searching for her at the shopping mall.

"I think that sounds like fun, Uncle Fred. Do you have everything you need? What about your glasses? Did you think to pack your medicine?"

"Yep. Got ever'thing I need. You want to drive me over there, son? She don't much like to drive at night." He nodded at Liza, who was obviously trying hard to disguise the increasing pain she was feeling.

It had been a long time since Beckett had suffered a skinned knee, but he hadn't forgotten how it stung, aside from the bruised aspect. Once the burning stage ended, she was going to be hobbling around, trying not to break the scabs and start it to bleeding all over again.

"I'll drive, Mr. Grant. Liza, you go start cleaning up your wounds. Better yet, just sit down and close your eyes for a few minutes and let me do it when I get back."

"Oh, don't fuss so, for heaven's sake. I told you I'm all right."

But as soon as they'd left, Liza drew in a deep, shuddering breath, far more shaken than a simple tumble would ordinarily cause. It was more than the fall, she realized as she watched Beckett escort her uncle out to the car, holding his arm and skirting wide of the front walk. It was…everything. The expectations she hadn't dared admit when she'd set out earlier tonight. The way the man had managed to impress her so that she couldn't stop thinking about him, even when he was hundreds of miles away. Especially then. It was almost as if he exerted some sort of gravitational pull on her.

My God, how could it have happened so quickly? It felt remarkably like her first teenage crush, only magnified a hundred times.

She hooked the screen, remembered to unhook it in case Beckett came back, and turned toward her bedroom. He had family in Charleston. Bay View was only a few miles up the road, but what if he decided to keep on going, since he was headed in that direction?

He said he was coming back, didn't he?

Lifting her sodden skirt—it was muddy, but not torn as far as she could tell—she winced at the sight of her filthy, bleeding knees. She didn't even want to think about how they were going to feel while she was scrubbing away the mud and grit. Good thing the medical frontier had advanced beyond those old antiseptics that burned like fire. She had a tube of something or other in the medicine cabinet that would soothe and disinfect.

No Band-Aids large enough, though. She'd just have to bind her knees up in gauze and learn how to walk stiff legged.

"You klutz, you stupid klutz," she muttered as she hobbled into the bathroom. Using only her fingertips, she unbuttoned the waistband of her skirt and let it fall to the floor, not even attempting to tackle her top. If it weren't soaking wet she might even sleep in it rather than use her stinging hands to change into something else. The sooner she got them cleaned and smeared with something to keep the air from touching them, the sooner they'd stop hurting.

Clumsy. Stupid. Embarrassing. She thought all that and more as she braced herself and turned on a stream of warm water. Turning an ankle might not have been so bad—even fainting. *Swooning,* as it had been called back in the days when it had been considered romantic.

There was nothing the least bit romantic about taking a damned pratfall. Even knowing she would never see him again once this debt thing was settled, she had really, really wanted to make a good last impression. Her romantic side, small and withered though it was, would have liked to think that somewhere in the world, an attractive man might occasionally remember her and wonder what would have happened if they'd met under different circumstances.

He'll remember you now, all right, she told herself, picturing the way she must have looked from his perspective. Biting her lips against the fiery pain, she thrust her hands under the water and winced as pain zinged all the way up to her armpits. Then she reached for her washcloth and soap.

Even though she tried to ignore the pain and do what had to be done, the process took longer than it should have—the cleansing, medicating and bandaging. The heels of her hands were the biggest problem. Even though they weren't quite as damaged as her knees, it made using her hands difficult. She applied the last of the gauze to her knees, then sat on the edge of the claw-footed bathtub wondering whether to put on a pair of gloves—if she could even find a pair of gloves—or risk getting her hands infected. Not to mention smearing antiseptic ointment on everything she touched.

"Well, crud," she said, fighting tears.

And then she heard the car pull up in front of the house. Had she left the door hooked or unhooked? She couldn't remember. Everything had been so confused at that point. Uncle Fred and her suitcase; the hurricane; Beckett carrying her in his arms as if she were Sleeping Beauty instead of the world's greatest klutz.

Being holed up during a storm might have been romantic under other circumstances, but not when she looked like an accident victim.

"Come in if you're coming," she yelled over the wail of the wind. The rain was beginning to blow through the screen door. She was embarassed and hurting too much to be polite.

"I'm shoving the ladder under the house for now, okay?" came the voice from the dark. The yellow porch light didn't carry far enough to see more than a shadowy figure struggling to lower the ladder without being blown over.

"Whatever," she muttered. The thought of climbing a ladder made her flinch.

A moment later he burst inside, flinging rain from his face and hair, and slammed the door behind him. "Whew! It's getting wild out there," he said, grinning as if he relished the challenge. It occurred to her that he would probably be right at home on the deck of a ship, pitching and rolling in mountainous seas. "Are you all right?" he asked. "Have you taken care of your…"

His voice trailed off as he looked down at her bandaged knees, reminding her of what she must look like in her ruined blouse, with wet hair hanging in ropes around her shoulders and her skinny, wounded legs hanging out.

Some women—the pretty, petite ones—could play the helpless heroine for all it was worth. Not Liza. She came off as a hapless clown. Okay, so she had gone overboard with the gauze. At least her knees were well padded. "Crud," she said again. Couldn't even do profanity with any style.

"Jeez, sweetheart, are they that bad? I wouldn't have left if—"

"They're skinned, all right?" she snapped. Sympathy was the very last thing she needed. She was feeling sorry enough for herself without his piling it on. And, dammit, she hurt more thinking about his walking out of her life than she did thinking about her increasingly painful injuries. Skinned knees healed in a week's time. Bruised hearts took longer. Broken hearts, she refused even to consider. She hadn't known him long enough for him to break her blasted heart.

Bracing herself, Liza took command of the situation. She might make a lousy tragic heroine, but she could play the role of gracious hostess to the hilt. She'd had plenty of practice back in the bad old days. "Come in, don't worry about tracking up the floor.

Let me get you a towel and I'll see about heating us some soup. Do you think Uncle Fred will be all right there? What if he decides he wants to come home in the middle of the night? Was it very crowded? Do you think he's acting…well, rationally? Maybe I should have insisted he stay here where I could keep an eye on him. I mean—''

So much for gracious hostess. She was falling apart, pure and simple.

Beckett took her arm and steered her toward the living room. ''Go sit down, let me heat us some soup.''

Liza let him take charge. Just for the moment, she told herself. Just until she could stop babbling and pull herself together. She was shivering, and it certainly wasn't cold. She was simply…

Well, hurting, for one thing. And hungry. And for no reason at all she suddenly felt like crying. ''Did you bring in the groceries?''

Beckett smacked himself on the forehead. ''I don't know about the meat and bread, but the milk and canned goods will probably be all right.'' He'd had a bag in each arm when he'd seen her stumble. No telling what had happened to them—he hadn't noticed them when he'd walked the old man out to the car. But then, he'd been holding on to his arm, watching both their steps.

On the way back, he'd been too anxious about Liza, worried that she was more shaken up than she'd let on. For a man who was generally considered pretty cool under pressure, he was flat-out losing it.

Nor did he care to define the meaning of the word *it*.

While Beckett found a basket and went out to retrieve the sodden groceries, Liza made her way from room to room, making certain all the windows were closed as tightly as possible. They were rattling in their frames, so she didn't hold out much hope, especially as the rain seemed to be coming from all directions.

Which meant the house would be stifling. If the power went off, she wouldn't even have her electric fan for comfort.

Probably wouldn't sleep, anyway.

Beckett insisted on cooking supper. He said something more substantial than soup was called for. While the ground-beef patties, seasoned with soy sauce, were cooking, he gathered up all her empty containers and filled them with water. "Just in case," he said. "If you've got a barrel or an empty garbage container, I'll set it under the eaves to collect flushing water."

"The gutter's down on the front."

"Right. Okay, the back then. If it keeps on at this rate, we won't even need a downspout."

While he was seeing to all that, Liza turned the burgers, then searched the drawers for spare batteries. She remembered reading somewhere that water and spare batteries were important.

"I don't suppose you have a weather radio," he said, coming in through the back door. She stared at him. With his clothes clinging like a second skin to a body that was muscular and whipcord lean, it took a minute for the words to register.

"A weather what?"

"Radio. You know, a dedicated NOAA receiver." He pronounced it "Noah."

She said, "You're not talking about Noah and the ark. No, even I know better than that."

She was standing by the stove. He came and removed the spatula from her fingers, skillfully turned the meat and replaced the lid. "What do you mean, even you?"

Shrugging, she moved away to stare out the window. "Nothing. It was a figure of speech, that's all."

He looked as if he didn't believe her, but then, that was his problem, not hers. She knew her shortcomings as well as she knew her longcomings. And while the former might have once outweighed the latter, she'd come a long way in the past two years. What was it they said in academic circles? Publish or perish?

In her case it had been survive or perish. She had chosen to survive.

The burgers were surprisingly tasty, even without buns. James would have been horrified—he'd fancied himself something of a gourmet. At least, he subscribed to the magazine and left it lying around along with her copies of *Art and Antiques* to create a certain impression on the people he invited to their home. If he'd ever done more than glance at either publication, she'd be very much surprised.

Beckett cut her meat for her, shushing her when she'd protested.

"I suggest you get ready for bed while I clean up the kitchen. If you don't mind, I'll commandeer your sofa again."

"Have you called home yet?" He's not leaving tonight, she thought gleefully.

"Checked in before I left Bay View. Nice place, by the way. Have you ever seen it?"

"A few times, when I drove Uncle Fred to visit some of his friends. It's a beautiful location." She'd heard it had been endowed by an elderly philanthropist. Certainly none of Uncle Fred's friends would have been able to afford it otherwise. "How are things in Charleston?"

"Wet. Mama's roses caught hell again, but other than that, everything came through just fine. My cousin Carson says hello, by the way. He was there when I called."

"Well. I know you're relieved." She was standing awkwardly beside the kitchen door, painfully aware of what she must look like. Neither of them had changed into dry clothes. It was extremely hot in the house, particularly in the kitchen.

"Uh…Liza? Do you need any help? I mean, with your hands and all…?"

But supper was over now. They could either sit in the living room watching TV as long as they had power, or go to bed and lie awake staring into the stifling darkness while the storm wore itself out and passed on up the coast. As tired as she was, she knew she wouldn't sleep.

And it wasn't the thought of the storm that would keep her awake. It was the thought of the man just a few feet away.

Beckett of the chiseled bronze features, the pewter hair and the quicksilver eyes. Becket of the square-palmed, long-fingered hands, the comforting shoulders and the hard, flat abdomen.

She quickly lifted her eyes to the ceiling. "The attic. I need to set out buckets under the leaks," she blurted.

"Stay here, I'll do it. Where do you keep your buckets?"

The buckets were all filling with rainwater, so she supplied pots and plastic wastebaskets, then waited at the foot of the stairs while Beckett set them under any drips he found in the cramped attic space. The thought of climbing the stairs was too painful to contemplate.

She tried to imagine how she'd be feeling if she'd been seriously injured—broken a leg or worse. She was one of those fortunate individuals who had never been seriously ill. Good thing, considering she'd turned out to be such a wimp.

"That's done." He descended, grinning and brushing his hands together. "Now, what do you say we switch on the fans and try to get some sleep?"

"You know where the linens are. You'll pardon me if I don't offer to make up the couch for you? I've just learned that I despise physical pain."

They were standing too close in the narrow stair landing. She could smell his shaving cream—he had obviously showered and shaved just before picking her up to go out for dinner. All that seemed aeons ago, but only a few hours had passed.

"Remind me never to accept a dinner date with you again," she said dryly.

"Remind me never to ask you for another date." He smiled, but the intensity of his look lingered after the smile had faded. She averted her face, her pulse suddenly kicking into overdrive.

Instead of moving away, he continued to stand in the attic doorway. "Liza?"

Just that. He said her name, and that was all it took. When he opened his arms, she moved into them as if he were a magnet and she a splinter of steel. No words were needed. Lifting her, he carried her to the bedroom door, then had to back up and reposition himself to maneuver her through the opening without bumping her legs.

"It never happens this way in the movies."

"Wider doorways," he said gravely. She snickered and he grinned, but the tension remained unabated. Carefully he lowered her to the bed. She held her breath. If he left her now, she didn't know what she would do. Beg him to stay? Swear at him? She was no better at begging than she was at cursing.

He reached for the tail of her shirt, eased it carefully over her head and draped it over the foot of the bed. "Liza? Are you all right with this?"

Was she all right with what? Letting him undress

her? That depended on whether it was an act of pity or an act of seduction.

Mutely she nodded. His eyes narrowed, and then he asked, "Where are your scissors?"

"My scissors," she repeated. She was sitting here naked except for a skimpy bra, matching panties and three miles of gauze, and he wanted a pair of *scissors?*

To cut off what?

"Kitchen shears in the third drawer down beside the sink, nail scissors in the medicine cabinet. Take your pick."

He left, returning a moment later with the nail scissors and a roll of adhesive tape. "Might as well get you more comfortable before we…"

Before we *what?* she wanted to scream at him.

Gently but methodically, he removed several yards of gauze from her knee, retaped the rest and used the excess to bandage her hands, wincing at the sight of her raw flesh. Finally, setting the scissors and tape roll on the dresser, he said, "There now, that's better."

She started to make a crack about playing doctor, but thought better of it. Obviously, she'd misread the signs.

But then he reached for his belt. While she watched, hardly daring to breathe, he shed his khakis and tossed them across a chair.

Neat, but not overly so, she couldn't help but notice. James would have spent minutes brushing off imaginary specks and wrinkles, draped his trousers carefully over the mahogany clothes rack and then spent even more time taking care of his shirt and tie. It was no wonder their sex life had never been terrific. By the time he was ready to come to her bed, she'd usually been half-asleep.

He was tanned all over, from his feet upward. And upward led past some breathtaking scenery. In a pair of navy boxers, he was visibly aroused. Aroused and perfectly in control. That was somehow even more exciting than being aroused and out of control.

They were adults, Liza reminded herself. He was probably better at this than she was—he had to be more experienced. She tried to swallow, but her mouth was too dry. Other parts of her body were damp and throbbing. She felt like a nervous virgin, unsure of how to act, wanting so much to please, terrified that she wouldn't. Dressed in a designer gown, with her hair professionally done and her face carefully made up, she might have felt more confident, but stick-skinny and practically naked, with big, clumsy bandages on her hands and knees, confident was the last thing she felt.

"Liza, stop it," Beckett said quietly. "If you don't want to do this, then just say so. I might not be able to walk upright for a while, but I'll survive. All you have to do is tell me to leave, and I'll spend the rest of the night on your potatoes."

She blinked. "On my *what?*"

All innocence, he said, "Don't you store your excess stock of potatoes in your sofa cushions? I could've sworn…"

She sputtered, then burst out laughing. Before she could recover, he came down beside her, kissing his way up her throat while he skillfully unhooked her bra and peeled it off.

And then his mouth found hers and all rational thought fled. Her breasts, modest at best, swelled to his touch, her nipples rising to his kisses. Her thighs first clamped together, then fell apart and she forgot all about her injuries. His back felt warm and slick as she stroked it with her fingers, wishing her hands weren't swathed in gauze so that she could stroke him with her palms. She was still smiling when he removed her panties, carefully easing them over her knees. She felt an urge to giggle. In her wildest imagination she could never have come up with a seduction scene like this, but, oh, it was working. She lay there, helpless to take a much more active part, and relished every single sensation as he brought her to the brink, allowed her to drift back, then swept her up again. First with his hands, then with his mouth, he took her places she had never before been.

By the time he moved over her, she was frantic with need. "Please, please," she gasped.

Swearing softly, he swung himself up and reached for his pants. "God, I hope it's still here." His wallet hit the floor. Rolling onto her side she curled around him as he ripped open the foil packet. Moments later he was back, positioning himself over her again, and she reached for him, never mind her bandaged hands.

It was everything she had ever imagined and more. Within minutes she climaxed not once, but twice.

Later, when she could think rationally again, she thought of the times she had accused the authors of all those romances she'd read of exaggerating. The truth was, they hadn't done it justice.

Sometime later Liza awoke, sore but relieved to find him still there beside her, curved around her back, his arm around her waist. She had never been prone to messy emotions, but suddenly her eyes were burning and her throat had that thick feeling that meant tears weren't far away.

She knew what she wanted. She wanted it to go on this way forever.

It wasn't going to happen. He'd be leaving today; she'd known that all along. She could take his money or not. She'd done nothing to earn it, yet if she refused, he might construe it as a means of holding on to him. There was nothing she'd like better than to hold on to him, but not that way.

Meanwhile, she reminded herself, there were buckets to empty in the attic, and windowsills to mop up. Hard, blowing rains always leaked through. Maybe she could take the money and use it to buy storm windows…although the whole house was so far off square, she doubted if she'd be able to find any to fit.

What on earth was she doing, lying here beside the man who had sent her over the moon again and again—thinking about *storm windows?*

There's no hope for you, Lizzy, none at all, she jeered silently. Here she'd been priding herself on the progress she'd made since her whole world had fallen apart, and now this. Now she'd gone and fallen in love with a—with a pirate chaser, of all things.

Oh, God, I don't believe this. She groaned—silently, she hoped.

"In pain, are we?" said a sleepy voice from beside her.

"No, we are not in pain," she snapped. "At least I'm not, I don't know about you."

He lay there, staring up at the ceiling, a slant of sun highlighting his bristles on his jaw. Evidently, he was one of those men who needed to shave twice. "Not a morning person, hmm?"

She was so a morning person, but it seemed childish to insist. Sitting up, she pulled the sheet over her bare breasts and braced herself to swing her legs out of bed.

"Easy," he cautioned, reading her intentions. "I wouldn't be surprised if you don't have a few bruises to show for your fall last night."

Which one? When it came to which fall would hurt the longest, there was no contest. "At least there's no point in hurrying out to the stand this morning. Why don't you shower and get dressed, and I'll make you some breakfast before you leave."

He was quiet for so long, she stole a look at him. Surely that wasn't anger she saw on his face? Lips clamped tight; jaw squared; those coal-black eyebrows that contrasted so dramatically with his hair practically glowering at her. "Beckett? Are you all right?"

"You're dead set on getting rid of me, aren't

you?'' he asked, his voice silky enough to put her on guard.

''I only offered—''

''I know what you offered, dammit.''

All right, Liza, time to take charge. She might not be used to waking up with a man who was practically a stranger in her bed, but it was no more disconcerting than what had happened to her back in Dallas. She had taken charge then; she could do it again. The storm was obviously over. Her one-night stand had been terrific. But it was just that: a once-in-a-lifetime thing. He hadn't offered more and she was too proud to beg.

She said, ''Give me a minute in the bathroom first, okay?'' Gritting her teeth, she eased out of bed, took a deep breath and stood, waiting for the pain to ease. Then she hobbled, stiff legged, toward the door.

''Hurts, huh?''

''I'll live.''

''Trouble with injuries like that, you can't sew 'em up, you just have to grow new skin.''

''If your shirt's still wet, you might want to hang it on the line. It should be dry by the time you're through with breakfast.''

He was watching her, dammit. She could feel his eyes on her backside as she hobbled to the door, clutching her damp shirt in front of her. *Idiot! It's not your pitiful boobs he's staring at, it's your scrawny rump!*

The mere thought of having to bend her knees to step into a pair of panties made her cringe. She'd simply have to find something to wear that would cover her decently without much underneath.

"You won't be able to drive for a while, you know," he said so close behind her she jumped. She hadn't heard him, but then, breathing through clenched teeth was a rather noisy process.

"I'll manage."

"Don't be a damned martyr, Eliza. Would it kill you to ask for help?"

Nine

Beckett took a moment to gather his thoughts after clipping his cell phone onto his belt. His last call to Carson had relieved him on several points. PawPaw was holding his own and might even be allowed to go home in another week or so if a private nurse could be found.

And one could, of course. When it came to seeing to the welfare of her family, Rebecca Beckett was more than a match for any five-star general.

The storm had passed by offshore, doing little more than surface damage. "Your end of the coast probably took more of a beating than ours," Carson had said early this morning. "How'd you and your fair lady fare?"

"Fair. A few minor scrapes, a few leaks, a few

branches down. Nothing too serious." He wasn't about to elaborate, not until he'd analyzed the data and decided on a course of action.

As to how Beckett himself had fared, that might be another story. He'd set himself up for what had happened, coming back again and again on a mission that had waited a hundred years and could easily wait another hundred.

Except for PawPaw. He couldn't go back and report failure; neither could he lie about it. Which meant he was stuck here until they reached an agreement regarding the money. If nothing else, he could set up an account in a local bank in her name. It would help to know where she banked, but it wasn't the sort of question a man could easily work into a conversation. From the looks of things, she probably didn't have much left to deposit after the usual monthly outlays.

Despite the fact that his family had always had money, Beckett was no snob. At least, he didn't think he was. Still, it struck him as all wrong for a woman like Liza Chandler to be eking out a living selling fruits and vegetables. She was no Eliza Doolittle. The woman had style. She had class. She had intelligence and integrity.

Not to mention sex appeal that was all the more potent because it was so understated. If she'd done anything to attract his attention, he might have been able to resist, but she hadn't. Just the opposite, if anything.

Granted, he had a weakness for needy women.

Maybe it was genetic; maybe it was an acquired trait—he didn't know. He did know he had trouble refusing any woman who'd ever asked for his help.

Liza Chandler was needy as hell, only she refused to admit it, much less accept his help. What woman in her right mind, with a roof that was about to fall in, would turn down ten grand, no strings attached?

"I'm out of the bathroom if you want to shave before you go. Didn't you mention something about seeing someone up in Virginia?"

Virginia. Newport News. McKee Shipping. He'd forgotten all about it. "I'm in no hurry," he called back. He'd never even gotten around to making an appointment. "I'll bring down the buckets from the attic."

"Just empty them out the window, it's a lot easier than trying to bring them down the stairs."

She was stalking around the house like a giraffe, mopping up windowsills and throwing open windows. Barefoot, with her hair in an off-center ponytail, she was wearing something that looked as if it was made to go over a tent pole. And all he could think of was taking her back to bed, making love to her until they both collapsed.

Great. Just bloody, blasted great. He was damned if he stayed and damned if he left. He had a feeling that Dublin wouldn't be far enough to cut him loose from her spell.

Worse, he didn't know if he even wanted to be cut loose.

Beckett knew from experience that he was bad

news to any woman looking for more than a brief fling. Maybe it was a conditioned reaction, a defense against his weakness for needy females, but it didn't change the facts. He'd been running from commitment far too long.

Not that Liza was looking for anything long-term. Not from him, at any rate. Over the years he'd gotten pretty good at reading the signals, and the only signals he'd picked up from her were confusing, to say the least. On the other hand he knew damn well that she was as conscious as he was of the physical awareness that had sprung up so unexpectedly between them. Uneasy, awkward and inappropriate as it was, recent circumstances had only served to heighten that awareness.

Once they'd ended up in bed, he'd put her awkwardness down to her injuries. Now he was beginning to wonder if there hadn't been something else behind it. The woman had been married for what, eleven years? Had the jerk been a eunuch as well as a crook?

From a few things Fred Grant had said that first night, Beckett had learned that she hadn't gone out on a single date in all the time she'd been living here. Which probably meant she was lonely. And lonely women were vulnerable. Lonely women had been known to latch on to the first reasonably healthy, solvent and available man who showed an interest in them.

Beckett qualified on all counts. Add to that the spice of the sexual attraction that had unexpectedly sprung up and it was trouble waiting to happen. A smart man would have been gone before things got out of hand.

Trouble was, he had never claimed to be smart where women were concerned. Wary, was more like it. His first experience had set the stage for that. At twenty-two he'd thought he knew it all. He'd thought that because his family was prone to long, happy marriages, it would happen for him whenever he was ready.

And he'd been ready. Ripe for the picking. Fresh out of college with family money behind him, he'd been ready to launch a career. It hadn't taken much to convince him he needed a wife at his side. Someone to help him keep his eye on the ball.

What a pathetic jerk he'd been. Shows you what comes of having a happy childhood, he thought now with no real bitterness. You grow up with unrealistically high expectations, and then one day, whammo! You wake up in the real world. There ought to be a vaccination.

Even now he could remember the scene. Both families already seated in a church that was overflowing with guests, the whole place reeking of flowers and carpet cleaner. The organist giving it her all while he stood there wondering if his collar had somehow shrunk a full size since he'd put it on less than an hour earlier.

The organist paused, waiting for a signal to launch into the pièce de résistance, when a kid about five or six years old darted in through a side door, slipped him a note and ducked out again.

Puzzled, Beckett had read the few lines in growing disbelief. He'd stood there for what seemed like an eternity, and then he'd looked up at all the curious faces: friends, family—people he'd known all his life—and told them calmly that the wedding was off.

Pam's family had blamed Beckett; his family had blamed Pam. Never mind that she and her new conquest, a middle-aged drugstore mogul, had already left for Bermuda. He never did know what happened to all the postfestivities food. He'd ripped the tin cans and ribbons off the back of his car and headed out of town with no particular destination in mind. Eventually he'd wound up at his best man's cottage on Kiawah Island, where he'd gotten royally soused on vintage champagne and been sick as a dog for days afterward.

Since then, the word *commitment* hadn't been in his vocabulary. He'd enjoyed a number of brief, mutually satisfying relationships, but he wasn't about to do to any woman what Pam had done to him. In retrospect, he figured she'd done him a big favor.

Now it was time to pass on the favor by moving out before any real damage was done. He both liked and respected Liza Chandler for the way she'd pulled herself through what had to have been a grueling experience. The last thing she needed, he told himself, was to get involved with a guy who would take all she had to offer and leave her to deal with his absence.

No way. The biggest favor he could offer her was

to get out before things got too complicated. Now that
the storm had passed he would simply thank her and—

Wrong. She might take his thanks the wrong way.

Okay, so he wouldn't thank her, he'd just explain
why he had to leave and—

Oh, hell. Why not just hand her the money and go?

But first he had chores to do. She would have
enough to handle without having to climb those stairs
half a dozen times. Anything that required bending
those knees was going to be a problem for the next
several days. Which meant he'd have to offer to bring
the old guy back home.

He'd better check out the stand, too, else she'd be
out there struggling with that section of tin roof. It
would never occur to her to hire someone to do the
work. Dammit, why couldn't she take the money and
build something decent, as long as she insisted on
staying here?

And she'd stay, of course, as long as the old guy
needed her. That was something else about her he
liked. Loyalty.

By the time he came downstairs with both hands
full of empty containers, she was standing on the back
porch, gazing out over the flattened cornfield beyond.
He turned over the buckets on the edge of the porch
and came to stand beside her.

"Did you ever see such a gorgeous sky?" she murmured.

"Yeah. Matter of fact, you see those colors a lot
in the tropics. Don't ask me why."

She was holding her hands up in postscrub position

again, palms inward. The bandages were damp and filthy. He couldn't see her knees for the denim tent that touched her shoulders, skimmed her breasts and flowed around her like a circus tent. "Want me to look at your hands before I go?"

"No point in it," she said airily. "I'm all out of gauze. I'll get some more while I'm out."

"Out? You're planning on driving in that condition?"

The look she shot him could be described as haughty, but he recognized defensiveness when he saw it.

Damn.

"Uncle Fred's probably dying to get home by now. I thought I'd wait until the grocery store has had time to restock and stop by on the way home."

"Why don't I go for you?" Beckett heard himself asking, just as if he hadn't planned on making his excuses, thanking her for her hospitality and hitting the road before he got in any deeper.

She hesitated, then said, "Thanks, Beckett, I'd appreciate it. You'd better get several rolls of gauze and some more of that ointment while you're out, too, if you don't mind. I'll reimburse you for everything when you get back."

He wouldn't argue with her now. Instead, he would strike a bargain. He would take her money if she'd take his. "Sure. Make a list."

"But pick up Uncle Fred before you go shopping, will you? He likes to sit in the parking lot and watch people come and go."

"As good as holding a reception." He'd seen the way the old guy held court out at the roadside stand.

By the clear light of morning, she looked even paler than usual, with shadows around her eyes and a faint pink rash on her throat where his beard had rubbed against her. Her hair was still shower damp, with red-gold strands curling on the surface. Remembering the warm weight of it in his hands only a few hours ago gave rise to a reaction that was both untimely and inappropriate. Not to mention downright embarrassing.

"I'll go make that list," she said, sidling past him to escape inside the house.

Thank God one of them still retained a few grains of common sense.

He gave her enough time to make a list before he followed her inside. She was in the kitchen, awkwardly digging a spoon into a jar of peanut butter. Neither of them had taken time for breakfast. Of all crazy things, it was when he saw the guilty look on her face that Beckett knew he was fighting a losing battle.

"You know what they say about emergencies," she said with that too quick, too bright smile again. "You need more fuel. The last time I got caught eating peanut butter from a jar, I was twelve years old."

It wasn't fuel he needed, it was enhanced powers of resistance. Crossing to the silverware drawer, he took out a tablespoon, then held out his hand.

By the time the red pickup pulled into the driveway, the jar was half-empty, Liza was holding up her skirt and frowning at the frayed bandages on her knees, and Beckett had surrendered to the inevitable: no way was he going anywhere, not until they had dealt with all the unfinished business between them. And this time he wasn't thinking about the damned money, either.

The doorbell rang.

Liza dropped her skirts, mumbled, "'Scuse me," and stalked off to answer the door. Beckett figured either a neighbor or someone from Bay View must have brought the old guy home.

"Patty Ann!" He heard her exclaim from the front hallway. "What on earth…! Come inside. We're in sort of a mess right now on account of the storm— did you know about the storm? Well I guess you did, with all the rain and wind we had last night."

This was obviously not the time to settle things between them. Waiting until she herded her company into the living room, he'd intended to poke his head through the doorway and tell her he was leaving and would be back in a couple of hours. It would take that long to get the old guy's things together, get him out to the car and then stop for the groceries and first aid supplies.

Patty Ann—whoever she was—was not alone. Seated beside her on the potato-stuffed sofa was a big guy with rookie cop written all over him. Brush cut, small eyes busy taking inventory of the shabby old room.

Something triggered a silent alarm. Not danger,

just…trouble. Stepping inside the room, he said, "Morning, folks. You headed back to the beach?"

"Oh, Beckett, this is Patty Ann Garrett. She used to work for me back in Dallas, and this is—Mr. Camshaw?"

Big guy. Wrestler's torso, thick neck, face like a high-school heartthrob. Beckett stepped inside the room and extended his hand, first to the woman, a pocket Venus with freckles and a minor overbite—then to the man who rose slowly to tower a couple of inches over Beckett's own six-one. Mutt and Jeff, he thought, wondering what the devil they were doing here at this particular time.

"We were, um…in the neighborhood and thought we'd stop by," Camshaw said. "Patty Ann, she's been sort of worried about you, Ms. Edwards, not knowing where you was and all."

"How *did* you know where she was?" Beckett asked, taking care not to let his growing suspicions show in his voice. For some reason these two were hedging. He knew guilt when he saw it, and it was guilt he saw in the girl's eyes. The way they darted around. The way her blue-tipped fingers kept stroking nonexistent wrinkles from her miniskirt.

It was the guy who answered. "Patty Ann, she come across this address book mixed up in some old magazines she brought home. It had this address in it, and she was pretty sure Fred Grant was a cousin or something."

"He's my great-uncle," Liza murmured. "But how

did you know...I mean, how could you possibly know...?''

Beckett read the growing doubt in Liza's face. Putting two and two together, he came up with...two. The hang-up calls and the letter she'd told him about. A blank sheet of paper with a Dallas return address.

Oh, yeah, this pair was up to something all right. But what? Could they have been mixed up in some way with Edward's business?

Camshaw's eyes were never still. He was sweating, but then the temperature was already in the high eighties. The girl looked as if she wanted to be anywhere but where she was.

Liza asked how her mother was and got a monosyllabic reply.

''She's fine. Real good.'' The girl squirmed. Either she needed to go to the bathroom or she had something on her mind.

Beckett turned to Camshaw. ''You're in law enforcement, right?''

The girl brightened. ''How did you know that?''

He shrugged. ''Lucky guess.'' He'd been working with law enforcement types for years.

''Cammy's just a security guard now, but he's studying to be a detective. We're going to open us this agency—you tell 'em about it, Cammy.'' And without pausing, she rushed on to say, ''We're going to call it Camshaw and Camshaw, Private Investigations at Bargain Rates, and we thought—that is...'' Her enthusiasm leaked out like air from a punctured balloon.

Beckett was beginning to get a glimmer of what it was they'd thought. Make a connection to a high-profile case, wait awhile, revisit the principals, then reap the publicity. It would be tabloid stuff, at best, but when you were trying to launch yourself as a P.I., any free press was welcome.

He wondered if either of them was aware of the fine line between jumping on a perceived opportunity and taking advantage of an innocent victim.

"We appreciate your stopping by, don't we, Liza?" He moved closer to her chair and rested his hands possessively on her shoulders.

"What? Well, yes, of course. You didn't say where you were going, Patty Ann. I wish I could offer you hospitality, but as you can see, we're in a mess here. My uncle's coming home as soon as I can go get him, and—"

"That's all right," the freckled blonde said, jumping up and reaching for Camshaw's ham-size hand. "We can't stay, can we, Cammy? I just wanted to— That is, long's we were in the neighborhood…"

Yeah. Sure you were, Beckett thought, wishing he could have just five minutes alone with the guy. While he was pretty sure they were no real threat, he had no intention of heading south while they were still in the area. It wasn't as if Liza had anything of value to steal—all the same, something didn't smell right.

"At least let me offer you some refreshments before you go," Liza said. "Coffee? Iced tea? Fruit?"

Ragged bandages, baggy tent dress and all, she was

totally convincing as the gracious hostess. Real dignity, he told himself, had little to do with outward appearances.

The phone rang, and he excused himself. "Might be for me," he said quietly as he headed for the kitchen.

It wouldn't be for him. Car would've called on his cell phone. Just as he reached for the instrument, his glance fell on the peanut butter jar with two spoons in it, and he had to smile. The lady was a constant surprise, not to mention a constant delight.

"Grant residence, Beckett speaking."

Ten

"**H**ey? Speak up, I can't hear ya. Is this Liza?"

It took a while, but Beckett managed to get the message. Uncle Fred would like to stay a few more days. Could Liza please pack a few more things and bring them out to the home? Don't forget his Bible and the picture on the mantel. Oh, and a bag of those orange-flavored prunes.

Beckett stood on the porch and watched the younger couple off before passing on Fred Grant's message. Liza said nothing. She sighed, turned and leaned her face against his chest, murmuring an apology she didn't mean and he didn't need. His arms came around her, and he held her for several long moments, savoring the feel of her, the scent of shampoo and peanut butter. "You all right?"

"No. Yes. Well, of course I am." She leaned back to look up into his face. "You know, the strangest thing…I think those two were up to something and for some reason they changed their mind. I mean, I've known Patty Ann for years, and I've never seen her so…so squirmy."

Squirmy. He'd have put it another way, but yeah…that pretty well described it. "Any ideas?"

"Nope. You?"

"A few. I think it might've had something to do with what happened a couple of years ago in Dallas. The guy's trying to launch a business, right? I doubt if they'd be spending money on a cross-country jaunt if there wasn't something in it for them. You saw what they were driving."

Her smile turned into a grin. With the sunlight sparkling on her auburn hair, highlighting her creamy complexion, she was totally irresistible. "Their truck, you mean? I think it's a year younger than my car."

Liza wished the moment could never end. Wished she didn't have to think about things like flooded vegetable bins, and leaky roofs. "But you know the sweetest thing? Patty Ann asked me to show her to the bathroom, and while we were out in the hall, she offered to lend me money. She said she'd been saving up for when she and Cammy got married, but she didn't really need it now. She said I could pay her back when I got on my feet again. Did you ever hear anything so sweet? I nearly cried."

"I thought you looked a little weepy there."

"Who called? Not another hang-up call—that's only at night."

With his hands roaming over her back, easing the stiffness she'd felt ever since she got up this morning, Beckett said, "Your uncle wants to stay on a few more days. That okay with you?"

"Well, of course. You think he really wants to stay? He's not just saying that because he knows I'll have my hands full cleaning up around here?"

"I think he really wants to stay, and I'll help you clean up."

Closing her eyes, she savored the moment. If she was lucky there might be a few more such moments before he left. She intended to savor every one of then, and shed not a single tear when he drove off. In a matter of a few days, he had brought her more happiness than she'd ever expected to find. Contentment was one thing; sheer, mindless bliss was something else. Scarcer than hens' teeth, as Uncle Fred would say.

"You know what? I think they did it," she said suddenly.

"Think who did what?"

"Those calls—you know, the hang-up calls? I think it was Patty Ann, or at least her boyfriend. But why wouldn't she just call and say they were coming East, and ask if they could come for a visit? It's almost as if—oh, I don't know, I just had the strangest feeling about the whole thing."

Beckett said nothing. He leaned against the porch support, holding her loosely in his arms. She went on.

"I know, I know, it's crazy. Honestly, I've never been paranoid—well, not very. All the same, I got a funny feeling they were, um, looking for something? What on earth did they expect to find here? And then offering to lend me money."

He waited for her to work it out in her own mind. She had most of the pieces of the puzzle. "I think you're probably right. Whatever they were looking for, whatever they were up to, the girl's all right. She'll keep him in line, and I seriously doubt if they'll bother you again."

His hands continued to stroke her back slowly, caressing her nape under the heavy fall of hair, moving down to curve over her hips. When Liza leaned away to look up at him, he smiled that slow, lazy smile that never failed to curl her toes. To think she'd once thought those silvery eyes were cold.

If she'd had a grain of sense she would have run the minute he stepped out of that big green SUV. Now, here she was, in love for the second time in her life—or maybe the first time, because this felt so much deeper, so much richer than anything she'd ever felt for James.

And this time she was mature enough to know what to expect. Tears, followed by curses, followed by bitterness, she admitted with painful honesty. Followed by a few more vows of "never again."

"Beckett, could we please go back to bed?" she asked suddenly.

He was still for so long she wanted to drop through

the floor and disappear. "Liza? Are you sure you want that?"

"Oh, I can't believe I said that," she whispered, eyes shut tightly. Opening just one, she said, "I'm sure, but if you're not— I mean, if you're in a hurry to leave…"

He laughed aloud, the sound ringing out clearly in the fresh morning air. One more time, Liza told herself, just one more memory to savor in the years ahead, is that too much to ask? She would tuck it all away together in her memory book: the sound of his rich, baritone drawl, the feel of his hands, gentle on her body.

Two spoons side by side in a jar of peanut butter….

He led her inside. There was no pretense on either side; they both knew what was going to happen. Last night the tension that had been growing between them for days had reached flash point. This time would be slower, more deliberate. They were both tired; they could take time to savor the moment.

In his own way, L. J. Beckett was every bit as much a thief as her late husband had been. He'd stolen her heart without even trying. Now that the deed was done, she might as well enjoy it while it lasted.

Thus spoke the new Liza Chandler. James had been a real education.

In the sunlight that slanted through the east-facing bedroom window, she could see the texture of his skin, the tiny creases that fanned out from his clear gray eyes, the crisp texture of his hair. Before he could inventory all her flaws, she reached up and pressed her mouth to his. He certainly wanted her—wanted sex, at least. That much was dramatically evident.

Coals of banked desire began to glow. Tiny flames began licking in the pit of her belly. She savored the now familiar taste of him, the soft tug of his teeth on her lower lip that opened her to a deeper invasion. She was lost. Light-years beyond the reach of reason. His tongue skillfully engaged hers in a game of seduction, and she gloried in every nibble, every thrust. Any remaining defenses she'd possessed had gone down without a whimper. This was her choice. She would take the lead and live with the consequences.

His hands tangled in the fabric of her denim float as he lifted it over her head. She hadn't bothered with a bra. Stepping into underpants had been painful enough without struggling to fasten a hook behind her back. She didn't know which was worse—bandaged hands or stiff knees, but if she broke loose every scrap of gauze and adhesive tape, she was not going to let herself be handicapped. This time she intended to do more than let it happen.

For long moments after he eased her clothes off, he simply held her. She loved being held. Until Beckett had come along, it had been years since anyone had held her this way. Since anyone had held her at all. She had never even missed it, never given it a thought, until this man had walked into her life.

Beckett was here, and he was nothing at all like James. Instead he was warm and caring, strong and honorable. She couldn't look at him without wanting to touch him, and it occurred to her that she had never felt that way about James, not even in the beginning.

A rash of goose bumps broke out as Beckett nuzzled the sensitive place at the side of her throat. Her head fell back and she whimpered. Slowly, slowly... make it last, she told herself, wanting nothing more than to drag him closer and feel him on every part of her body, inside and out.

His hands, unbelievably gentle, covered her small breasts. When his thumbs feathered the tips, making them rise like small pink acorns, she gasped, inhaling his clean, musky scent. She licked the skin of his throat with the tip of her tongue, felt him shudder and knew a small surge of power. He tasted slightly soapy, slightly salty.

Mmm, delicious. She wanted more.

And so she did it again and felt his arousal surge against her. *Yes!* She exulted, this is for me! Bandaged knees and all, it had to be more then merely physical.

Although the physical alone was almost more than she could bear.

Overflowing with love, she offered him one last chance to escape, if only to prove to herself that she could handle whatever did or did not come next. "Beckett, are you sure? I mean, this probably isn't very...ohhh, smart."

"Shh, honey, no one's checking IQs."

On an emotional razor's edge, she couldn't help it—she laughed aloud.

She stroked his chest under the knit shirt that clung

to his chest and shoulders with her padded palms, feeling like a molten puddle of liquid desire.

Beckett stripped quickly and efficiently, removing something from his hip pocket first. He kept a first-aid kit in his car. It was equipped for all emergencies. "Honey, are *you* sure? I don't want you to have any regrets…ever."

In other words, Liza interpreted, he wasn't making any promises.

She hadn't expected any. Hadn't asked for any. Quickly she stifled the last shred of doubt as to the wisdom of what she was about to do. There were times when wisdom was a highly overrated quality. She held out her arms, and he came down beside her.

Sunlight gleamed on the sharp angles of his tanned face, glinted off his white teeth. She said, "Let's not talk. I can't talk and have sex at the same time. It just doesn't work that way."

"Doesn't it? Sweetheart, you could lie there reading aloud from the yellow pages and I'd still want to jump your bones, bandages and all."

"Hand me the phone book, then," she demanded, and he laughed. Laughed and nuzzled her throat, then moved up to begin kissing his way down her body. Just before he reached her navel, he lifted his head and said, "Read on—don't let me stop you."

Ignoring his teasing words, she arched her hips, oblivious to the pain of her knees. All too quickly the tension reached flash point. One more touch and she knew she would go up in flames.

And then he made that one more touch. Liza, who

had never been particularly sexual until this man had come along, opened herself to his explorations, gasping as he closed in on her most sensitive flesh. What had happened to her? She wasn't like this. Until last night she had never felt this! Never *ever* gone off like a...like a firecracker! "Please...I can't stand it," she gasped.

It built swiftly and exploded just as suddenly. Spiraling rainbows, arching and dissolving, arching and dissolving, until she was nothing but a shimmering beam of white heat.

Beckett watched her ecstasy, feeling great pride and, oddly enough, an even greater sense of humility that he'd been the one to bring her this gift. And then his own control broke and he moved over her, and when she welcomed him, it began all over again.

He began to thrust, slowly at first, but all too soon he was racing out of control. There was only the sound of groans and whimpers. The sound of his rasping breath and her shuddering, gasping sighs, and then the world went up in flames again.

Twice within minutes, Liza marveled later, when her brain began functioning once more. Until last night that had never happened to her before. Usually, once didn't even happen. Sex had always been... pleasant. Something men and women did together that meant more to the man than it did to the woman.

Last night she'd been stunned by the magnitude of her climax. Today...

How on earth was she going to get through the rest

of her life without this man? Because she knew for a
fact that sex with any other man, even if she could
bring herself to the point, would wither in comparison.

Beckett didn't sleep afterward. His body was exhausted, his mind racing. Every particle of self-
preservation he possessed was clamoring, urging him
to get the hell out of her bed before it was too late.

Studying the woman sleeping in his arms, he was
reminded all over again of the reasons why this never
should have happened. He'd promised himself he
wouldn't let things go this far—that he would settle
the debt, help her get through the storm and leave.

Almost from the first time he'd seen her there in
that crazy little stand of hers, looking like a down-
on-her-luck duchess in her calico apron, he'd been
stunned by his own reaction. It was that attitude of
hers—part pride, part vulnerability—that had gotten
under his skin. It had irritated the hell out of him the
first few times he'd tried to do business with her.

What he hadn't known until she had come apart in
his arms was how totally, devastatingly defenseless
she really was. He didn't know much about that jerk
she'd been married to, except that he was a crook. He
sure as hell hadn't been much of a husband. Newly
widowed, she'd evidently walked away from an up-
scale address with little more than the clothes on her
back, only to devote herself to taking care of an old
man and his rinky-dink roadside stand.

And now, along with all else she had to deal with,
she was going to start piling on guilt, because what-

ever she said to the contrary, Liza Chandler wasn't the kind of woman to take sex lightly. He'd been with enough of that sort to know the difference. When it came to sex, she probably knew less than today's average teenager.

A drop of water plunked down on his forehead and ran off onto the pillow. The rain had stopped hours ago, but it would probably continue to drip through the ceiling for hours, maybe days. No wonder the damn roof was rotted. The whole house was probably about to fall down.

He needed to shop for her groceries, rebandage her hands and knees, make sure Rambo and his groupie were gone for good and wouldn't be bothering her again—and then he could hit the road with a clear conscience.

It wasn't going to happen.

Lying on the petrified foam rubber mattress, listening to the soft purr of her breath beside him—feeling the heat of her bottom pressed into his groin, Beckett tried to rationalize his way out of the mess he was in. He'd been a practicing adult for the past twenty-odd years. Liza was only a few years younger than he was. She knows the score, he told himself.

Nope. He'd seen her, wanted her and seduced her. Some women took a broader view of life than others. She might consider herself experienced, but she was as green as any kid—more so because she didn't realize how vulnerable she was.

With wry humor, he wondered what the chances were of pretending he had amnesia. "What? We had sex? Never happened, honey, you must have me mixed up with some other guy.''

For a supposedly intelligent man, he had managed to pull some real blunders in his life, but this one was in a class by itself.

Easing out of bed, he located his pants and headed for the shower. It had to be going on noon, and he still had a few things to do before he could leave. Damn. You'd think he was deliberately looking for reasons to stick around.

From the bed, Liza watched him grab his clothes and make his escape. She hoped, she really did, that her last view of L. J.—Lancelot Jones Beckett— wasn't going to be him scurrying out of her bedroom, his clothes clutched in his arms and a guilty look on his face.

She got up, slipped on a T-shirt and loose jeans and stared at herself in the mirror. Yuck. Magic hadn't happened over the past hour. She was still plain old Liza, bony face, messy hair and all, only now she had a look in her eyes that shouldn't be there.

Sadness. She was finished with sadness. She'd sworn off sadness when she'd left Texas and headed east to start over again.

How many fresh starts was one woman allowed? She'd made her first one when, hungry for the close family she'd been missing ever since her mother died and her father had remarried, she had married James.

She'd made another start when she'd moved to North Carolina.

Another new start wasn't going to happen, because

Uncle Fred needed her. He'd been barely hanging on when she'd turned up on his front porch, uninvited. Somewhere he had a nephew—his wife's kin, not his own, but family was family. The nephew was a sailor of some sort, and evidently he wasn't into family relations.

Bracing one hand on the iron bedpost, Liza slid first one foot and then the other into a pair of sandals and set out to put things back in order. They still had produce out there that needed spreading out to dry. Some of it would be beyond salvation. Then there was that blasted roof....

The bathroom door opened and Beckett joined her in the kitchen. Pretending an intense interest in the list she was making, she ignored him. She'd managed to blunder through seducing the man. Trouble was, she hadn't a clue when it came to postseduction protocol. Neither of them smoked. Besides, that probably only worked in old movies.

Maybe she could come up with a smart quip, something like, Well, my, that was fun, wasn't it? Do you want a cup of coffee before you hit the road?

Yeah, that ought to do it.

He came to stand behind her chair. "Is that the list?"

"Is that what list?"

"The stuff you want from the grocery store. What about the things your uncle wanted?"

She stole a glance at him, gaining some small satisfaction from the fact that he seemed as ill at ease as she was. "This is all I can think of now. I'll get together the things to take to Bay View, but, Beckett, you really don't have to do this. I know you're eager to get back to Charleston.''

"Am I?''

Scraping her chair back, she stood and glared at him. "Stop it. Just stop it right now. I know this is awkward and embarrassing, and if you're looking for an apology, then here it is. I'm sorry, okay? Sorry I— that I—''

"I'm not,'' he said quietly. "Now give me the list and go round up whatever you want me to take to Fred.''

Without another word she stalked off, plastic bag in hand, and filled it with the things her uncle had requested, throwing in several apples and a peach that wouldn't last another day.

"Here. Thank you very much,'' she snapped.

Her temper seemed to have a peculiar effect on him. He started to smile. The smile broadened to include flashing teeth and sparkling eyes.

Liza's eyes narrowed. Her jaw clenched, and then he confounded her completely by saying, "PawPaw's going to flat-out love you, honey. I'll stop somewhere on the way back and bring us a couple of barbecue sandwiches, okay?''

Eleven

To Liza it seemed as if days should have passed, but actually it had been than less two hours. The sun shouldn't be shining so brightly, she thought. The sky shouldn't be that incredible shade of blue, but it was. Glaringly bright, setting millions of diamonds to sparkling on emerald-green grass that was littered with storm debris.

It could have been worse, she told herself as she circled the house, surveying the damage—mostly minor—and making a mental list of what needed doing immediately and what could wait.

Another section of gutter had come down last night and was lying across the hood of the old Packard. More shingles blown off—no big surprise there. One of the oaks had lost a big limb, and the front yard was littered with leaves, twigs and green acorns. She would have to rake and tote, as Uncle Fred called it—but not today. Today she had other priorities.

Such as seeing Beckett off with a smile that would linger in his heart long after he'd said goodbye.

Oh, sure. ''Grow up, Eliza,'' she muttered, hurling a short, dead branch over into the cornfield.

Her immediate concern was the stand. Everything inside the security fence would be drenched, but otherwise more or less intact. She had covered the cash register—her roadside antique—with a large plastic garbage bag. The three country hams she'd taken to the house, along with the soft goods. Water shouldn't hurt the produce as long as it dried off quickly enough.

In other words, she had her work cut out for her.

By half past noon, her stomach reminded her that she'd skipped breakfast. Peanut butter didn't count. And then she had to go and remember just why she'd skipped breakfast.

A few minutes later she found herself sitting in Uncle Fred's rocking chair, a sack of wet Mattamuskeet sweet onions on her lap, with tears overflowing her eyes.

It wasn't because of the onions, either.

''Well, damn,'' she growled, scrubbing at her cheeks with the now-filthy apron.

Carefully setting aside the onions a few minutes later, she climbed up onto her stool, hammer in hand, and managed to remove the last few nails anchoring the strip of tin roof. Once the place dried out thoroughly, she might replace it with a heavy tarp, but for now the fresh air was welcome.

She was carrying out the last few ears of corn and arranging them on the twisted tin to dry in the sunshine when Beckett pulled up in the graveled parking lot.

Oh, damn. She was filthy. Her hands…her apron. Her shoes were caked with mud, and her hair was, too, where it had escaped her clip and she'd raked it back again and again.

"What the hell do you think you're doing?" Beckett demanded.

"What does it look like I'm doing?" she returned, hoping there was no visible sign of her recent tears.

"That could've waited until I got back."

"Fine. I should've stayed in the front parlor sipping tea and reading the *Ladies' Home Journal*."

They were glaring at each other like a pair of feral dogs. Beckett held out a paper sack. "I brought lunch."

"I'm not hungry."

"Don't start with me, Liza, I've got a category-four headache."

That brought on a smile that was patently false. "Oh, what a pity. Take two aspirin and call me in the morning, all right?"

"And then you'll start with me?" The twinkle of a smile crept into his eyes, into his voice.

"You wish." Getting up off her knees, she winced, shook the wet grass and gravel from her apron and reached out for the paper sack he held tauntingly just out of reach. Her empty stomach reacted audibly to the tantalizing aroma of pit-cooked barbecue with a light, vinegary sauce.

Instead of handing over lunch, Beckett grabbed her hand. "What the hell have you been doing?" he growled.

"What do you think I've been doing?" She looked around at the onions, potatoes and cantaloupe, the watermelons and squash and corn, all of it spread out in the sunshine like a huge, colorful quilt. Some of it wouldn't make it—the rest would serve as hog food for the farmer who lived down the road. But whatever she could salvage would be produce she wouldn't have to restock.

Her shoulders drooped, and she sighed. "How's Uncle Fred holding up? Did he say when he wanted to come home?"

"As a matter of fact, we had a long talk about that. Let me get the groceries out of the car and we'll go inside and eat."

"What do you mean, you had a long talk about that? Is he coming home this afternoon? Because I really would like to do a lot more cleaning up before he sees the place. At his age, something like this can be upsetting."

Beckett steered her past the rumpled section of rusty tin roofing. He should have known she'd tackle it the minute he was gone. "Dammit, Liza, would it have killed you to ask for help?"

"I asked. You helped. What did you expect me to do, cry on your shoulder?"

Whatever he'd expected, he'd got more than he'd bargained for. A hell of a lot more. Trouble was, he didn't have it yet, not signed, sealed and delivered. "Let's get you cleaned up and rebandaged, then we'll eat, then we'll talk."

He was tempted to sweep her up in his arms and carry her up the front steps—whether on account of her scraped knees or his newly awakened caveman tendencies, he couldn't have said. Instead, he took her arm and steered her toward the house. It was time the lady learned to let someone take care of her. He was going to have a devilish time trying to convince her of it, though.

After putting a pot of coffee on to brew, he sat her down at the table, lifted her voluminous skirt and folded it back over her lap. "Hell of a thing to be working in," he grumbled, careful to keep the concern he was feeling from his voice. "Climbing up on stools, you could have—"

"But I didn't, all right?"

He grunted. "Okay, let's see how much damage you've managed to inflict on yourself."

It was a mark of how exhausted she was that she didn't protest. Beckett took full responsibility for some of her tiredness: he hadn't let her get a whole lot of rest lately.

The damage was mostly superficial, but just to be on the safe side, he bathed her injuries. When tears sprang to her eyes, he said, "Oh, hell." Laying aside the towel, he reached for her, toppling her forward. Holding her, he did his best to soothe away the fresh pain, drawing from dim memories of the way his mother had held and comforted him back when he was a brat in short pants, daring the devil and quite convinced he was invincible.

"I know, I know—hurts like hell, doesn't it? Let me pat it dry, and we'll put some more of that gunk on it. Seems to be doing the trick."

Liza took a deep, shuddering breath and nodded. He smeared antibiotic ointment on her knees and the heels of her hands. Digging into the sack of groceries, he produced a big box of gauze and proceeded to bind her wounds with yards of the stuff.

"I feel like a mummy," Liza said, feeling shaky all over again. Not from any great pain, other than the pain of seeing Beckett kneeling before her, and knowing this was probably the last hour she would ever spend with him. In which case, she would much rather have been wearing something filmy and romantic.

Or at the very least something clean.

Candles would have been a nice touch, too, although candles in a kitchen at high noon might be overdoing it. Still, a woman could dream, couldn't she?

"Poor Uncle Fred," she said, making a determined effort to shift her mind away from the mess she'd made of things. "At his age he shouldn't have to come home and find everything all torn up. He can't do much of anything himself, and he probably knows we can't afford to hire anyone. Although he's not real good when it comes to managing money. Maybe I can convince him—''

''Liza, about Uncle Fred.''

''Oh, I know, I know, he's a lot tougher than he looks, but all the same, I wish—''

''Liza, listen to me. Your uncle's been through a lot worse than the little blow we had last night. He might not be good at handling money, but he's handled more than most men—wars, depressions, grief.''

''I know that. I'm whining on his behalf because he won't. All the same...''

''All the same, there comes a time in a man's life when he wants to shed a few responsibilities, settle back and enjoy the things he can still enjoy, preferably with friends.''

''Didn't I just say that? That's why I want to get everything all cleaned up here. Then maybe I'll suggest he invite a few friends over for baseball and supper. Or maybe we'll drive down to Manteo and watch *The Lost Colony*. He told me he hasn't seen a performance since his wife died.''

Rising, Beckett shoved aside the first-aid materials just as the coffee gurgled its last gurgle. He took down two cups. Liza watched him, but made no effort to interfere. Good, he thought. He was going to need a docile Liza to get through what he had to tell her.

Over barbecue sandwiches, he brought up the first topic under consideration. ''About Fred...Liza, you do know he has a nephew, don't you?''

She reached for a French fry. He snagged his lower lip with his teeth, trying to think how best to break the news. "Well, sure. I know his wife had—has—a nephew," she said. "I told you that, remember? I've never actually met him, but he calls to talk to Uncle Fred whenever he's in port. I think he works on one of those big container ships, I'm not sure."

"You're right. But he's thinking of retiring as soon as he can get on with his plans here."

"Here where?" She took a big bite of her barbecue sandwich, closed her eyes and sighed. "Heavenly. It's even better than Texas barbecue, and if that sounds traitorous, Texas can sue me."

"The lot next door?" Beckett indicated the east-facing window. To the west and north of the Grant house were cornfields. On the east side was a cleared lot surrounded by several hundred acres of soybeans.

"What about it?" she asked with her mouth full.

Leaning across the table, he brushed a streak of barbecue sauce from beside her mouth, then licked it from his thumb. "Yeah, well, the thing is, all that belongs to Fred's nephew."

"Fred's wife's nephew," she corrected. "I'm his only blood kin."

"Dammit, Liza, I'm trying to tell you that this place—the house, the lot next door—they belong to Solon Pugh. The nephew."

"In-law," she supplied, frowning.

"Right. The thing is, they don't belong to Fred."

She stopped chewing. Her eyes went round, narrowed, then widened again as she absorbed the full impact. "You mean this Pugh fellow—he's just letting Uncle Fred live here?"

This was going to be painful. He figured it was best to get it over with quickly and let the healing begin. "Fred's wife's folks built the house. It belonged to her, and when she died, it went to her nephew, with Fred retaining a lifetime right."

"So?" She had carefully laid her sandwich on the napkin. Her freshly bandaged hands were resting on her lap. "I don't see that that changes anything."

"It doesn't. You did."

"I don't think I want to hear this. If you don't mind, I'm going to go back out to the stand and—"

He caught her by the arm before she could leave. "You're going to have to hear it. Honey, Fred was all ready to move into Bay View with his friends when you turned up one day, needing a place to stay. Needing someone to help you get started again. Fred recognized that. His hearing might not be what it once was, but his mind is as sharp as ever. He called Pugh and told him he'd changed his mind and was going to stay on awhile longer. As he told me this morning, you needed something to latch on to to get you back on your feet, and he didn't mind helping you out."

"Helping me out?" Liza repeated, a stricken look on her face. "But I'm the one who was helping him. He couldn't have stayed here without me—without someone…"

He came around the table and knelt beside her, holding her while she sucked in great gulps of air. "I'm not going to cry, don't worry," she said. "Just give me a minute, will you?"

"All the time in the world, sugar babe. Go ahead and cry, if you need to, sweetheart."

That got her attention. Rearing back, she glared at him, her elegant, patrician features no less beautiful for the smear of grime across her forehead.

"What, I can't call you sweetheart?" he challenged.

"Sugar babe?"

"Hey, it's what the men in my family call the women—and the women call them that right back. It means 'I love you.' Don't people in Texas talk that way?"

"Not the people I knew."

He waited for her to pick up on what he'd said. It might come as something of a shock. It had shocked the hell out of him, but once he'd realized it had happened, he'd accepted it. Felt pretty damned good about it, matter of fact. No more running away. This was it—this was what he'd been running toward all these years.

Now all he had to do was convince Liza.

"You see where I'm going with this, right?"

"Uncle Fred wants to stay on at Bay View so that his nephew can move in here." She nodded slowly. "I understand."

Beckett's reputation as a negotiator had never been in question. He was among the best. But negotiating with hijackers—modern-day pirates—was one thing. Reaching a mutually satisfying agreement with a woman who was both proud and needy…that called for an altogether different set of skills.

For a guy who had commitment avoidance down to a fine art, he was digging his own grave here. Never had a grave been dug more willingly. "You heard what I said, then?"

She nodded. Her fingers, which were the only parts of her hands not swathed in gauze, walked their way up his chest and latched on to his collar. She still refused to meet his eyes.

"All of it?" he pressed.

"All of what?" She lifted her face then, and he caught a glimmer of what was going on behind those whiskey-colored eyes. Satisfaction began to glow inside him like banked coals.

Emboldened, he said, "You want the full, complete translation? *Hon* and *honey*—now those can mean either one of two things, depending on who's saying it to whom. It can mean either 'I love you,' or 'I'm content with who I am and hope you're lucky enough to be the same.' As for the rest—*sweetheart*—that's pretty self-evident."

"And *sugar babe?*" She was getting into the swing of things.

"Ah, yes...well now, that can mean a couple of things, too. There's the *sugar babe* that means, 'Wow, I'd sure like to get in your pants!' Then, there's the *sugar babe* that means, 'Me and you, hon—better or worse, thick or thin—side meat or sirloin, we stick together.'"

"I'm afraid to ask," she said, and darned if he didn't believe her. How the hell could she still have doubts? Hadn't he just told her he loved her? Maybe he'd circled around it a time or two, but then, he hadn't had any practice in the past couple of decades.

"Look, how about we pack up what Uncle Fred wants to keep, take it to him, then we come back here and pack up everything you need, and then we'll lock up and head south. You need to meet PawPaw, you need to meet all my folks, and then, if you'll still have me…."

Liza thought, *Oh, Lord, don't let me hyperventilate.* "I think I've just been proposed to. If not, you'd better set me straight real fast."

"Hey, I'm down on my bended knee, aren't I?" It was hard to tell under his deep suntan, but she could almost swear he was blushing.

"If you're waiting for me to get down on mine to accept, then you're going to have to give me more time."

"Sorry, time's up. What about we both get horizontal and continue this conversation?"

Liza had to laugh at that. So did Beckett, because they both knew there would be little conversation in the near future. "Know what? I can hardly wait to take you home to show PawPaw. If I didn't know better, I'd think he'd set this whole thing up on purpose."

* * * * *

Find out how the Beckett family debt started with the linked Historical—Beckett's Birthright, written under the name Bronwyn Williams— on sale in February 2004.

▼ SILHOUETTE®
DESIRE™ 2-IN-1

AVAILABLE FROM 16TH JANUARY 2004

LIONHEARTED Diana Palmer

Texan Lovers

Virgin Janie Brewster had always been in love with Leo Hart. But he'd never noticed her as a woman—until she decided to tempt him beyond *all* reason.

INSTINCTIVE MALE Cait London

Heartbreakers

Past experience had taught Mikhail Stepanov to keep his boss's dangerously alluring daughter at arm's length. But once the desperate single mother turned to him, how could he resist?

KISS ME, COWBOY! Maureen Child

Career-woman Nora Bailey was planning to lose her virginity—with relationship-shy, sexy single dad Mike Fallon! This was a challenge Nora would take on both day and...*night*.

THE TYCOON'S LADY Katherine Garbera

The Baby Bank

When Angelica Leone stumbled off the stage at a charity auction and into the arms of tycoon Paul Sterling, she knew he would stop at nothing to get what he wanted—and he wanted her!

CINDERELLA & THE PLAYBOY Laura Wright

When C K Tanner got Abby McGrady to pretend to be his wife to snare a business deal, he never expected the attraction between them—let alone wanting to turn this into something permanent.

QUADE: THE IRRESISTIBLE ONE Bronwyn Jameson

Chantal Goodwin had never stopped wanting ex-love Cameron Quade. So she thought they could have one night of passion and then walk away. But that was before she found out about their baby...

AVAILABLE FROM 16TH JANUARY 2004

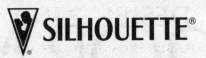 **SILHOUETTE**®

Sensation™

Passionate, dramatic, thrilling romances

ONE OF THESE NIGHTS Justine Davis
MOMENT OF TRUTH Maggie Price
BENEATH THE SILK Wendy Rosnau
PRIVATE MANOEUVRES Catherine Mann
THE QUIET STORM RaeAnne Thayne
HONKY-TONK CINDERELLA Karen Templeton

Special Edition™

Vivid, satisfying romances full of family, life and love

MICHAEL'S DISCOVERY Sherryl Woods
HER HEALING TOUCH Lindsay McKenna
TAKING OVER THE TYCOON Cathy Gillen Thacker
BABY 101 Marisa Carroll
THE WEDDING BARGAIN Lisette Belisle
THE MISSING HEIR Jane Toombs

Superromance™

*Enjoy the drama, explore the emotions,
experience the relationship*

SUBSTITUTE FATHER Bonnie K Winn
THE NOTORIOUS MRS WRIGHT Fay Robinson
THE FIRE WITHIN Kathryn Shay
SHOOTING THE MOON Brenda Novak

Intrigue™

Danger, deception and suspense

DADDY TO THE RESCUE Susan Kearney
PHANTOM LOVER Rebecca York
FAKE ID WIFE Patricia Rosemoor
UNDER LOCK AND KEY Sylvie Kurtz

0104/51b

SILHOUETTE®
SPECIAL EDITION™

proudly presents

a brand-new series from
GINA WILKINS

THE McCLOUDS
OF MISSISSIPPI

*Three siblings find their way back
to family — and love.*

THE FAMILY PLAN
January 2004

CONFLICT OF INTEREST
March 2004

FAITH, HOPE AND FAMILY
May 2004

0104/SH/LC81

are proud to introduce

DYNASTIES: THE BARONES

Meet the wealthy Barones—caught in a web of danger, deceit and…desire!

Twelve exciting stories in six 2-in-1 volumes:

SILHOUETTE® SPECIAL EDITION™

proudly presents

a brand-new five-book series from
bestselling author

SHERRYL WOODS

The Devaneys

*Five brothers torn apart in childhood,
reunited by love!*

RYAN'S PLACE

December 2003

SEAN'S RECKONING

January 2004

MICHAEL'S DISCOVERY

February 2004

PATRICK'S DESTINY

March 2004

DANIEL'S DESIRE

April 2004

1203/SH/LC75

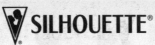

2 FREE

books and a surprise gift!

We would like to take this opportunity to thank you for reading this Silhouette® book by offering you the chance to take TWO specially selected titles from the Desire™ series absolutely FREE! We're also making this offer to introduce you to the benefits of the Reader Service™—

- ★ FREE home delivery
- ★ FREE gifts and competitions
- ★ FREE monthly Newsletter
- ★ Exclusive Reader Service offers
- ★ Books available before they're in the shops

Accepting these FREE books and gift places you under no obligation to buy, you may cancel at any time, even after receiving your free shipment. Simply complete your details below and return the entire page to the address below. *You don't even need a stamp!*

YES! Please send me 2 free Desire books and a surprise gift. I understand that unless you hear from me, I will receive 3 superb new titles every month for just £4.99 each, postage and packing free. I am under no obligation to purchase any books and may cancel my subscription at any time. The free book and gift will be mine to keep in any case.

D4ZED

Ms/Mrs/Miss/Mr ....Initials................................
BLOCK CAPITALS PLEASE

Surname ....

Address ....

....

....Postcode................................

Send this whole page to:
UK: FREEPOST CN81, Croydon, CR9 3WZ
EIRE: PO Box 4546, Kilcock, County Kildare (stamp required)

Offer valid in UK and Eire only and not available to current Reader Service subscribers to this series. We reserve the right to refuse an application and applicants must be aged 18 years or over. Only one application per household. Terms and prices subject to change without notice. Offer expires 30th April 2004. As a result of this application, you may receive offers from Harlequin Mills & Boon and other carefully selected companies. If you would prefer not to share in this opportunity please write to The Data Manager at the address above.

Silhouette® is a registered trademark used under licence.
Desire™ is being used as a trademark.
The Reader Service™ is being used as a trademark.